Content Warnings

This story includes themes of addiction, family struggle, and healing. There are scenes involving alcohol abuse, difficult parent-child relationships, and emotional trauma, as well as pregnancy, childbirth and coercion of abortion.

If any of these topics are sensitive for you, please take care while reading.

The Hidden Score

G. KESPA

Contents

CHAPTER 1

Dylan

"I can't believe you talked me into going to some rando's house party."

"He seemed nice when I met him at the bar last night."

"You're not helping your case, Sierra."

Big brown eyes bore into mine. "Come on, Dylan! Do *not* back out on me now. We look hot AF, and you swore we're going to go all out for this trip. We're supposed to be up for every adventure and..."

"I know!" I say, interrupting her rant. "I said we'd go, and we are. I'm just warning you, I won't be partying too hard considering we're far from home, and in a complete stranger's house."

"Okay, cool. Just a couple of shots, then we'll just chill and have a good time. Dance a little... maybe meet some new guys." She says, wiggling her brows suggestively.

"What about the guy from the bar? Casey?" I ask, avoiding the shots comment completely.

I can't even think about another shot after last night. I spent the majority of the night and some of the morning puking them back up after we found a bar that bought our fake IDs.

No, thank you!

Looking at her nails now, she says, "He's an option for sure, but playing the field will only make him want me more." Then tosses her long, wavy blonde hair behind her.

Sierra isn't normally the "playing the field" type of girl, but she's determined that she's not upset from her breakup, and I'll support her moving on from that douche anyway she needs to.

I shake my head at her. "Okay, so we grab some *beers,*" I eye her meaningfully when I say beers. "Call in the hot guys with our sweet dance moves, pick the most eligible bachelor for the night and head back home in a couple of days."

"Now we're talking. Who knows? Maybe I'll find my cowboy love and take him with us." She fake-swoons against the door of the Uber.

I roll my eyes. "Have fun with that."

She quickly sits up, points, and yells at our driver. "That has to be it up there."

Our Uber parks as close as he can to the house that's obviously throwing a party, due to the influx of vehicles centered on this particular section of the block.

We get out and take it all in as the driver pulls away behind us.

I link my arm with hers, and we start walking down the sidewalk. The door is wide open to a view of a house full of people overflowing onto the front lawn.

The porch has setups for flip cup and beer pong on opposite ends with matches already going. Music and party noise join, creating the perfect atmosphere for a pretty decent party.

"Let's go find Casey so he can show us to some *beer*." Sierra snarks the last word, side-eyeing me.

I chuckle, then follow her lead into the house.

I can't believe we're at a house party in the middle of freaking Texas.

Sierra came up with this harebrained idea after her breakup with Jake. She's a bit of a hopeless romantic and stuck it out with Jake for way too long.

She began swearing she's supposed to be with a cowboy or rancher or... whatever.

She probably just finished a cowboy romance and got it in her head that Texas is where she'd find hers.

As my childhood best friend, she's always been the spontaneity in our relationship. Whereas I kept us in reality, balancing our friendship perfectly.

We're both out for summer and I don't have to show up for the internship at my dad's firm until August. So, we packed our bags and drove the long drive to Texas.

We started in the bright lights of Dallas and then worked our way around. We got the Buc-ees t-shirt, tried the

Whataburger, visited the Alamo, and ended up in a bar out west.

That's how we ended up in Dry Creek, Texas.

"Hey, y'all made it." I hear Casey yell over the music while pushing his way through the crowd. I'm not sure if he's the true 'cowboy' Sierra's looking for, but I have to admit there's something attractive about his worn-in boots and jeans paired with a nice shirt.

Sierra leans in and tells me, "I'm really loving these accents." Then yells back to Casey, eyes sparkling. "We figured we'd see how you native Texans like to party."

I was going to say hi to him too, but he's really all eyes for Sierra. Ignoring their flirtatious chatter, I scope the scene.

It seems a little loud for a neighborhood like this, but maybe they're used to it here. I'm pretty sure this is a college town.

There's dancing in the living room, but mostly just groups of people clustered together, talking to each other.

I spot a group of guys that are being extra loud and bro-ing out, a few girls wrapped up underneath muscular arms, claiming them for the night.

I notice a guy standing outside of the huddle, hands in his pockets with a bored expression, like he doesn't really want to be here.

He catches me staring at him but neither of us look away. His eyes hold mine, green on hazel, and I'm a moth drawn to the flame.

He lifts one side of his mouth in a crooked grin, making me smirk at his confidence.

He has short, messy brown hair to match his sun-tanned skin. Athletic shorts and a muscle shirt on, like he doesn't want to or doesn't need to dress for the occasion. He's tall but thick with muscles, accented by his lack of sleeves, like he works out on a regular basis.

When I finish my perusal, I end with his eyes again, and he shoots me a quick wink. I flash him a sultry smile of my own, and his shoulders shake with silent laughter.

"Y'all just grab whatever you want from outta here. This is my ice chest." I hear Casey say while handing us each our own bottle.

Snapping away from the guy's gaze, I mutter my thanks.

"Well, I'm going to take my dance that this little number promised me. Try to find me later, yeah?" Sierra says coyly, pulling me to the living room.

I turn my head one last time and I think I catch a peek of the guy still staring at me, but there are bodies blocking my vision as I'm pulled to the unofficial dance floor.

Casey shouts to Sierra. "You can count on it."

Sierra has a giant smile plastered across her face, but she doesn't reply.

We start shaking and grinding off-beat in our cutoffs and crop tops to the today's hits mashup that's blaring from the speakers.

"Casey seems to be really into you. I think he should at least take the top contender position of our bachelors." I say just loud enough to be heard over the music.

"Yeah. He is, but it's more fun to keep him guessing." She tells me right before she meets eyes with him again and drops seductively to the floor and bringing it back up in time with the music.

"Are you actually going to hook up with him tonight?" I ask her, thoroughly impressed. She's definitely the better dancer of the two of us.

"If it happens, I won't be mad about it, but right now, I just want *us* to have fun. Maybe one round of beer pong?" She shoves her bottom lip out in a pleading pout. "I need my partner."

"One round." I say, holding up a finger, and she beams with satisfaction. "*After* a couple more songs, please?"

"Your wish is my command." She waves her hand in circles and does a little bow.

We both laugh and keep dancing like we'll never see these people again.

♡ ⤜⤛ ♡

I'm rapping—badly—into my pretend microphone about one shot and spaghetti, leaning in way too close to Sierra as she tries to concentrate at the table.

"Now's not the time for Eminem lyrics, Dylan. You know I

hate the last cup pressure!" Sierra throws her head back, groaning her frustration.

I laugh, feeling bubbly now that I have a few drinks in me.

I may get slightly loud and annoying, even with a simple buzz going.

"Okay, I'm sorry. No pressure, but if we both make it, they'll never be able to come back from it and we win."

We met these two girls while dancing—Kelsey and Sadie. We hit it off talking and dancing together and decided they'd make perfect opponents.

They agreed and kept up with us damn near shot for shot. But Sierra and I are a well-oiled machine. We've been playing with water cups together well before we were old enough to play with actual alcohol.

Sierra gets a little more focused than's necessary for a beer drinking game, steps up to the table and sinks her shot.

We erupt into our celebrations, and everyone surrounding the table cheers along with us.

Sierra's high-fiving one of the guys standing around the table when Casey walks up.

"Looks like I found you." He says with a big grin, cutting in between Sierra and the other guy.

Seems her plan worked after all.

She takes him in with a smile of her own. "It took you long enough."

"Well, I didn't want to distract you with my charm and good looks." Casey tells her, stepping a little closer to her.

Getting a third-wheel vibe, I tell them. "I'm going to get myself another drink and find someone to dance with. I'll catch up with you later."

Sierra pulls me in for a sloppy hug and whispers in my ear. "Don't panic too much, my Dyl-pill, if you can't find me."

"Go get him, girl." I tell her with a wink.

Finally finding Casey's ice chest, I grab another bottle and take a long swig.

I see Sadie dancing again and make my way to her.

Her long blonde hair is bouncing behind her. "Are parties like this where you're from?"

"Well, they aren't as hot." I answer, fanning myself and bobbing along to the music.

"Yeah, summers here can definitely be intense, but you get used to it or find a swimming hole to cool off in. There's a lake nearby that we go to a lot. There's a beach area that we all hang out on."

"We have Lake Erie, obviously, but we also have so many creeks and rivers that we float down. With school, I haven't had a lot of time to go the past couple of years. Sierra and I will have to check it out."

"Y'all definitely need to."

We dance together for a few more songs, each of us taking turns asking questions about the other.

After a while, I get tired and feel like I'm sweating off my perfectly made-up face.

"I'm actually going to check on Sierra real quick. I'll be right back." I say over the music, and she nods her head, turning to the person beside her, never missing a beat of her dancing.

I walk back onto the front porch, and Sierra's nowhere to be seen.

Good for her.

She needs a one-night stand to get Jake out of her system.

Honestly, I prefer a casual hookup.

No attachment. No distraction. No hurt.

I'm just about to head back to the living room when I see those damn red and blue flashing lights.

Shit!

I cannot get caught for underage drinking a month before I turn twenty-one.

My mother will kill me.

I have no idea where I'm at, so running isn't an option. I just have to hide and pray they'll just break it up and leave.

I yell Sierra's name several times in case she happens to be close by and I just don't see her. She's either gone or can't hear me over the chaos of everyone scrambling.

I run for the hallway and try to open the first door I get to.

Locked.

Luckily, the next door I go to isn't. The lights are turned off, so I close the door behind me and hurry for the bed.

I lift the blanket to jump in and *smack*...

right into another body.

CHAPTER 2

Dylan

"OUCH!" I hear a deep voice burst out.

"I'm so sorry! I was just trying to hide. Shit! I'll find somewhere else." I whisper-talk, moving to leave the safety of the bed.

A warm hand wraps around my wrist, pulling me back down.

"You're fine. We can hide together. If the cops walk in, we might get them out faster if they think we're hooking up." His voice draws me in more than his light tug does.

I search his face, now that my eyes have adjusted, and notice it's the guy from earlier with the gorgeous green eyes.

"Oh. Umm... Okay. Yeah, that's an idea." I stammer.

What the hell, woman? Get it together. He's just a guy.

A ridiculously attractive guy, but still.

"Why are you hiding?" I whisper settling in beside him.

He hooks his arm around me casually, like he talks to all girls for the first time, basically cuddling.

He hesitates for a moment. "I've had a few run-ins with the cops, and I'm not looking to be on their radar."

"Oh no. Did I just fall into bed with a bad boy cliché?" I push a little at his chest with my hands, like I need to get away.

His low deep chuckle vibrates my whole body, then he pulls me back in a little closer than before.

"You're hiding too. Did a bad girl cliché just throw herself at me?"

"I don't throw myself at guys. I don't need to." I tell him with a smirk. "I'm actually trying to avoid a MIP."

I'm *actually* trying to pretend like the massive pecs under my palms aren't doing things to my head right now.

His body goes tense and his hands loosen around me. "Oh shit. How old are you?"

"I'm twenty. I'll turn twenty-one next month."

His hands relax back into place, and his thumb starts moving slowly up and down. "That would suck. But it would be good for your bad-girl rep."

"You're right. What the hell am I hiding in here for?"

My mystery guy flashes a smile, with a perfect row of white teeth, framed by full lips.

"Getting caught making out with the bad boy could score you some points." He says, staring at my mouth.

I gasp. "You really just shot your shot without even knowing my name?"

He drags his hand off my back, fingertips leaving hot trails in their wake, to move a stray red curl behind my ear. Leaving his hand there, he looks intensely into my eyes and asks softly. "What's your name then?"

I have to swallow before telling him, "Dyl..."

A knock and a voice saying, "This is the police." interrupts us. When the door starts to crack open, bad boy jumps into action.

His mouth goes straight to my neck. His hand that's on the side of my face slides quickly to the small of my back to pull our bodies flush against each other.

My entire body lights up like a live wire the second I feel his lips on my skin. The hand that's trapped between our bodies clutches his shirt to bring him closer while my free hand snakes around to the nape of his neck.

I moan, rolling my body into him, feeling him hard *everywhere*. He slides his hand onto my ass at the same time I feel his tongue slip out to lick and suck down to my collarbone.

I hear someone clear their throat, and we pull back, both of us breathing heavily already. I can feel his warm breath on the wetness of my skin, sending a fresh wave of goosebumps.

The cop barks, "The party's over. Everyone needs to go home."

"Yes, sir. We'll leave right now." Bad boy replies, laying his forehead on mine, either for strength or for cover from the cop's sight now that the lights have been flicked on.

After the cop walks off grumbling about horny kids, we remain where we are, just breathing each other in. I open my eyes to find him staring at me. Everything in me wants to lock the door and finish what we just started.

"I need to get ahold of my friend that I came here with. I need to figure out where she is," I whisper, lifting up out of the bed, while he does the same.

He runs a hand through his hair. "I have a truck here. I can take y'all home if you need me to, and you can call her from there if you need a charger or something."

"No offense, but I'll just call an Uber or something. I don't like to ride with people who have been drinking." I try to soften my rejection with a small smile.

"I don't drink." He tells me.

I tilt my head and let the grin widen on my face. "Not very bad boy of you but okay. Thanks."

"Yeah, I guess I'm not your typical bad boy." He says, shooting me a wink.

Geez. I can't take too many winks from this guy or I'm going to be a puddle on the ground.

He takes my hand and pulls me out the back door and around the house. He scopes the place for the cops before we take off to his truck.

It's an older model Ford. It isn't messy but has a layer of dirt on the floor, like maybe he works out of it. The radio, he had to have put in here himself, looks out of place in the older truck, with all of its bright lights and modern technology applied to it.

The door creaks loudly when I shut it after sliding into the passenger seat beside him.

I pull out my phone and click call on Sierra's contact. She answers after three rings.

"Hey, Dyl. I know I just sorta took off. Sorry, I should've sent a text. I left with Casey. Is everything okay?"

"Well, the party got shut down by the cops. You two had to of just missed them. I wanted to make sure you were okay."

"Oh shit! You didn't get in any trouble, did you?" She pulls away from the phone, voice sounding far away when she tells Casey to bring them back.

"Oh no. I'm fine, and I actually have someone to take me home. Don't worry about it. You guys do... whatever you're doing. I'm going to go home and call it a night."

"Are you sure? I really don't mind coming back for you." She says earnestly.

"Go have your fun and give me all the details when you get back."

"Alright. Well, I love you."

"I love you too."

I stare at my phone, worrying about her. Casey seems like such a nice guy. He's been nothing but sweet and completely doting to Sierra for the past couple of nights. But it's hard not to be concerned when we're in such a strange place to us.

My mystery guy starts his truck and looks at me expectantly.

"We're staying at the Dry Creek Hotel. Hopefully that's not too far out of your way or anything." I inform him, just wanting to get back in my bed at this point.

"It's no problem. I guess you're not from around here, are you? You don't sound like it." He grins that crooked grin again before throwing it in drive and taking off down the road.

"No, we're from Ohio. We decided to take a trip before I have to start my internship and we have to go back to school. We're going to start heading back in a couple of days." I lean back into his old cloth seats making myself comfortable.

"Internship? What are you going to school for?"

I huff out a breath. "I'm pre-law." He lets out a low whistle. "I don't really want to bore you with all that, though. What do you do? Are you from around here?"

"I'm from a couple of towns over, basically born and raised here. Been going to college at Dry Creek University. Studying for petroleum engineering." He answers, never taking his eyes off the road.

I just stare at him, surprised. He looks over at me.

"What?" He asks almost defensively.

"I'm just impressed. Not so cliché after all, bad boy."

He rolls his eyes and shakes his head, grinning.

"Do you want to go somewhere before I bring you home?" He asks suddenly. "This is kind of the first night I've been out in a while and not really ready for it to end."

I narrow my eyes at him with playful suspicion. "Where do you have in mind?"

A low chuckle rumbles through the darkness. "It's a surprise."

I should probably have more caution than I do but something about him just seems so... safe.

I think about it for a second and realize I'm not ready to go home either. Or just not ready to leave him. "Why not?"

When we pull up to the lake a few minutes later, he moves to get out of the truck, then pauses to say, "I swear I'm not going to murder you and leave the body out here."

"Oh, I didn't think you were a murderer. How crazy would it be for us both to be murderers?" I look at him with faux-crazy eyes.

He laughs at my lame joke and shakes his head. "Get out of the truck, you dork."

We walk over to the edge of the lake, and I look down when he locks our hands together and pulls me off the path. We have to move some branches as we move through a few trees. We finally make it to the waters edge and sit on a fallen tree trunk.

I look out over the moonlit lake and breathe in the quiet. Taking in the peace and letting everything else fall away.

"I thought you might like it out here." His low voice rumbles out beside me.

"It's so serene. Like you could sit for hours and just let all of life's problems float away." My cheeks heat in embarrassment and I drop my gaze to my feet before sneaking a glance at him through my lashes.

He has a small smile as he watches me. "That's why I come out here. Just to get away from," he hesitates. "...it all. It's quiet and no one really comes out here that often."

He looks back out over the lake with a heaviness I wasn't expecting.

I know I don't really know him, but he looks like he's carrying the weight of the world on his shoulders.

I don't know why, but I want to hug him and tell him everything's going to be okay. I squeeze his hand with mine, only just realizing he never let go.

He turns back to me, confidence settling back into place as he clears his throat. "And to fish."

"There's a park back at home. It has lots of biking trails, hiking spots and camping sites. There's a river that runs through there with a really old bridge. I like to sit out there during the fall. The leaves are so bright and look almost like confetti when they land in the water." I share my spot with him the way he just did with me. Then, to lighten the mood, I add, "But I do *not* fish."

"You don't like to fish?" He tsks. "Damn, for a second I thought I was riding around town with the perfect girl. I was so wrong."

I scoff in mock hurt. Then I realize everything he said and smile. "You think I'm the perfect girl?"

He smiles, showing all of his teeth. "I did. Looks like I'm not a very good judge of character."

Feeling a need to defend myself, I turn to him completely. "Look, I can throw the line all day, but I can't touch the fish. They're slimy and pokey, and don't even try to get me to put the bait on the hook. Squishing a worm in half is just disgusting." I shudder at the thought.

He gives me a beaming smile and proclaims, "Alright, I can work with that. As soon as I get you to fall for me, I'll always be around to bait your hook and hold your fish for you."

"Hold my fish? Is that your idea of how to make me fall for you?" I ask playing along with his game.

"Well, I have a backup plan if that doesn't work."

I toss my head back, laughing at the gall of him. "Oh yeah? What's your backup plan?"

He looks down at me with those intense green eyes of his. "Whatever it takes to keep you laughing like that."

♡ ⅜⅜⅜⅜ ♡

He pulls up to the hotel, and I point him in the direction of my room. When we park, I find myself not wanting to get out.

I open the door and tell him, "Thank you for the ride. And for sharing your hiding spot. Both of them."

I move reluctantly to get out, but he grabs me by the wrist like he did earlier, keeping me in place.

I turn back and find him looking troubled, drawing his thick eyebrows together.

"You could stay in here and we could talk." He clears his throat and fixes his face into a confident smile. "I mean, I can keep you company until your friend gets back or until you get tired."

I bite my lip to contain my excitement. "Or, you could come inside and we can see if there are any good movies on?"

His grin stretches across his face, revealing a dimple. "That sounds good."

We both get out, and I can feel my heart beating a mile a minute as we approach my door together. I run the card through the lock, and he reaches over me, holding the door open to let me in first.

Walking inside and setting my stuff on the tiny table, I hear the door click shut behind me.

I begin my hunt for the remote and start rambling to fill the silence. "It's not the nicest hotel in town, I'm sure, but it's good enough for the two of us for a couple of nights..."

I turn to find him, hands in pockets, watching my every move. I gulp and turn to search for something on the guide.

How does this guy have the ability to knock me so hard off my game?

It's a good thing we're leaving in a couple of days. This boy is serious trouble.

CHAPTER 3
Lane

I step into the little hotel room and glance around before settling my gaze back on the beautiful girl who's completely enthralled me since the moment I laid eyes on her.

Her barely contained mess of dark red curls, her light hazel eyes, tiny nose sprinkled with freckles, pouty lips... the view of her bent over in those cutoffs.

All of it has every ounce of my attention right now.

I need to go back home, but I can't make myself leave her yet. I'm not someone who normally hooks up that often, and not completely sure that's what this is. But I definitely want to.

I'd been dying to kiss her earlier, but I refused to take that mouth for the first time and have her think I was only doing it to put on a show.

When I kiss her, I want her to know it's because I want to.

She turns around and catches me staring at her, but I refuse to look away. I smile when she waves the remote at me and then starts searching through the guide.

"Looks like there's an *Austin Powers* marathon on. Does that work for you?" She asks. When I nod, she adds, "I'm gonna go change. I'll be right back."

She walks back outside to her car, parked just outside the door, and digs clothes out of her luggage in her back seat.

"Why don't you bring all of your stuff inside? Wouldn't that be easier?" I chuckle at her wrestling with closing her suitcase again.

"We tend to sleep in pretty late... on this trip, not all the time or anything... so it's easier for us to just have the car ready to go. We run out of the hotels just in time not to have to pay for another day." She explains heading back inside to the bathroom.

I look around the room again, noticing it does seem untouched, like they hadn't even slept here. Nothing to give me clues to my mystery girl.

Eventually, she walks out of the bathroom in a simple pajama short set. Her hair's piled on top of her head in one of those lazy buns girls do, and she's wiped all the makeup clean off her face, revealing even more freckles on her cheeks.

She was breathtaking before but seeing her like this. She's adorable.

"You ever going to tell me your name?"

She giggles and scrunches up her nose. "I don't know. I kind of like being a mystery you'll never solve. I'll leave in a couple of days, and you'll wonder for the rest of your life, 'Who *was* that almost-perfect girl?'"

Damn, she's going to ruin me.

♡ ⚡ ♡

"...and the manager ran out screaming, 'You can't be on the beaver statue like that!' So, we ran and we took off in our car without even getting gas." She told me her story, throwing her head back in laughter when she finishes.

We'd raided the snack and drink machines before we splayed out on the bed to watch the show. I don't think we've even watched any of it. We just started talking and never stopped.

"Sierra sounds crazy." I muse. "How long have y'all known each other?"

"Pretty much our whole lives. And yeah. She's definitely the fun one of the two of us. If she'd told you that story, you would've actually laughed. She's always been more of a people person than I am."

"I like the way you tell stories." I shrug my shoulders at her. "I just think you enjoy 'em more than anyone else in the room."

"Ha ha. That's because I'm so funny." She slaps at my chest. "It's just that everybody else isn't as funny as I am. Thus, my humor is misunderstood. It's a genuine tragedy in my life."

I laugh at her ridiculous explanation. "That must be it."

She scoffs, then tosses a piece of candy at my face, and I catch it in my mouth.

Yes! That was smooth.

A cocky grin spreads across my face and she rolls her eyes at me and then checks the clock.

"It's pretty late. I guess Sierra's not coming back tonight." She looks my way with a frown on her face. "You don't have to stay. I wouldn't want you driving back too late, or for you to be tortured by my tales."

I probably should get back, but the way she keeps glancing at my mouth makes me think it's now or never. And with this girl, I can't let it be never.

So I slowly lean over, pinning her with my gaze, until I get to where our lips are almost touching.

"Or I could stay."

Her answering smile is all I need to close the gap. My hand moves to the curve of her neck, tilting her head so I can take her mouth fully.

I kiss her slowly at first, just enjoying the taste of her, but when I feel her tongue slide out to join mine, I lose it.

My hand moves down to palm her ass and pull her underneath me. She arches her hips to meet mine and lets out a groan at the unmistakable evidence of how much I already want her.

I feel her hands pulling at my shirt, so I lean back to take it off.

I know I look good. I work out a lot, and the hungry look in her eyes when she takes me in makes it all worth it.

The corner of my mouth turns up on one side. "Your turn."

My perfect mystery woman doesn't disappoint. She pops an eyebrow, giving me a sultry smile, and takes her shirt off next.

Her pale skin gleams in the dim light, only accented by the dark lacy bra she's wearing. Every curve draws me in and leaves me undone.

I'm going to devour every single bit of her.

I drop my mouth back to hers, partly to wipe that smug-ass look off her face.

Don't get me wrong. Her confidence is sexy as hell, but I need her drooling over me, not the other way around.

Her fingers dig into the nape of my neck while her other hand runs down my chest and around to grab at my back. I press in deeper between her legs, savoring the way her body molds to mine.

My lips trail down the curve of her neck until they find the soft swell of her breasts. Sliding her straps aside and pulling the cup of her bra down, I take her nipple into my mouth.

Soft sounds escape her pushing me forward.

Every time she lifts of her hips to meet mine it surges through me like a jolt straight to my core.

I trail one hand down and slide her shorts to the side, finding only smooth, bare skin. A low chuckle slips out. "Commando? Huh? Personal choice, or did you just think I was a sure thing?" I mutter into her skin.

She starts to snark back at me. "Oh, I knew you were a sure thing..."

I silenced her sass when my fingers slide through her slick folds, finding her sensitive clit.

"Oh God." She presses her head back into the pillow with a groan, one hand clawing at my hair.

Fuck. She's drenched.

A feral part of me can't wait to taste her.

I work my fingers and tongue in sync to completely unravel her. I move from one breast to the other, occasionally thrusting a finger into her tight, dripping heat.

Every moan and whimper she makes stokes the ache to be inside her.

Her body squirms beneath me, her core tightening until I finally work her to completion. Screaming at me not to stop, she wraps herself around me, pulling me closer as she rides out her orgasm.

I feel like a man starved.

I lick and suck my way back up her throat until we're face to face.

Deciding I can't help myself, I suck her juices off of my fingers and watch her eyes widen and mouth part.

While she catches her breath, I tell her. "We can stop now or… I have a condom in my wallet."

She grabs my face with both hands to quickly kiss my mouth. "Go get the condom."

After untangling her body from mine, I stand to the side of the bed and pull the wallet out of my shorts.

"Oh no, is that what I felt the whole time?"

I look down at my dick, standing firmly at attention, then back at her with an eyebrow raised.

She giggles, waving both of her hands at me. "Sorry, bad joke."

I laugh at her, pulling the condom out of my wallet. "You really do think you're so funny, don't you?." But her giggles come to a halt when I pull my shorts down to slip on the condom.

I glance back over at her, and point two fingers at my face. "Excuse me, my eyes are up here." She lets out a nervous laugh, but looks back up into my eyes. "See, I make bad jokes, too." I grin down at her.

She narrows her eyes at me and stands up out of the bed. Never breaking eye contact, she takes off all of her clothes with a small smirk, in challenge.

It took every ounce of my willpower, but I win this round by never sneaking a peek. I just let out a big grin before I lean in to steal her lips once more.

I fall back onto the bed, pulling her with me, where she's laid out on top of me.

I let out a groan of my own when I feel her bare breasts pressing into my chest.

My hands travel where my eyes couldn't, while she moves to plant her knees on each side of me.

She lifts to reach between us and wraps her hand around my cock. I let out a hissed breath when she strokes up and down, creating the friction I desperately needed.

"Fuck! That feels so good." I say into her mouth before she moves to nibble on my neck, sending shivers all over me.

She lifts up and I feel her hips shift. She hovers her entrance over my tip, teasing us both.

Slowly, she lowers herself onto me, clenching my jaw as her tight pussy wraps around every inch of my cock, and I never take my eyes off of her.

I watch her soak in the feeling of being full, and I drink in every detail of her face. Her eyes are heavy, and her pink plump lips are just slightly parted. Both my hands are on either side of her waist while hers rests on my sternum.

"Damn. You look almost perfect up there."

Fucking perfect riding me like this.

"Almost?" She breathes out with a smile at our inside joke.

Then she starts moving.

I stay still at first, just wanting to enjoy the feel of her, only encouraging her movement with my grip on her sides.

I feel us both getting closer to the edge. Then I use my feet, still planted on the floor, to meet her thrusts, to push deeper inside of her.

"Fuck. Yes!" She groans out, matching my pace.

I could feel myself getting close to the edge, so I move a hand for my thumb to rub circles on her clit.

"Come for me, baby. I'm so close. You're driving me fucking crazy."

She yells out and feel her tighten around me. I drive into her a few more times when her orgasm stutters her movements, then I fly over the edge with her.

She falls into my arms, resting her head on my chest. We both lay there catching our breaths, before I roll us onto our sides.

She watches me when I lift my hand to straighten out a curl that had broken free from its restraint. I grin when it bounces back into place, then I tuck it behind her ear and let my hand rest there.

"It's Dylan." She tells me so softly I almost can't hear her. "My name is Dylan."

The grin on my face deepens.

"Lane. Nice to meet you."

I wake up the next morning reaching for her, but the space beside me is empty.

Maybe she had to pee.

I can't believe how incredible last night was. I know she lives in Ohio, and I have some shit on my plate, but I can't let her go without trying something. We can still talk, and I don't know... just try something.

Oh shit. What time is it? I really need to get home.

I yell out for her to hear in the bathroom. "Hey, I know how this will sound, but I really need to go home. I really think we should exchange numbers, though. I know you have to go back. And maybe one night is all you wanted, but.." I trail off listening for any noise or response.

I get up and walk to the door that separates us, slowly twisting the knob, easing it open in case she's in there.

It's empty.

Did she go get breakfast?

I look outside, and her car's gone. I put on my clothes and wait for a bit. I get a sinking feeling that I know what happened, but I go to the front desk.

"Hi, I was wondering—did you happen to see where the girl from room 122 went?"

The lady gives me an embarrassed look and answeres, "She came in this morning and paid for one more day, saying you might still be asleep past the 11:00 a.m. checkout." She can't look me in the eye when she continues, "She also told me that if you came here asking about her, I absolutely couldn't tell you anything about her."

CHAPTER 4

Dylan

"So you just left him there!?" Sierra screeches at me from the passenger seat.

"I know, but what else was I supposed to do? It was a one-night thing, two at best. We're leaving anyway." I reply, exasperated.

"So why the melodramatic exit?" Sierra asks, looking at me in utter confusion. Shock flits across her face before the pointed accusations follow. "You really like him!"

I stiffen. "I just met him."

"Yeah, but you hook up all the time and you've never been weird about it. You even stayed friends with most of them. You just *ran...* from him, from that town, from that freaking state, Dyl! You must've really, *really* liked him."

I sigh, staring ahead at the long road leading us back home. I managed to wake up before him this morning, and I knew I had to get out of there.

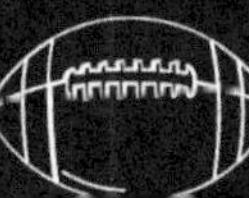

After grabbing the few things I had in the room, and paying for an extra night, I took off to find my friend, and we started our way back to Ohio.

Everything about him was just so... intense. I knew that I couldn't stay.

He's the type of guy you'd give up everything for, and I just can't do that to myself.

I can't end up like my mother.

She'd given up everything for my dad and me—her career, the best years of her life, even her heart. And in the end, she was left with nothing but bitterness and loneliness.

Mom was in law school when she met my dad and fell head over heels. Not too long after that, she wound up with little ole' me and dropped out to take care of her family.

And we were a good family... for a while.

My dad isn't a bad guy, he's always been there for me my whole life for whatever I needed. But... he loves love. Unfortunately, not the true everlasting kind, the kind that'll fight through all of the hardships and monotony of a marriage. My mother's the closest he ever got to that.

He loves the chase and rush of all the firsts. The roller-coaster of emotions, with the lows that make the highs feel higher.

My mother just fell in love, and when he left her for the next chase, she never got over it. She also never let me forget how he ruined her life.

By example and endless warnings, she sketched out the life

I'd have if I quit school and never became what she should've been.

I took it to heart and swore to myself I'd never repeat her mistakes.

My plan is simple. College. Law school. Career.

A family?

Someday, but not until every duck is lined up perfectly.

"It doesn't matter. We'd never work. I have so much I need to focus on, and long distance never works. Best just to let it drop." There's no use in denying it, she knows me too well.

"I knew it! We have to go back. You have to at least try. I've never seen you like this over a guy ever."

"No."

"Yes!"

"NO!"

"YES!"

"No! That one night is probably all he wanted, anyway. Why else hook up with the out-of-towner?" She looks defeated, as if she hadn't even thought of that. "I know you love a good romance, but this isn't one of your books. This is real life, and mine and his happen to exist on opposite ends of the country."

She crosses her arms and looks out the window. "Fine. Maybe I romanticize things a bit, but at least I don't just avoid it altogether."

I jerked my head toward her, a little in shock at the anger exuding from her.

"You know I have a plan."

"Yeah. Yeah. The plan of living out the life your mom never had. But what if you let the love of your life pass you up one day because you're too focused on not being your mom? You may have your career, but you'll still be alone." She softens the blow at the end by laying her hand on my shoulder.

I know Sierra has the best of intentions and is only concerned about me, but she just doesn't understand.

Not really wanting to fight or dive too deep into this particular conversation, I say, "Well, I'll always have you so I won't be alone." I look at her with a half-smile I'm using as a white flag. "Unless you ditch me for your cowboy. How was last night? Is it true what they say about everything being bigger in Texas?" I ask, wiggling my eyebrows suggestively.

Lips pursed, and a brow arched, she lets me know she knows exactly what I'm trying to do. Still, she lets it go and answers my questions with enthusiasm.

After a grueling few days of driving, we finally make it home.

Sierra walks home across the street, dragging her luggage

behind her, after I hug her goodbye and tell her I'll see her later.

"Mom, I'm back." I shout walking through the front door of my childhood home. I drop all of my bags at the entryway before walking towards the kitchen. The wide space as familiar to me as it was grand.

Tall arched ceilings lead me to my destination. The marble counters and stainless steel appliances make this room look like it belongs in a magazine.

It wasn't too long after my father's career took off that my parents got their divorce, but my dad moved us into this huge house a couple of years before he left.

He kept paying the mortgage afterwards, probably out of guilt. So, we got to live in this mansion of a house while my mom worked a clerical job at a law firm.

It was a little much for two people, but with Mom and Dad both coming from money, they're used to a pretty cushy life, and my mom never thought twice about us living here.

She's pouring herself a glass of lemonade when I find her.

"Hey, Mom."

"Oh, honey. I'm so glad you're back. I missed you. How was your trip?" She asks before wrapping me in her arms with a quick hug.

My mother and I share the same hair color, and that's pretty much where the similarities end. Hers is sleek and straight, mine wild and curly. She's small and petite, while I carry fuller curves. Her dark brown eyes warm her features, and unlike me, she barely has any freckles.

While I'm usually a little more relaxed in my dress, she's the picture of posh. Always put together perfectly.

"We had so much fun! You won't believe how long it took us to drive across Texas. It's massive!"

"I've been absolutely sick thinking about you two, all by yourselves." She dramatically proclaims, placing a hand over her heart.

"Mom, you shouldn't worry so much." I pause before adding, "The guy who gave us all those drugs swore it wasn't laced with anything." I tease her with a mischievous smile.

"Dylan Sterling Whitlock! You'd better be joking." Fists resting on her hips now.

Ouch, not two minutes in the door and I'm already getting the whole name?

"Yes, Mother. No drugs were taken on the trip in question." I roll my eyes. "We had a few drinks, and that's it." A lot of drinks, but she doesn't need all of the gory details.

"That's your father's sense of humor coming out of you." She huffs out.

My face falls in aggravation, not wanting her to get started on the bashing dad conversation. That could go on for a while.

"We were safe, I promise. We paid for rides if we knew we were going to drink and stuck together so no stranger would kidnap us or anything."

"Well, that's good. Now that you're back, maybe you could talk to your father about starting your internship a little earlier. He may have screwed me out of my career, but at least he's helping you with yours." She replies with a pointed look.

Once again ignoring the father comments, I hedge, "I don't know, Mom."

Her eyes widen in horror. "What do you mean? You're not having second thoughts, are you? Baby, you've worked so hard for this. You don't want to give up now."

I look into her panicked eyes. I'm not sure how to explain to her how I'm feeling or why I'm suddenly pushing back against her. I don't really understand it myself, or where this reluctance is coming from.

I've just had this feeling since even before the trip, that it all just feels wrong. It's probably nerves, so I let her know just that.

"No second thoughts. I'm wanting to wait until after my birthday. I think I'm just a little nervous about going to work at Dad's office and what everyone else will think about me being his daughter." I let out a heavy breath, knowing that isn't quite what I'm feeling but definitely a part of it.

"None of that! You've worked so hard. You were top of your class and still are. Nobody handed that to you. You're going to be the best." She grabs another glass cup out of the cabinet and fills it up before handing it to me.

"I'll be sure to let them know my mom said so." I crack a grin before taking a sip.

"Oh, you're such a pain. I'm trying to help you. I could do

without the smart-ass remarks." She sighs, letting her head fall into one dainty hand. "Are you sure that's all?"

I hesitate a moment before answering. "Of course, Mom. I'll get over my nerves. Why would I care what anyone else thinks, anyway? I just want to wait until after my birthday. Sierra probably has big plans, so I don't want to take time off right after starting."

"Okay, I just don't want you to quit this when you've made it this far. Especially over something as trivial as worrying about what other people will think. You have a plan, you need to stick with it. Everything will work out just fine." She says, cupping my face with one hand, and driving her point home with those piercing eyes of hers.

She's right. I'm not sure where all of this just came from. Maybe I let Sierra get in my head a little bit.

"You're right. I'm going to go put my things away in my room and maybe rest for a while. That was a very long drive."

Mom walks around the bar grabbing her glass and flipping through a magazine. "Sure baby. I'll let you know when I have dinner ready."

"Thanks, Mom."

I gather all of my things before heading upstairs to my room.

I open the door to see that everything is neat and in its place. My canopy bed is draped in sheer white lace down to my fluffy sage green comforter.

My vanity sits between two windows, with curtains to match my comforter, and my desk sits off in the corner on the other side of the room.

I make my way to my walk-in closet and begin putting away all the clean laundry and sliding shoes into their homes on built-in shelves.

I dump all of the dirty clothes into the basket in my bathroom, looking longingly at the tub. I consider taking a bath, but my bed is just too tempting.

Leaving behind my jetted tub, I make my way back into my room. I fling myself onto my bed with loose limbs sprawled out wide like a starfish.

Green eyes run through my head, making me groan out loud.

This is ridiculous. I have to get him out of my head. It's done. I left with absolutely no way to contact him again, so there's no point in dwelling on it.

I have to get back to my own life, just like I'm sure he's already gone back to his.

Right?

CHAPTER 5
Lane

Fuck! I can't stop thinking about Dylan. I don't know where I went wrong and what made her so determined to leave without so much as a goodbye.

I tried everything I could to find her or just learn more about her. I went back to the house where we met. Nobody knew a Dylan or a Sierra.

I wish I could've found the guy Sierra was with that night and beg him for her number.

Maybe if I'd been able to drag my eyes off of Dylan dancing, I might have recognized any of the people she was dancing with.

I sink into the rhythm of the bench press, pushing to better myself and trying to press away the thoughts of her.

"Man, keep sulking over some girl like *this* and you'll end up training yourself into a first-round pick." Nate grins down from where he's spotting me.

I met Nate my second year in college, when he strutted onto the football team as a cocky freshman receiver fresh off his high school glory days. As the team's starting cornerback, I thought I could shut down some of that ego when I knocked him on his ass after he caught the ball on a hitch route.

When we lined up for the next play, he smiled at me around his mouth guard and said, "Nice hit, old man. Now let's see if you can keep up."

When the snap was made, he slipped past me down the field with lightning speed I wasn't expecting and made the catch before I knocked him out of bounds.

Laughing, I hauled him up with one hand. He smirked at me, all arrogance, so I snapped at him, "Don't get cocky freshman, you're still out of bounds."

"Yeah out of bounds halfway down the field after smoking your ass."

And just like that, our reluctant friendship was born.

Racking the bar, I sit up breathing heavily, I answer Nate. "You know I'm not chasing the draft. Football's just scholarship money. My career will end with college. And I always train this hard. I'd never let my teammates down."

I do love football. It's always been my way out. My way out of my house when I was younger, my way to college, my way out of my head.

Four quarters at a time... it's just me and the game.

NFL just isn't in the cards for me.

"I'm calling bullshit, Lane. Nobody works this hard at something that they don't care about. Just like you don't spend weeks chasing down a mystery girl that you pretend to have forgotten."

Deciding to bypass the football argument we'd hashed out a dozen times, I reply, "Well, what am I supposed to do? She left, making damn sure I had no way to reach her."

"Doesn't really sound like a problem to me." Nate chuckles.

I groan out my frustration and make my way around the bench to remove some weight before sliding into place to take my turn spotting.

Nate lays out on the bench, gripping the bar before saying, "You met her once, man. One night. What did she do to get under your skin like this? Any girl who can leave my best friend high and dry doesn't deserve this much headspace."

"You're one to talk. You leave every girl high and dry." I throw at him defensively.

"I leave 'em… not dry though." He gives me a cocky smile, punctuating the line with the lift of the weights.

I can't help but laugh at him.

"You're right. It was just one night. It doesn't matter. I've got more important shit to deal with, anyway. I mean, at this point, if I don't let it go, I'm going to start looking like an obsessed psycho-creeper."

"Start?" he grunts, face red from exertion.

"Yeah, fuck off." He drops the bar back into its place and stands up to lean on one of the neighboring machines.

"Look, it meant one thing to you, and something different to her. It doesn't make her a bad person, Mr. Defensive. It just makes her gone." He slaps me on the shoulder. "All this suffering-in-silence extra training is going to do wonders for your game, though. Might even be able to catch me soon."

I can't stand this asshole.

I check him with my shoulder on my way to do leg presses. "We need to hurry. Your dad said we need to have that fence fixed by the end of the day."

"I'm not the least bit worried about the wrath of my dad," Nate tells me, brushing me off. "Now if one of those cows gets out upsetting my mom, we may have some problems."

I shake my head and start my reps.

I know I'm being crazy. It makes zero sense for me to be hung up on this girl. But she's all I think about. Every time I lay my head down at night and all throughout the day.

I can hear her stupid jokes, her laugh that made her throw her head all the way back... the way she moans.

I can see her skin glowing under the moonlight by the lake, her dark auburn hair that refused to be contained, her eyes heavy with longing, drinking me in like I was all she needed.

I think mostly I long for the way she made me feel that night. It was like how I feel when I play. An escape. Only with her I didn't feel like I was running from something. She felt like something to run to.

Unfortunately, neither was going to be an option for my future.

Not the game. And certainly not the girl.

CHAPTER 6

Dylan

I t's July 24th!

My favorite day of the year!

My Birthday!

HAPPY BIRTHDAY, BEST FRIEND!!! I LOVE YOU 🥹

> Thank you!!!! I love you too 🤍

Get up and go get us some alcohol for your party tonight! You're finally legal!!

TWENTY FREAKING ONE!

>  Come over before so we can get dressed together and pregame.

I'll be there soon 👍

I swipe through my phone, looking through texts and socials, thanking everyone for my happy birthday messages.

My mom walks in right when I finish sending my last thank-you message.

"Happy birthday, baby." She comes for me, arms open, and wraps me up. She pulls back teary-eyed, grasping my face with both hands. "How can you possibly be this grown? I swear I just took you home from the hospital, bundled up in a tiny blanket."

"Thank you, Mom. And it felt like a hundred years to me. I can't wait to finally buy my own alcohol...well legally. Speaking of," I look at her innocently. "When are you heading to Nonnie's?"

"Please don't destroy my house tonight." She demands, shooting daggers at me.

"We won't. There'll only be a few friends over, and I'll keep it all in the backyard."

She sighs loudly. "Yeah sure. I was in college once too, you know. Just don't go crazy."

"I swear!" I throw up three fingers in a Scout's honor salute. "I'll be on my best behavior-ish."

Rolling her eyes at me, she answers my question from earlier. "I was actually coming to tell you goodbye. I wanted to get an early start on the trip so I could get there at a decent time. Since you're too old to hang out with your old bat of a mom on your birthday now, I'll go be with mine."

"I don't think you're an old bat. You should stay. You can

be on my team for flip cup." I tell her, hoping that it would dissuade her from staying.

She looks completely disgusted. "Absolutely not. I'll see you in a few days."

I hug her again, giggling at her horror-filled face. "Okay. I love you, Mom. Drive safe."

♡ ⥫⥫⥫⥫ ♡

The toaster jumped with my toast, and I already have the avocado mashed and waiting on the counter.

After smearing the mushy green stuff all over the toast and sprinkling on some seasoning, I pour myself a glass of milk.

I flop down on my living room couch and flip on the TV. I sink my teeth into the toast, moaning with pleasure. I go to wash it down with my milk and take a sip before halting in my tracks.

The milk had gone bad.

The smell hits my nose, and a sour, curdled taste coats my tongue. Gagging, I bolt to the bathroom, hand over mouth, barely making it in time to hurl everything into the toilet.

I hear Sierra yelling through the door after my second round of upchucks. "Birthday girl, where are you?"

I gag out the last of it, the sound echoing way too loud.

A second later, she bursts into the bathroom, eyes wide

with worry. "Oh no, Dyl-pickle. Are you sick?" She kneels beside me, pulling my hair out of the way.

I lean back, wiping the back of my hand across my mouth.

"Milk was bad." I croak out.

"Oh shit. That's disgusting." She shudders. "How about I go clean up your breakfast and you go take a shower and get cleaned up?"

"Yeah, thanks. I'll be right back."

I shuffle my way up to my bathroom and turn on the hot water. After tossing my dirty clothes into the hamper, I step into the steady stream.

I lean my head back, letting the water cascade down the length of my body.

Memories of his calloused hands running up my side to cradle my face flash through my mind.

"Fuck, Dylan. I didn't think you could be any more beautiful, but your soaking body is going to be burned into my mind for the rest of my life." He murmurs into my neck.

I pull at his wet hair at the back of his head so I can drag his mouth back to mine.

He lifts me by my ass to push me up against the cold wall. I gasp at the loss of the warm spray of the shower, but quickly lose myself in him again.

I wrap my legs around his waist, pressing my heels into his back to hold him as close to me as I can. I can feel the rigid heat of his dick brushing against the curve of my cheeks.

He has one hand holding me in place while the other traveled all over my body. I have to pull my head back and catch my breath.

He lays his forehead on mine, keeping our eyes locked. The sheer force of him sears through me, heat spreading from the inside out.

I want to run from this feeling, but something about him holds me steady. Like the best kind of anchor, keeping me in this moment.

"You feel like something I'm not supposed to keep... but damn it if I don't want to."

"Dylan? You good in there?" I hear Sierra yell out over the rush of the water.

"Yeah, just washing my hair." I rasp out, my throat dry and rough.

I finish getting the shampoo out of my hair, throw in some conditioner before shaving everything and completely rinsing everything off. I step out of the steam of the shower and wrap a towel around me.

"Sorry about that. I just got so grossed out. I certainly won't be able to drink milk for a while." I apologize to Sierra, stepping out of my bathroom into my room.

"I'm just glad you made it to the toilet. You know I'm a sympathy vomiter. If I'd seen it, I would've been done for." She covers her mouth as if just the thought might have already got to her.

"Mom already took off, so we have the entire house to

ourselves for a couple of days." I tell her as I search through my drawers for underwear.

"Sweet!" She exclaims while bouncing on my bed. "Let me do your makeup tonight... and hair... and pick your outfit. I want you looking hotter than hot, not your 'I'm-an-uptight-lawyer-so-I-have-to-dress-like-I-file-taxes-for-fun' thing you do."

"Hey, I look hotter than hot every day, no matter what I wear." I argue with her, but take a seat at my vanity for her to work her magic.

She snorts, reaching for my hair products first. "The confidence is crazy."

"You aren't going to dry my hair and straighten it?" I ask, when she begins running the cream through my damp locks.

"Absolutely not... your curls will be as wild as I expect you to be tonight. Like on our trip. I also have this fancy wing I want to try with your eyeliner. Ugh, wait. Let's go pick out your outfit first so I know what color eyeshadow."

I wrap the towel tighter around me and tuck it so I can use my hands before sauntering over to my closet.

"I actually have two outfits I couldn't decide on. I have your basic but cute little black dress." I tell her holding out the first option in front of me.

"I love it. What's the other option?"

I hold out the outfit I picked for my first day of interning. "This adorable khaki pantsuit. I could even leave the top button undone. Party mode activated." I hold my face together as long as I can, but Sierra's look of horror is too much.

"You almost had me for a second." She pulls the dress off its hanger to throw it at me. "Try this on, you butthead."

I put on my matching black lace bra and thong first. "It may still be a little 'I-do-taxes-for-fun,' but like in the hottest way, right?" I ask when I get the dress in place.

"Holy shit, your boobs look amazing! Did the dress come with a push-up bra?"

I step up to the full-length mirror and take in the tutu bottom that lands perfectly on my thighs. Not too short, but not too long either. It pulls in at the waist, shaping me into an easy hourglass. And... holy knockers!

"Damn, maybe I should've tried the dress on first. It's a little tight on top, isn't it?"

"I think you look perfect. Don't overthink it." She rushes to say.

"Okay. I'm going to change back into this later. For now, I'm going to throw on some clothes to go use my actual license to get us some alcohol." I squeal in excitement.

Sierra jumps to attention. "Oh, I'm going too. I want to film it."

"No." I deadpan, pulling a shirt over my head.

"Fine," she huffs. "But I still want to go. I can at least be a witness."

I roll my eyes at her before I finish getting dressed and head for my keys.

♡ ⚡ ♡

I have the speakers turned up loud enough for everyone to hear the music, but not loud enough to piss off the neighbors. The smell of chlorine hangs heavy in the air, kicked up with every splash and dive.

I slip through the crowd with a tray of jello shots and make my way to the patio table my best friend has claimed as her stage.

Sierra is mid-sentence when I catch her attention. "Behold the birthday queen!" She slams into my side, reaching for the tray. "And she brings us offerings."

"Seems you've had your fair share of 'offerings.'" I say, laying the tray on the table for everyone to take a shot.

"Uh-oh." Her eyes go wide.

"What do you mean, 'uh-oh'?" I ask, wary of where this is going.

Sierra loops her arm through mine. "Somebody's having trouble getting out of stick up ass mode. Come on, it's your birthday. Do a damn shot."

I look at the jello shots she's reaching for, and my entire body revolts at the idea.

But she's right. I need to start somewhere to get out of this mood I'm in. I really don't want to be a party pooper when she worked so hard to get all of this put together.

"Alright," I smile indulgently at my adorable best friend. "Hand me one."

"Yes!" She pumps her fist like it was a huge accomplishment for her.

When Sierra has everyone in our immediate vicinity a jello shot in hand, she lifts hers up and yells out, "To Dylan! Happy 21st birthday!"

Cheers erupt everywhere as we slam our plastic cups together and all slurp down the cherry-flavored slime.

I swallow down a violent shudder, the taste-memory of that rotten milk slamming into me like a freight train. Nope. No way. Jello shots could go to hell. I won't be doing any more tonight for damn sure.

I put on a good face and slip into full party mode. I cheer when everyone else cheers. I laugh when someone did something funny— even when it's only drunk-people funny, the kind that's annoying when you're the only sober one.

I try sipping on a beer but my stomach is just not having it.

When the last person finally stumbles out, I nearly cry with relief.

I pick up a couple of cups to clean up before deciding... Nope, absolutely not.

Sierra is currently starfished across my bed, drooling on my pillow. Her ass can help in the morning.

After pushing Sierra to her side of the bed, I roll onto my belly and cradle my head in my pillow and immediately fall asleep.

The next morning I wake up to a churning stomach and bile in my throat. I sleepily dash to the toilet in my bathroom just in the nick of time.

Sierra groggily stumbles to the entrance and starts laughing at my expense. "Looks like someone partied hard for their birthday."

When I finally finish up, I sit on the floor and lay back against the cool wood of my cabinets. "Sierra, I shouldn't be throwing up right now."

She waves a hand dismissively. "It's fine. You're allowed to get as sloshed as you want on your 21st birthday, dude. I'm pretty hungover right now and it wasn't even mine."

I shake my head at her. "You don't understand. I didn't get drunk."

My mind is racing, trying to figure out how bad of food poisoning you can get from rotten milk.

I continue to explain. "I did that one jello shot with you and had one beer. That's it."

"Umm Dyl?"

"What? Do you think that milk could've poisoned me? Should I go to the emergency room?" I ask, trying to think of everything that could have me in this situation.

"Dylan!" She yells trying to get my full attention.

"What?"

Sierra looks at me carefully.

"I think you need to remember the last time you had a period."

CHAPTER 7

Dylan

"**N**o!"

I'm shaking my head in denial.

"No, that can't be it. I mean, it was a couple of weeks ago on our trip." I start panicking, trying to piece together memories with dates. "Remember, I had to throw away a pair of panties at that gas station with the dinosaur?!" I yell at her to fix this for me.

"Umm, yeah…that was at the very beginning of our trip. We hadn't even made it to Texas yet. That was exactly six weeks ago."

She moves towards me slowly, as if I'm a wounded animal that you need to be careful around. She sits beside me and holds my hand.

"Look, don't start freaking out and thinking the world is ending and your lifelong plan is in shambles. I'll go get you a test." I jerk my head up to meet her eyes. "Or two. Just to make damn sure."

"Sure, okay. It's probably just stress from the internship or something. No big deal."

"Yeah, I'm sure that's it." She tells me with a forced smile.

"Just go get the test so I can show you. You're coming off super condescending right now." I huff out.

"Geez, okay, I'm getting dressed." She gets up and walks out of the bathroom door and whispers loud enough for me to hear. "Pregnancy hormones: check."

♡ ⫘⫘ ♡

POSITIVE!

"Holy shit! It's fucking positive!" I yell at Sierra. "What the hell am I going to do?"

I take one of the other ones she bought and dip it in the cup full of my urine.

Two pink fucking lines.

"Is it Lane's?" Sierra asks softly from behind me.

"Well yeah. I haven't had sex with anyone else." I answer still entranced by the pregnancy tests I'm holding.

"You didn't use protection?"

"Of course we used protection... the first time." I mumble out the last part quickly and quietly.

"THE FIRST TIME?! JESUS! First of all, you held back on me. There was no mention of multiple penetrations—"

I make a face. "Eww, don't call it that."

"Second: Why in the hell did you not use protection both times?"

"Fuck! I don't know. We were just in the shower, and it just kind of happened. I wasn't thinking at all. I mean, I'm on the pill. That should've done the job, right?" My voice cracks on the last word.

She looks at me with pity. "It should've." Then she snaps her fingers at me. "The shots!"

"I wasn't going to do the pill and the shot. That's a bit overkill." I tell her, exasperated.

She looks at me like I'm the crazy one. "No, you weirdo. The shots from the night at the bar. You spent all morning throwing them up."

My eyes widen. "Shit, you're right."

For the first time in my life, my entire world has changed in an instant. I don't think I truly understood that statement until this exact moment.

"Holy shit. I'm having a baby. I'm having his baby." I can feel the tears building in my eyes, blurring my vision.

Sierra's arms go around me before she softly asks, "What are you going to do?"

What *am* I going to do?

This is going to ruin everything. My whole life I've worked toward one goal, and this is the one thing I was always told would derail the whole thing.

What an idiot I am to let this happen. My mom has always said... SHIT!

"My mom's going to lose it! She's told me my entire life how having a baby ruined her career." The tears are a steady stream now, while my fingers are clawing through my hair.

"That's such bullshit!" She grits her teeth in frustration. "Lots of women have kids and a career."

"Yeah, well, I seriously doubt the firm wants a pregnant intern. And what then? How am I supposed to raise a kid, stay in school, and pass the BAR? As a single mom? Or with a guy I basically don't know! That's impossible, Sierra. I can't... I think I should..." The words catch in my throat. The logic feels obvious, but the reality of it is so heavy.

"Dyl, are you thinking about getting an abortion?" She asks me softly.

"Does that make me a terrible person?" I'm scared to look her in the eyes and see what they might reveal about her thoughts of me.

"Of course not! Look at me." She grabs my face in both hands, forcing my eyes to meet hers. "I'll NEVER judge you or think less of you if you decide that keeping the baby isn't the right decision. Do you understand?"

She's looking at me so intensely, like every part of her needs me to believe that. And I nod my head, letting her know I believe her.

"What I'm scared of," she continues in a gentler tone. "is that you're making this decision based on a fear that, personally, I think's more your mom's than yours. Just make sure you think about this before you decide anything for sure. I'll be there for you either way."

She holds me close to her and I wrap my arms around her needing her to be my strength for a moment.

When I get myself together, I pull out of her arms and look at the two bright pink lines, and it feels like they're rewriting my entire future in permanent marker.

"Thank you, Sierra. I love you for that." And I do. I know she'll have my back through all of this.

"If you don't mind, I think I just want a little time to myself. Maybe take the day to process before I have to tell my mom tomorrow morning." Sniffling, I go in for the hug I desperately need and take a few extra seconds of comfort from her but pull away before I fall apart completely.

"Absolutely! Just be on the lookout for my texts. I'll be super worried about you, so please just answer me back, okay?"

After she leaves, I connect my phone to the speaker in my room and let my music play. I don't really pay much attention to the songs. I just lay on my side on top of my comforter and let my racing mind calm down a little.

All I can think about is how this is going to ruin everything. Everything I've done in my life has been done with one goal in mind.

I've always been at the top of my class. Joined multiple clubs and organizations, even sports, so that my college applications would shine.

When I got into the college I wanted, it was the same thing. I rarely partied, denying any distraction. I studied constantly, planned, networked, and did everything by the book so I could land an internship at a good firm.

Yes, I did end up at the one my father is a partner in. His happens to be the best.

Now it feels like all that hard work was for nothing. Like I'm standing at the edge of becoming exactly what I swore I'd never be: a resentful, bitter mom with a dream that died in her hands.

Calm green eyes, sparkling from the lights off the lake, flash in my mind, making me wish I was back in that place. Like maybe *there* I could find the answers I can't seem to find here.

Then I remember the look in his eyes when he thought I wasn't watching him. He clearly has a life and problems of his own. Even if I could find him, he almost certainly wouldn't want to add this to whatever burdens he already carries.

I think it's obvious what I should do.

Everything can just... go back to normal.

Mom won't have a conniption about history repeating itself, or about me "ruining my life."

I can stay on track. Keep my internship, crush law school, and maybe even make partner one day.

And a boy over a thousand miles away, will never have to shoulder the weight of a baby... or the fallout of a decision he never asked for.

♡ ⊶⊷ ♡

"Dylan!"

A familiar voice is sing-songing through the hall into my room.

I lift my face out of the drool that had gathered on my pillow. I must've drifted off at some point last night.

I quickly grab my phone that's facedown on the bed beside me, and check the time.

10:30.

How did I sleep so long? I must've stayed up later than I thought.

"Mom, I'm in my room." I groggily yell out, followed shortly by the sound of my door swinging open.

"Oh my goodness! How much did you drink on your birthday? Are you still hungover? You look terrible."

"Thanks, Mom." I say with little emotion while I sit up.

"I see my house stayed intact and everything was cleaned up."

Oh no!

That must've been Sierra. I completely forgot about the cleanup. I'll definitely need to remember to thank her for that.

"Nothing crazy happened anyway. Just a few of our friends hanging around the pool." I was stalling, and I knew it.

Letting her keep having a casual conversation with me like I wasn't carrying around her biggest fear in my belly.

It was best just to rip the band-aid off, but once I tell my mom, it just seems like it will make it all too real.

"How did that dress we picked out look? I wish I'd have seen you in it before I left. Did you get a picture?"

Fuck it just do it. Get it over with.

"Mom."

"Yeah?"

I open my mouth but nothing comes out.

Damn it, come on you pansy just say it.

"I, uh... have something... I ummm... I need to tell you." I fumble through my words not sure how to start.

"This can't be good if you can't even manage to get it out." She sinks down on the end of my bed and rubs my feet through the blanket for encouragement, but readies herself for what I'm about to tell her.

I feel the stupid tears in my eyes again for the billionth time in not even two whole days.

"Mom, I'm pregnant."

She stiffens, going completely still. Even her rubbing comes to a complete halt after my words drop in the room like an atom bomb.

My stomach begins to twist. Morning sickness? Fear? Maybe both?

"Mom?"

"Is this one of your stupid jokes?"

I flinch at the anger in her voice. "No Mom." The tears were starting to fall now. "It was an accident. There was this guy in Texas... and we were safe, but it happened anyway, and I'm thinking I should probably get an abortion, so everything will go back to normal..."

I race through my explanation to her. My words falling onto the one person I need to make this better for me.

"Well of course you're getting an abortion. How many times have I told you that a baby will completely ruin your life? I can't believe you did something so stupid." She says harshly.

I bristle at her demand to get an abortion, like I didn't even have a choice. "Geez, Mom. Believe me, I know. You've never let me forget that having me was your biggest regret, but I thought maybe you could ask me how I was feeling about all of it. I know you're upset, but this is hard for me."

"Oh, don't be so dramatic. And I don't have to ask how you feel. I know, remember? I made the same mistake you did. At least I wasn't dumb enough to make it with what I'm assuming is some hillbilly with no money to help. Luckily for you, you do have me, and I'll help you fix your problems before they're problems."

It feels like she's physically slapped me. I just stare at her in horror. Does she even hear herself? I knew she wasn't going to be happy about this, but the callous way she talks about the little thing growing inside of me is sending me over the edge and bringing out a strange amount of protectiveness inside of me.

What if I can't go through with it? Would she always feel the same way about my baby as she does about me?

My baby?

My baby!

I can't do this with her. It'll never feel like my choice if I have her standing over me.

I jump away from her and out of my bed. Grabbing whatever I can on the way to the door.

"Please don't do me any favors. I wouldn't want to burden you anymore than I already have." She's following me as I move out of my room and to the front door. "You know? I don't know if I can or will go through with this, but I can promise you one thing. If I do have my baby, it'll know every day of its life that I chose it and that I wouldn't have it any other way. It'll NEVER feel like a mistake." I slam the door in her stunned face and run to Sierra's house.

Maybe everything's falling apart, and who knows what the right decision is, but I'd be the one to make it, and I'll damn sure stand by it when I do.

CHAPTER 8

Dylan

"You actually said that to her?" Sierra asks stunned.

"Yeah, and I'm not gonna lie, I'm still shaking a little bit. You don't think she'll come over here, do you?"

"So you want to keep it?"

"I don't know. A baby changes everything. I can't imagine throwing away everything I've worked for... but I also can't imagine going through with an abortion."

My eyes drop to my fingernails, all uneven and torn, a perfect reflection of how shredded I feel inside.

"Every time I talk myself into believing an abortion is the smart choice, I picture a little girl with his eyes and my hair... or a boy with his crooked grin and my freckles splashed across his nose. I imagine holding a baby that's mine and loving it with everything I have. And suddenly I can't do it. I can't choose. Is that insane?"

"It's not insane. I'm so glad you're really thinking this through. I'm really glad you're taking your mom out of the

equation! I really want to say something, but I also don't want you to think I'm trying to sway you one way or another."

"You might as well just say it."

She studies me, really *seeing* me. "You can do it, Dylan. You can have both if that's what you truly want—the career *and* the baby. It's not impossible. I've watched you take on every challenge like it's a dare. Valedictorian. OSU. This internship. You decide something and the world just... bends."

She pauses, softening. "But is being a lawyer what you actually want?"

I open my mouth, ready to fire back, but she holds up both hands defensively.

"I'm not saying you're some dimwit who doesn't know her own mind—don't look at me like that. I'm just saying... somewhere along the way your parents put this idea in your head, and your determined little brain said, 'Hold my beer and watch this,' and then you went and freaking did it. But is it the challenge or is it something you actually want?"

My knee-jerk reaction is to get defensive, to tell her I wouldn't have busted my ass for something I didn't want. But my thoughts are a tangled, doubtful mess right now, so I swallow whatever sharp comment is about to slip out and make myself sit with her words instead.

"Honestly, I think I'm just overwhelmed right now. It feels like I suddenly have a hundred decisions to make, and then decisions beyond those decisions. Can we just pretend for the rest of the night that I *didn't* find out I was pregnant yesterday and just binge-watch *New Girl* until we fall asleep?"

She looks at me full of concern for just a moment before a smile slides on her face and she grabs the tv remote. "Alright, you go pick out snacks and drinks, and I'll set up the tv."

I roll out of her bed and head toward the kitchen, knowing every step of the way like it's my own house.

When I pull open the fridge, I spot leftover crunch rolls—my favorite. I reach for them automatically, already tasting the crunchy bits drenched in soy sauce.

Then it hits me.

Shit. I can't have this. Can I?

What can I have?

I groan out loud and shove the container back into the fridge like it personally offended me. I keep digging, but nothing looks appealing. So I move to the pantry and scan the shelves. Chips. Random snacks. A giant tub of popcorn that already has my stomach doing somersaults just imagining the smell.

Absolutely not.

Fuck it. I grab a couple bags of dried fruit. That has to be fine for the kid, right?

I reach for a soda for us but freeze halfway.

Can I even drink this?

Great. I'm already drowning—and this is the easy stuff.

Snacks. Drinks. Literal basics. If I'm already this confused, how the hell am I supposed to handle the rest?

I give up and pour us both water before heading back upstairs with my pathetic little haul.

Sierra hesitates for only a heartbeat when I hand off her half the snacks and drinks. There's an amused flicker in her expression. Then she settles back onto her side of the bed, like we're doing what we always do—like nothing about me has changed.

We watch our show in almost complete silence, but even one of my favorites can't pull me out of my spiraling thoughts.

I can't imagine the firm being thrilled about my being pregnant.

I barely get enough sleep during the semester as it is. A newborn will eat up whatever scraps of time I have left.

And I know it's stupid, but...

I can already hear what people will say.

That girl.

The one who got knocked up by a random guy she met once.

The one who can't even find him now.

A sharp, ugly guilt slices through me.

If I go through with this, Lane may never know he has a kid out there because I was too much of a coward to face him the next morning.

Or maybe he wouldn't care. Maybe he'd prefer not knowing—prefer being blissfully unaware and never having to handle any of it.

I don't know which possibility is worse.

Sierra laughs out loud, and it brings my attention back to her. I'm clearly not paying any sort of attention to this show, but she's carrying on the charade until I'm ready to talk it out with her.

I look at our poor excuse for movie snacks that would've normally been an array of cavity-inducing treats and carbonated drinks full of corn syrup.

Am I capable of sacrificing so much? Capable of that kind of love?

I meant it when I told my mom that if I went through with it, I'd never regret my decision. I'll never, *ever*, let my child feel like it's not wanted.

My hand lands on my belly before I realize I'm doing it, like I'm trying to shield it from that kind of emotional hit—from knowing that no matter how hard you work to be the best, one of the people you love most might still look at you and only see a disappointment.

Am I overcomplicating this?

Like Sierra said, I can do both.

People do. Women do.

There's no rule that says you can't be a damn good lawyer and a good mom at the same time. It was my mom's choice not to do both, but that doesn't mean it has to be mine.

And maybe I won't end up as the very best, highest-paid attorney in the entire state.

But no one's telling me I *can't* be.

Not really.

And I can sure as hell try.

"I'm gonna do it."

The thought and the words collide, bursting out of me before I even know I've decided.

Sierra's head snaps toward me immediately, like she's been on the edge of her seat, just waiting for the moment I finally break open and say something.

"Which 'it'?" She asks tentatively.

"Have the baby." I reply, looking for an opinion on the matter to be shown on her face. She stoically and calmly reaches for the remote to pause the show.

"And this is your decision? I didn't influence you, or your mom? This isn't about rebelling against your mom?" Sierra presses me.

I scoff. "Uhh, no?"

"Are you asking or telling me?"

"Yes... I mean no. Damn it! I want to have this baby. Me. Like you said, when have I ever let a challenge stop me from getting what I want? I can do both. It's not an either-or situation, and I don't think I could go through with the abortion. I already feel so stupidly protective of the tiny future tax deduction."

She immediately perks up and starts ranting, "Well, I hope you work on your terms of endearment, but I'm so happy for you! We need to find a doctor, some vitamins-"

"The father." I say because we're both thinking it.

"Yeah, I was going to give you a little time before I asked what you're going to do about that." She tells me, chewing on her lip.

"I was wondering if you could message Casey and ask if he knew Lane?" I ask her with a pleading look.

She groans but gives me a nod and pulls out her phone to send him a text.

"How do you think I should do it? Call him? Text him? What's the proper way to tell a guy you ran out on 'Hey, dude. Sorry I dramatically ditched you a month ago, but I'm having your baby. Please don't return the favor because our kid deserves a father.'?"

"We'll work on it." She never even glances up from her texting.

"Is he messaging back?" I ask, turning to face her and crossing my legs underneath me.

"He is. He said he didn't know any Lanes at the party. I asked him if he knew a Lane at the college, but apparently he doesn't go there. He just knows people who go to school there."

"Fuck."

She finally looks up from her phone and throws it to the side.

With brows drawn together, she says, "I told him to be on the lookout for me, but he seems like a dead end."

"Do you have any other ideas?"

"Google? We can try to put Lane and Dry Creek College together on all the social platforms." She picks up her phone again and starts typing.

"I've tried that already. Couldn't find anything." I tell her absentmindedly, chewing on my thumbnail.

"But you just found out." She lifts an eyebrow and smirks.

My cheeks burn in embarrassment. "I may have tried to search for him in a moment of weakness... before I realized I was carrying his spawn."

She snorts while making a sorry attempt to hold back laughter. "No need to be embarrassed. We've all been there."

A couple of weeks ago, I couldn't stop thinking about Lane. I told myself I was only looking him up to prove he'd already moved on. That he was back at parties, not giving a second thought to his out-of-town one-nighter.

Then, it was a challenge to find him. Nothing I looked up worked on any of the social media platforms. I even searched through the whole college website in hopes of finding a picture of him.

The only way I think I'd be able to find him is to wander around the town until I found him.

I swallow hard before asking, "Would it be crazy to swap colleges?"

"What?!" Sierra gasps. "What about your life here?"

"It's not just my life now. I have a kid who deserves a dad. Besides, there's no way it's going to work out at my dad's firm." I shrug before adding. "Dry Creek has a surprisingly decent reputation for producing competitive law school applicants."

"Learned all of that in your 'moment of weakness,' did ya?" I throw my pillow at her. She catches it giggling. "And you don't sound too upset about the internship."

"You know, as crazy as it sounds, I actually feel relieved to have that option taken away from me. I hated the idea that people would think it was handed to me, and if I did fail, it would be right in front of my father. But what person in my position would turn down working at Whitlock & Danforth?"

Sierra looks down at her hands.

"Maybe this is your chance to take a step away from others' expectations and just do what feels right for you," she says a little glumly, as if I'm already gone.

I realize then that if I did this, I'd be losing my whole support system. My best friend, Mom, and Dad are all here.

"You know, I think you have a lot of wisdom buried under all that crazy." I reach over and squeeze her hand in mine. "I can't leave, though. I need you. I need all of my family. What if I still never find him, or I do and he wants nothing to do with us? I can't do this by myself. I need your crazy wisdom with me." I'm trying to slide some humor in there to mask the emotion I can feel building inside of me again.

"You can call anytime for my crazy wisdom. You don't need us, though. You're the most self-sufficient person I know.

You're going to be a great mom with or without anyone's help."

That did it. Tears are springing loose again without my permission.

I place a hand on my belly and draw strength from the action. My heart's full of fear, but there's a determination there too. It softens the anxiety of all the unknowns I'm facing. The plans that have been a steady anchor in my life are changing right in front of me.

I see the sad acceptance in Sierra's eyes and feel the warmth in my palm from my belly, and I already know this is something I have to at least try.

For both of us.

CHAPTER 9

Dylan

"You feel like something I'm not supposed to keep... but damn it if I don't want to."

I freeze.

He feels it too, I think. The sense of something more happening here.

But we both know what this is and how it has to be.

We linger in that feeling a moment longer until the tension in the room is something palpable. I gulp, feeling like everything inside of me wants to run.

Something in my eyes makes him pull back as if he were going to let me go. Let this moment go. Leaving me surprisingly upset.

I should be relieved. He's handing me the space that I was pretty sure I needed.

"Don't."

The words fly out of my mouth suddenly, and every part of me that was holding onto him clutches him tighter in a refusal to let him go.

I see the muscle in his jaw tick and the hand he has propped up beside my face balls into a fist. He looks as if he's caught in some internal battle.

He says nothing as he scrutinizes my face, his jewel-toned eyes bouncing between mine.

He takes a deep breath and, like a switch flipped, his gaze drops to my lips, the corners of his mouth turning up.

His easy confidence slides back into place, and the tension evaporates with the steam.

"I hope you weren't counting on getting a lot of sleep tonight." His husky voice touches parts of me his hands never could.

Relaxing at the change of pace, I give him a cocky grin of my own.

"If you think you can handle me, Tex."

—

My eyes shoot open and I'm lying beside Lane in the hotel bed. My hair, still a little damp, is sticking to my skin.

We must've dozed off at some point, and now we're wrapped around each other, skin on skin.

I listen to the sound of his soft snores, his chest rising and falling with each breath he takes, and I almost let it lull me back to sleep.

I wouldn't mind waking up like this all the time.

I pull back to look at his face, soft in his sleep. He's insanely handsome; long dark lashes rest on his strong cheekbones; pink puffy lips that are parted slightly.

I let my fingers trace the side of his face, and he pulls me closer to him in his sleep.

How can someone you just met feel like someone you've known your whole life?

Every time we'd finish a round of sex, I'd be drained and dying for sleep... but I needed more of him.

We kept talking and laughing and playing until it would start all over again.

I couldn't get enough of him... and that terrified me.

I lean over and press a soft kiss to his lips one last time.

Slowly, I wiggle out of his grip and put my clothes back on. It's still dark, but I can see just a bit of light through the curtains, telling me it's early morning.

I grab my keys and phone, then quietly open the door. I hesitate, looking back over my shoulder to get one last look at him, and I almost change my mind and get back in the bed.

Almost...

I wake up determined and, for the first time in my life, with a brand new plan. Well... if you can call it a plan. It feels more like a hopeful idea.

Sierra and I stayed up most of the night trying to find him online with no luck. I go back and forth several times about whether it's actually a good idea to move or not because, let's be honest, it's pretty freaking insane.

But eventually I came to a firm decision that I'll do my best to search for Lane for a month, and if nothing comes of it, I'll make the transfer to Dry Creek University.

If after a year I don't find him, I'll transfer back and hope that one day destiny, or fate, or whatever will step in.

I really hope it doesn't come to that. He may not want any of this, but I hate that I have no way to let him know.

He deserves to be told that he has a child.

I walk back into my childhood home, feeling like I don't belong to it anymore. My mother stands in the kitchen as if she'd just been waiting there the whole time to resume our discussion.

"I'm sorry. I really hope you don't think that I regret having you. I love you very much! I truly can't imagine my life without you. I just would've preferred to have you later in life. And I really hate that you have to deal with this decision at this time in your life. I'll help you, whatever your decision is. I'll be there for you, I promise."

I drop my things where I stand and run to her with my arms out. She embraces me as if I were a child again, laying her head on top of mine after kissing my temple. I don't think she even understands how much I need her support.

It's surreal to realize that I'll be to this baby what she's been to me. I can only hope I do it right. Right now, I'm still trying to figure out how to be someone's rock when I don't always feel steady myself.

I pull back and look at my mom with her matching tears. "Thank you for saying that. I'm sorry too. It was all so melodramatic. I know you love me, and I love you, too." I pause just to absorb some of the peace of the moment. She smiles, palming my cheek with one hand. "I want to keep the baby, Mom. I can do it. I can be a mom and finish law school."

"Of course you are," she smiles tenderly at first, then determination fills her eyes. "...and you absolutely can. I'll be right here with you to help the whole time. Babysitter, study buddy, whatever you need!"

I'm so grateful for my mom's turn-around. It feels so good for her to have my back in this.

"Hopefully, I can find Lane on the internet and won't have to transfer to Dry Creek. I'd definitely prefer to stay here so I can have you with me."

Mom's whole demeanor changes. "Excuse me?"

"What?"

"You think you're going to nowheres-ville, Texas, in the *hopes* that some boy you don't even know, will be there to help you raise a baby?" She steps back from me, throwing her arms in the air before letting them fall to her sides. "You're already giving it all up."

"I think he deserves to know. It's his baby too. And I'm not giving up. I'll still be going to school, and they actually have..."

"I knew it. I knew you wouldn't be able to do what needed to be done, so I sat here and told myself I'd do it all again. I'd raise another kid so that mine could be something. And you're telling me you're going to deliberately go out of your way to ruin everything?" She scoffs and shakes a finger at me. "No, absolutely not."

I stand there frozen in shock. I really thought she was supporting me and my decisions, but she just found another way to live out her dreams through me. I know she loves me, but she's so self-involved she can't see past her own issues.

I steel myself for the battle I thought for just a second I didn't have to fight. "I *will* be going. Not only should he know, but my baby deserves to have a father."

"Oh please, you would've been better off without one."

"I probably wouldn't be here if I didn't have one." I shoot back, sick of the venom she keeps spewing.

She hesitates, then tells me sharply. "I refuse to help you. I'm cutting off all of your cards, and you can forget about me helping you pay for college or anything to do with moving there. You want to destroy everything we've worked for, you can do it all by yourself." She spins around and walks straight to her bedroom.

I'm hurt, but this is what I'd expected. I go upstairs and start packing a suitcase, gathering the things that mattered —pictures, books, the small pieces of my life that felt irreplaceable.

Then I grab a giant duffel bag and stuff as many clothes as I can fit.

I take one last look around the room, unsure of what I was hoping to find. Things I didn't want to leave behind? Or pieces of myself I already had to?

I carry all my things to my car, and with nowhere else to go, I point it towards my dad's house and leave.

CHAPTER 10
Dylan

"**I**'m pulling up to the apartment right now, Dad."

"Just please don't tell your mother I helped you pay for it, alright? I really don't need the headache from that particular phone call."

I groan. "That would require us having a conversation. I don't see that happening anytime soon, so you're in the clear."

"Oh, kiddo. You two will work it out. You knew she was going to be upset about the little bun in the oven." He pauses, then adds, amused with himself. "She was pretty upset when I gave her one too."

I roll my eyes as I pull into the parking lot outside my building.

"Look how crazy she is about you now," he goes on. "I'm sure it'll be the same once the little bug is born."

"Yeah... I guess we'll see." I put my car in park and fall back into my seat. "Thank you, Dad. For everything. I know you

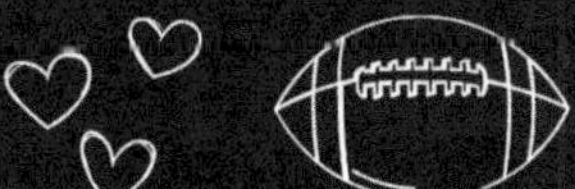

were looking forward to me working with you at the firm, and you're probably wondering how you ended up with a statistic for a kid, but it really means a lot to me that you've helped me so much."

"Always, kiddo. You'll see soon when your baby's here that there's nothing they can do that'll stop making you proud of them. Especially one like you."

Don't cry, don't cry, don't cry.

"Aww, Daaad," I drawl, stretching the word to hide everything I'm feeling. "Okay, I have to go. I'll call you later. I love you."

He chuckles at my sorry attempt to hide my emotions. "Love you too. Bye."

"Bye."

After a long month of living with my father and his new girlfriend, I'm certainly glad to have my own place.

They're both really great and accommodating, but watching them live out the honeymoon phase of their relationship was triggering my morning sickness too often.

My father told me he agreed with my mother and that I should try to do this with a little more financial independence. But he's always spoiled me, so I managed to snag my own apartment for a year, the first payment for this year at college, and his emergency credit card from him.

He's firm about me paying my own utilities and the rest of my school payments, so I'll be needing a job.

I've already set up appointments with my new OB-GYN and had my records transferred from my doctor back home.

There isn't much in them yet besides confirmation of the pregnancy and an estimate of my due date.

March 18th.

That's how long I have to get my shit together.

Now that it's August, it doesn't feel that far away.

When I walk up to my apartment, which is thankfully on the first floor, I hear my neighbor's door open up behind me.

I turn, waving a hand at her. "You didn't happen to be missing a package, did you?"

"Uh...yeah. I am, actually." Her eyes bore into me, waiting.

"I think I have it." I pull my door open wider and grab the box from inside. "They must've delivered it to the wrong door."

She takes it, flattening her lips into something that might've been a smile. "Thanks for not stealing it."

"Yeah. Anytime."

She quirks an eyebrow, only mildly amused.

Tough crowd.

"I'm Dylan." I hold out my hand. "Feel free to knock if you ever need anything."

She surprises me by taking it without hesitation. She's giving some serious don't-fuck-with-me vibes.

"Bexley. Same."

I can tell she's already done with the neighborly pleas-
antries, and honestly I'm not a fan of small talk myself. So I
give us the out by saying, "I'll keep an eye out for any more
mixed-up mail."

"K. Thanks."

And then she's gone.

Might take me a few conversations to win her over.

I walk through the door to a mostly furnished open living
area that connects to the dining room and kitchen I'm
standing in.

The hallway to the left leads me to two bedrooms and a
bathroom. Both rooms are pretty close in size, but one
has a little bit bigger closet, so I chose that room for
myself.

The other will be for my little peanut. I can't wait to start
filling it up with all of the tiny cute things that babies
require.

I sink onto the couch and turn on the TV, scrolling until
something starts playing.

A few minutes in, the quiet settles in anyway.

Like she was summoned by my depressing thoughts, Sierra's
name and picture pops up on my phone screen. Luckily, no
one's here to see how quickly I scramble to answer the
FaceTime.

"Hello." I chirp.

"Whatcha doing?" Her voice comes through bright and
familiar, like a piece of home I'm desperately missing.

"Just laying up on the couch watching some TV," I deadpan.

"Why?"

My face squeezes together in confusion. "What do you mean, why?"

"Shouldn't you be looking for your lost love?"

I scoff. "Where do you suggest I look in a town I know nothing about?"

"Well, you certainly won't find him under your coffee table." She peers at me pointedly. "Go grocery shopping or eat lunch."

"I don't really have a lot of money," I complain, lips pursed to the side.

"Job searching will get you out there too," she says smugly.

I narrow my eyes at the screen. "Did you just call to judge me? I *just* got back from getting all of my classes lined out."

"Okay, fine," she giggles. "I just don't want you to get there and live like a hermit for a year. Get out there and live your life. You're pregnant, not dead. You're allowed to have a social life."

I let out a slow breath. "I know, it's just hard to figure out where to start."

"I get it. It's going to be hard to find people who will live up to my sparkling personality. You're just gonna have to settle."

I laugh out loud before softening my expression to say, "You're right. There's no one in the world quite like you."

♡ ⊷⊷⊷ ♡

A week later, I'm officially a Dry Creek Mustang.

I'm starting to figure out the campus, having less trouble finding my classes. And now, I know which restaurant is closest and most used by students.

Creekside Diner, where I'm currently ordering my lunch in between my Legal Writing and Logic & Critical Reasoning classes.

I'm going to sit at a table to wait for my food when I see Bexley sitting in the back. I not-too-creepily sit at a table by her booth.

When I slam myself into the chair, she glances up and catches my eyes.

She gives me that half-ass smile and a quick flick of her hand.

I return both with a little more enthusiasm, but go back to waiting on my order. I can see out of the corner of my eye her looking up at me and then back at her food.

"You can come sit with me if you want." She eventually says.

"Oh thanks," I smile as I slide into the booth in front of her. "You go to Dry Creek too?" It feels like a stupid question, but you never know.

"Yeah, pre-med. Planning on pediatrics." When I can't hide

the shock on my face, she chuckles. "I'm more warm and fuzzy when I'm with kids."

"I can see it. Kids would break right through the whole lone wolf thing you've got going."

She rolls her eyes, flipping back cold black shiny hair, but I can see her fighting off a grin.

"You new or something? I haven't seen you around, and you clearly aren't staying in the freshman dorms."

"Transfer from Ohio." A waitress lays out my food in front of me, and I don't hesitate to dig in. In between bites, I add, "Pre-law."

She nods slowly, and a hmm slips out. "That explains it."

We continue our eating in silence, neither of us feeling the need to fill it while we enjoy our lunch.

Suddenly she jerks to check her watch. "Damn it. Gotta go. See you later."

"Later." I get out while she's passing me when she stops and turns back to me.

"Saturday is the first home game. Football is kind of a big deal around here. I don't know if you have anyone to go with or even want to go, but you're more than welcome to tag along with me and my friend."

I can feel my smile stretch across my face. "I'd really like that, thanks."

"Just walk over to my place a little after lunch, we'll pre-game." Then she takes off.

Did I just get my first friend date here?

I've always been confident, but this move has rattled me more than I want to admit. I'd started counting my losses instead of hustling for opportunities.

For just a moment, I can understand how my mother saw the world, and I know I have to do better. I refuse to ever look at my child and see a burden.

Only the person I'll choose to love every day for the rest of my life.

♡ ﹏ ♡

When Saturday rolls around, I'm way too excited. I spend most of the morning perfecting my outfit.

My blue jean shorts are a bit snug, but other than that, there are no signs of my little passenger.

I debate wearing the cowboy boots for a while. I bought some in town along with a team t-shirt.

Probably not what my dad would constitute as an emergency use of his card, but I'm still having no luck on the job front, and I really need these for my first night out with friends.

In the end, I decide on my sneakers. I need the comfort item to feel my best. I crop the T-shirt and I'm ready to go.

I make my way across the hall and knock on the door.

Someone shouts, "It's open." When I walk inside, Bexley and a guy I've never seen before are taking shots.

When their faces finally unscrew, they both smile and wave.

"Hi!"

"Hey, I'm Wes." The guy walks straight up to me and wraps his big arms around me for a hug. "Bexley said you just moved from Ohio. What's it like having seasons?"

Wes radiates warmth and kindness, I could see how he would've won over my guarded neighbor.

"The fall is nice, but it may not be worth the winters." I retort, falling into conversation with ease.

He gets a dreamy look in his eyes. "I'd love to go one day."

"We should all road trip to my home sometime." I say excitedly.

Wes beams at me. "We were just taking some pre-game drinks, wanna join?"

I start to panic. It's not that I'm embarrassed exactly. I just want them to get to know me before the whole I'm a mommy bit happens. "I, umm, don't really…"

Bexley steps in and says, "She already agreed to be my DD."

Is she covering for me? Surely not. There's no way she'd know. She must've thought she asked me when she rushed out.

"Yeah, I wouldn't want to be irresponsible. What time does the game start?" I swear I see Bexley smirk.

"3:30 is kickoff." Wes answers. "We need to get there early to see them doing their drills. Do you watch football?"

"Well, I'm no super fan or anything, but I grew up watching some with my dad. He's a Browns fan."

We settle into a banter that makes the time fly before we have to leave for the game. When we're finally in our seats in the stands, the crowd is a living thing.

The excitement is something tangible in the air.

"Holy shit, this is crazy!" I do my best to yell at them over the noise.

Bexley yells back, "I told you it's a big deal here. Especially these last couple of years. My brother and his best friend are really good."

My eyes light up. "No way! Your brother plays?"

"Oh yeah, I guess I never mentioned that. I'll show you when they announce the players on the screen."

Wes leans closer to me to say, "He's fine! And his best friend, the cornerback, Gavin. Fucking swoon-worthy."

I laugh out loud when Bex rolls her eyes and shoves at him. "Gross. One's like my brother and the other one actually is."

"I'm just stating facts, Bex."

"Here they are!" Bexley points excitedly at the giant screen.

I watch patiently as each player's called, clapping along with the crowd when they reignite with each new person.

When her brother flashes across the screen, she and Wes both start cheering extra loud as they announce Nate Maddox.

He's very handsome. You can definitely see the resemblance, with their dark black hair and bright blue eyes being the same.

Then they call out Gavin Kemp, and when his face fills the screen, my legs give out beneath me. I land roughly on the metal seat.

Wes and Bexley are screaming for him too. Bexley turns to say something to me, but I'm locked onto the emerald-green eyes that have haunted me for months.

"Lane?"

His picture flips to another player's, and I hear Bexley ask, "How did you know we call him Lane?" She looks at me perplexed, as she drops down beside me. "Do you know him?"

Still in shock, I twist in the bleachers and reply, "Y—yeah. I, umm... we met over the summer."

She keeps staring at me, her confusion only growing. Then her brows shoot up and her eyes go wide before they dip to my stomach, then back to my face.

"It's his, isn't it?"

CHAPTER 11

Lane

Being down at halftime is the worst.

You're stuck in the locker room, mentally exhausted and recalling every play that went wrong. Wondering how you could've done something better that would've changed the entire game.

It eats at you.

But it also lights a fire under your ass. If you can manage to pull your head out of your ass and say the right things, you can motivate everyone around you to take that frustration and turn it into determination.

That can give you an edge when you walk back out there on the field.

That's what I'm aiming for as I find the words I need to pull us back up and get us through this second half.

"They're a good team, sure. But this is *our* home. Those people in the stands showed up for *us*. And I know damn well we've got what it takes to finish this and get the win."

A round of masculine yells goes up, and the team's quarterback takes over where I leave off.

When our time's up, I'm standing with Nate in the tunnel.

"I saw that Bexley showed up tonight." He points to a specific spot in the student section of the stands.

This far away, I can't see well enough to recognize his sister in the sea of people, but... I do see a flash of red hair.

I let myself imagine the possibility of her actually being here. Of her driving across the country just to be at my game.

Yeah right.

That's not possible, so I shake it off and say, "Is she going to wait for you after the game?"

"Yeah. She said she's going to find Mom after the game and they'll wait for me." He jumps up and down, shaking his arms around.

"Nice. I'll probably stop by. We both know she's here to watch me, anyway." I shoulder-check him, and he stiff-arms me back.

"Whatever asshole. Just making sure you cover 88. I can't have him leaving this game with more yards than me." Nate glares across the field to the other team.

"You really can't stand Blackwood can you?"

"Dax Blackwood is an arrogant prick." Nate snarls. "Been that way since high school. I can't fucking stand him."

I give him a look but don't point out that he could be talking about himself.

I pull on my helmet. "I'll do my job. You get us in the lead again."

That gets him pumped up again. He slaps me on the side of my helmet.

"You'll be seeing my new end zone dance in no time." He gives me a shit-eating grin before throwing on his helmet too, and we take off to our side.

♡ ⸻ ♡

We're neck and neck in a tie ballgame. Our offense is on the field facing third and seven with one minute and thirty-two seconds left in the fourth quarter.

We need some kind of points here to get us in the lead.

I keep feeling like someone's watching me.

Which is stupid.

Everyone's watching me. I'm playing a game.

I scan the stands anyway, trying to figure out what's pulling my attention away at a moment like this. My eyes drift to where Nate had pointed out Bexley earlier.

I spot the wild strands of hair that look unmistakably like *hers*. I don't know why I can't get the idea of her being here out of my head. There's no way it's possible.

If only I could see her face.

I strain to look around the guy standing directly in front of her, desperate for a better look at the girl's face for confirmation, when the crowd erupts, snapping my focus back to the field.

I look up just in time to see Nate get shoved out of bounds.

First down.

And we're in field goal range.

I'm being ridiculous. She's not here, and I need to get my head in the game.

This is one of our toughest teams to beat, and I can't choose now to let anything outside of these lines distract me.

We get stuck at third and three, and our running back can't push through the line for a new set of downs. Luckily, our kicker comes in and sails it right through the middle of the field goal for three points to put us in the lead.

Special teams stop them at their twenty-five with fifty-eight seconds on the clock.

My turn.

When our defense gets together in the huddle, I shout, "Four downs. That's it. Keep them out of field goal range and we've got this game. Let's go!"

"Finish." They all yell in unison.

First, they go for a run play, which gets them four yards. When they try it again, the runner doesn't get further than the line.

On the next play, they throw a slant. Our linebacker, Jacob, closes fast and knocks him out of bounds just short of the first down—but the clock stops with nine seconds left.

Holy shit, we're doing it! One more to go.

They could try to steal the first down and hope for another step out of bounds since they're out of timeouts. Or they could take a shot at the end zone and go for the win.

When number 88 lines up across from me, he smirks.

"You better not blink, Kemp."

With that one line, I'm pretty sure this cocky motherfucker just gave himself away.

I sink into my stance, a slow grin tugging at my mouth. "You better not drop it, Blackwood."

His face falters at my words, then the ball is snapped.

He takes off downfield, and I'm right on him. The moment he turns his head and throttles down for the catch he's expecting, I don't slow with him.

I twist my body around quickly to track the ball and jump as high as I can to make the catch first and get the interception.

I pull the ball in toward myself, cradling it, before taking the jarring fall onto the turf.

The stadium explodes.

My boys swarm me to celebrate my interception as the clock ticks to zero.

Game over.

We win.

♡ ⚈⚈⚈⚈⚈ ♡

"I can't believe you got the pick right there at the end like that." Nate scrubs shampoo into his hair. "The girls and scouts are wetting their panties right now over that. But did you see me get them in field goal range?"

Mostly to hurt his ego a little, I tell the truth. "I actually didn't. I got distracted."

He jerks his head to the side, water droplets flying in all directions. "You didn't see me?" he asks, offended like I betrayed our friendship. "What the hell do you mean, 'distracted'? You're never distracted in a game."

"Well, I did in this game." I reply, trying not to laugh at his genuine hurt about me missing his play.

"I don't get distracted," he says as he rinses away all the suds. "I always watch when you play."

A chuckle slips out when I answer, "Sorry, buddy. I won't let it happen again."

I wrap a towel around myself and head to the lockers while ignoring the mutterings of my butthurt friend as I walk away.

Nate emerges from the showers, chatting with some of the players about the game as he makes his way to me.

He leans on the lockers in front of me, hair still dripping. "I know you saw that touchdown, right?"

I snort, pulling my clothes out of my locker, but indulge him. "Of course. Double teamed! That was a crazy catch."

"Thanks, man," he smirks. "If only you'd seen my crazy run game. That was a pretty big deal in the game." His expression shifts. "What the fuck were you looking at if not the play?"

I roll my eyes as I pull up my jeans. "Would you just drop it, dude? I was just in my head... or something."

Nate frowns. "You don't do that. You have a superpower for blocking your shit out while you're on the field. I've seen you play through some stuff that would've wrecked anyone else. Hell, even when your mom..."

"Yeah," I cut him off from finishing whatever the hell he was going to say. "I guess I couldn't today."

He pulls his shirt over his head, and he leans toward me with a look of concern. "You got shit going on?"

"No, nothing more than normal. It's all good." He studies me like he doesn't believe me. So I keep going. "I swear everything's fine. You *do* need to be concerned about your mom being more excited about my pick than your touchdown."

That earns me a smile, but it never reaches his eyes.

"Come on, Laney. Let's go see my family. Hopefully, my sister's in a good mood." He lets out a groan. "I never know whether she's going to be proud of how I played or bitch at me about the injuries football allows."

We finish getting dressed and head to the family waiting area.

"I like to let you feel her out before I decide how to approach her myself." I say with a grimace.

"Are you scared of my sister, you wussy?"

"I feel like 'scared' is a strong word."

He laughs out loud while we walk side by side to his family.

I'd never tell him this, but sometimes walking with him to his family sucks.

I wish just once I could walk out of one of these games with someone looking at me the way they look at him. I want a person of my own to share my happiness with.

Someone who shows up just for me and can't wait to see me so they'd rather stand outside patiently waiting while we finish up in the locker rooms.

As we weave through the crowd, scanning for his family, I swear I catch it again. That same flash of red that's been pulling at my attention since halftime.

I glance over at Nate to see if he's veering off to his family but his gaze is locked in the same direction I was just searching and he shouts, "Bexley."

We pass one more cluster of families and there they are... waiting for their player.

There they all are... plus one.

The girl who, even all these months, still finds her way into my thoughts more often than I care to admit.

Dylan.

She's here.

In my state and at my fucking football game.

And she's staring directly at me.

I can't even move. My legs have stopped working, refusing to carry me toward her. The girl I searched for, the one who's been stuck in my head for months.

She looks fucking stunning wearing my team's shirt. And those shorts that are showing off all of her curves and long legs.

She's even more beautiful than I remembered.

And I'm... still standing here like an idiot.

I'm not sure what's being said, but something causes her to glance away, breaking the trance we have on each other.

I can finally breathe again and force my feet to move.

Then I take my first step toward her.

CHAPTER 12

Dylan

I've never been this nervous in my life. I watch as a red flake of fingernail polish floats to the ground that I pick off thinking about what to say when I finally see him.

Is he going to be mad when he sees me? He'll probably think I'm some stalker who scoured the depths of the internet just to find him again.

I hear a throat being cleared, and my heart skips a beat. I jerk my head up to search for him and find Susan's imploring gaze.

"Where did you say you were from, darlin'?" Bexley's mother repeats her question.

I yank my hands apart and hold them at my sides. "I didn't," I reply with a smile to match hers. "I'm from Ohio. Luckily, I landed in the apartment next to your daughter's. She's been so kind to me."

Susan's brows shoot up, and she looks at Bexley. "*My* daughter?"

Bexley rolls her eyes, while checking her phone, ignoring her mother's teasing. "Wes said he just made it back to his dorm from the campus shuttle." At the sound of her name being called, she looks up and then points towards the crowd. "Here they come."

I can feel her eyes watching me when I turn to search for him.

When our eyes finally meet, the butterflies in my stomach kick into overdrive.

Lane freezes. He actually stops walking.

He looks even better than I remembered. His damp hair is pushed up as if he just ran his fingers through it and left it. His bright green eyes look breathtaking in the setting sunlight.

I can't tell what he's thinking or how he's feeling. He's just gawking at me, like he can't even believe I'm here. Which makes sense...

At least he remembers me. That would've been embarrassing.

We just keep staring at each other while the family beside me greets one another cheerfully. "Well, who do we have here?" I hear a deep voice say. I pull my gaze away from Lane's to make my introduction.

I look into smiling blue eyes that match the color of his sister's perfectly and reach to grab the hand he's extending. "You must be Nate, Bexley's brother. I'm Dylan, your sister's new neighbor."

I glance back at Lane and I gulp down my nerves and give him a small smile when he starts moving towards us again.

Nate loses his whole southern-boy charm act after he hears my name. He quickly releases our handshake and glances between his best friend and me.

"The runner? What the hell are you doing here?" Nate asks coldly.

I flinch at the instant look of repulsion in his expression but quickly steel myself just as fast. I smooth any emotion from my face and refuse to look away.

"It's Dylan, and last I checked I didn't need your permission to be here." I tell him flatly.

I'll be damned if I let a guy who doesn't even know me try to belittle me.

Nate opens his mouth to spew more venom my way but Lane takes this opportunity to finally find his words.

"Hey Dylan." He offers a polite smile, roughly nudging his friend out of the conversation. Then realization crosses his face. "Wait, did you just say you're Bex's neighbor?"

Susan breaks in before I can answer. "Y'all have already met?" Her eyes bounce between us, curiosity written all over her face.

Tom gently steers his wife away from the interaction with a simple, "Honey, I think we should let them catch up on their own, don't you think?"

I could hug the man.

When they start to walk off I say to Bexley, "Give me just a minute and I'll drive us home."

"Don't worry about it," she slaps Nate on the chest...hard. "This guy can take me back."

I give her a grateful look. "You sure?"

"Yep. Come over tomorrow if you want." Then she turns and walks off with her family.

Now it's just Lane and me.

"So you moved to Dry Creek?" He asks without preamble.

"Yeah, I just started at DCU." I chuckle nervously, pumping a small fist in the air. "Go, Mustangs."

He just stares at me, arms crossed defensively across his chest.

"You play really good, by the way. You never mentioned you played football." That might have helped my relentless search, I don't say out loud.

He rubs a hand down the back of his neck. "I guess I didn't, did I?" He lets his hands fall to his side and blows out a breath.

"Dylan, what's going on here? How the hell did you end up here?" He makes a general gesture towards the town.

He doesn't look angry that I'm here. Just a little confused... maybe guarded.

I start to pick at my nails again, unable to look him in the face. "I know it seems a little crazy." I try to hold it together and keep calm and collected, but something about him always throws me off my game. "I actually would really like to get together and talk about it. Maybe somewhere a little more private?"

I flick my gaze around and see several people watching us. Including his mean-mugging best friend.

"Hey, look at me."

He says it so calmly but sternly enough that I comply immediately. His thick eyebrows are drawn together in genuine concern. "Are you okay?"

My hands fall away from each other. His question catches me off guard.

I've been trying to figure out how to get him alone, convinced I looked like the psycho one-night-stand that followed him across the country.

But he seems concerned about me...not himself.

I relax just a smidge and let out a sigh. "Yeah, I'm okay. Everything's fine, I swear. I just wanted to talk to you, and Bexley happened to know you, so she fast-tracked the whole thing. Sorry if this all feels like a lot."

His face twists into his crooked smile that shows off his dimple. He pulls his phone out of his pocket and checks the time.

"I don't have anything going on right now, if you don't."

I wasn't prepared for everything to go down right now.

I gulp. "You don't want to go and celebrate your win?"

"I don't really do parties." He chuckles, "The only reason I showed up to the one we were at was for Nate."

Damn it. I really thought I could put this off a little longer. I was dying to find and tell him, but now that he's right here in front of me, the words are stuck.

"If you want, you can come over to my place. It's not too far." I fasten my hands to my sides to hide the shake in them.

He has to know something's up. It's written all over his face. The questions he holds back are burning behind his eyes.

"Yeah, that's fine. I've been to Bexley's apartment, so I know where it's at. I can just meet you there. Apartment number?"

"I'm in the one across the hall from hers." I stare at him, wishing for the ease we had that first night. "I guess I'll let you talk to your people. I'll see you in a bit." I gesture to the Maddox's. "Will you tell Bex I'm leaving now if she wants to go?"

I go to walk off, but feel the familiar tug at my wrist. "Dylan," I look back into his handsome face that has softened. "It was a nice surprise to see you today."

A small, breathy laugh bursts out of me. "It was a nice surprise to see you, too."

♡ ⊱⋅⋅⋅⋅⋅⋅⋅⋅ ♡

"I don't really have the right to ask, but you didn't tell your brother, did you?" I glance over at Bexley, my grip on the steering wheel a little too tight.

"Of course not. It doesn't feel like my place. Unless you're not planning on telling him," she says, lifting an accusing brow. She pauses, then adds, "But considering you moved across the country... in what I'm assuming was your attempt to find him, I don't think that's the case."

"He's coming over tonight for me to tell him," I say blandly, trying to mask my genuine fear curling inside of me. "I can't believe you knew."

"I saw you early on when you were moving in, carrying pamphlets. I was going to let you tell me on your own. But when you freaked seeing Lane, I kind of freaked too when it all clicked."

I stare straight ahead at the road. "Thank you for letting me talk to him. You didn't have to let me go back there with your family."

Bexley laughs outright. "Are you kidding? I didn't want to miss it. He was really surprised to see you. I don't think I've ever seen him shook up over a girl before." I look over and see her grinning. "My mom was sure living for the drama."

"Your brother certainly wasn't a fan." I deadpan.

Bexley snorts. "Yeah, he can be a dick, but he doesn't really have many real friends." She shrugs. "He's a little overprotective of the one he has."

I pull into our parking lot and put the car in park. I sink back into the seat.

"Fuck!" My emotions explode out of me with that one word.

"How far along are you?" She asks me gently.

"Ten weeks." I croak out.

She clears her throat. "So... you're keeping it?" She throws her hands up. "No judgement. Just wondering."

I feel a tear slide down my face. "Yeah, I want to keep it. Even if I have to do it alone." I look into her wide blue eyes, not judging, just assessing.

"Lane's a good guy. He has a lot on his shoulders, but trust me when I tell you that he'll do right by the two of you." She pushes her mouth to one side and lifts one shoulder. "No matter what it takes."

"What does that mean?" I ask, catching the weight in her tone.

"It means y'all just need to talk." Her tone softens again. "I know you've got a lot you're worried about right now, but whether that baby will have a father or not, is not a concern." She looks at me meaningfully. "Y'all are going to be okay."

I wipe my tears away and straighten in my seat. "Thank you." I pop down my sun visor and check for running mascara. "Either way, I gotta go do this part." I snap the visor closed and place a hand on Bexley's. "I really mean it. Thank you. It's really nice having someone to talk to about all of this... here."

I change into some comfy clothes and sit down on the couch, and try to find something to watch while I wait. I'm not even really sure what I'm watching with my mind going a mile a minute.

Then I hear the soft knock at the door.

I jump up, stumbling over my throw blanket, but catch myself on the coffee table. "Come in. The door's unlocked." I yell, still fighting the blanket around my feet.

I look up and suck in a deep breath when the door slowly creaks open.

He steps into my space, filling it by simply existing. His thick body takes up the whole of my entryway. His hair looks even messier now that it's dry.

I guess I was too nervous earlier to realize how handsome he looks in his jeans, boots, and a nice shirt. Something about the rugged, formal look is doing it for me, though.

Tension pulls tight along his chiseled jawline until he looks down at the tangle that my feet are in, and his face loosens into a small grin.

"Don't go falling for me already. I haven't even baited the first hook."

I roll my eyes but laugh at our joke from all those weeks ago.

I hear the door close and the stomp of his boots as he walks over to help me. "I believe my issue is falling on you, not for you."

As if the universe decides to back up my joke, one foot breaks free and I launch straight into him. He catches me easily, steady hands pulling me back onto my feet.

I tip my chin up to look at him and say, "See what I mean?"

I meant for that to be said with humor, but it comes out all breathy. His hands on my sides are burning holes through my T-shirt.

I clear my throat and press my hands to his chest, pushing myself back into my own space.

"I'm sure you're wondering how the hell I ended up here. I know I probably seem like a crazy person showing up like this." I look up at his face that's filled with humor. "Especially after leaving you alone that morning and hauling ass." His face falls at the mention of it, so I look away again. "There's been some stuff that's happened, and now I'm here..."

I'm stating the obvious, stalling while I gather my courage to just fucking tell him.

"Dylan."

His deep voice cuts through my rambling.

I look up at him again, these motherfucking tears making another appearance.

His concern is instant, and he takes a step toward me.

"I'm pregnant."

He stops moving.

Well, that certainly wasn't how I planned it.

CHAPTER 13

Lane

For the second time today, I'm frozen where I stand.

Except this time I'm not just frozen, I feel like I've been hit by a damn bus.

Pregnant?

With a kid?

My kid?

Holy shit.

I'm just staring at her face that's steady and patient, like she's giving me space to catch up.

Fuck. Say something, you idiot.

"You sure?"

Yeah, not that. She didn't cross the country on a hunch, moron.

She just nods, bracing for my reaction. The only sign she's

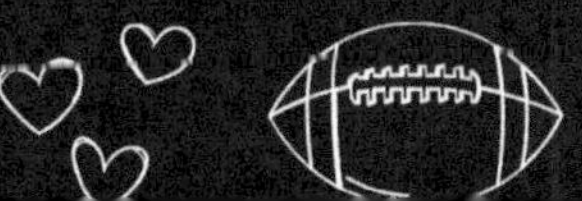

even showing of cracking right now are her stubborn tears she keeps quickly wiping away.

For a split second, I consider asking if it's mine, but that would be just as stupid as my first question.

I run a hand through my hair and glance around the room, needing something to focus on.

I look at her and gesture to the couch in question. She nods her head and moves aside for me to walk past her and sit.

"I'm sorry. Give me just a minute here." My palms are pressing into my eye sockets as I rock back and forth, trying to get my shit together.

She perches on the far arm of the couch, keeping her distance.

Damn. All the things I've been working toward… does this change all of that? My whole life just turned on a dime.

They're depending on me. All of them.

And now there're two more people who will need me.

Can I handle all of that?

Okay. Get it together.

I remove my hands from my face and find her watching me still.

"Are you okay?" I finally ask her. "Y'all…are healthy?"

She clears her throat, but it still comes out a little hoarse when she replies, "I think so. It's still pretty early, but I'm supposed to get blood work done at my next appointment."

"How long have you known?"

"I've known for about a month." She looks a little sheepish. "I tried to find you. We asked Casey about you. I searched every social media page I could think of. I had no way to tell you."

"Whose fault is that?" I snap, but instantly regret it when she tenses and her defenses go up. "Shit." I say quickly. "I'm sorry. I didn't mean that."

"No, it's fine. I deserve that." Her face is a cold mask, accepting blame while making no apologies. She sits straight as a board, waiting for my next question.

"No, you don't." I say, looking at her intently. "You've been dealing with this on your own, and I lashed out. That wasn't fair." Her walls lower just a fraction. "I can go to the appointment with you...if you want me to."

"Do *you* want to?" She asks hesitantly.

"I do." I reply earnestly. She takes me in for a beat and gives me one sharp nod.

My gaze drops to the belly housing my baby. "How big is it?"

She slides down the arm onto her side of the couch and pulls her knees into her chest.

"Apparently the size of a prune." A small smile tugs at her lips. "That's what my pregnancy app says."

"Does your app come with a how-to guide for dads?" I try to break up the tension but then realize I just referenced myself as a dad.

"Holy shit." I let out a huff. "I'm a dad."

"It took me a little bit to wrap my head around it too."

I shake my head at her in disbelief. "It just doesn't feel real."

She peers down, thinking and then back to my face. "I almost didn't go through with it... I almost didn't have the baby." She shrugs, and another tear slips down her face. "I just couldn't do it."

When I realize what she's saying a small sting of hurt hits me at the thought. Then I'm just sad that I wasn't there for her while she made her decision.

Her voice goes firm, and she lets her legs fall to the side.

"If you don't want to do this, please tell me now. You can go back to your life exactly how it was. Guilt-free out. I promise." Her shoulders slump, and she swallows. "Just... don't say something right now if you don't mean it."

I truly believe she means what she's saying. If I want out, she'd take it on the chin and carry on without me. Like she's used to doing everything alone, but me saying I'll be there when I won't be is more than she can take.

Something about that grounds me. And the decision I'd already made settles into place.

I grab her face with one hand and wipe a wet streak away with my thumb.

"Look, I can't promise I'll be any good at it, but I'm here. I'm not going anywhere. I promise."

She releases a heavy breath.

"Okay."

I reach an arm around her, and she leans into my side.

We sit there like that in silence for a bit, settling into our thoughts.

"So you moved all the way across the country. New place. New school. All on the chance you *might* find and tell me?" I let the awe show in my tone. "What if you couldn't find me?"

"I was going to stay here for a year. Go back home if I couldn't find you." I feel her tense. "I wanted you to have the chance to be a part of the baby's life, but if I couldn't find you, I didn't want to stay away from my family forever."

I rub small circles on her arm. "I can't believe you did all that."

"I sound insane, huh?" She asks relaxing into me a little more.

"Just a little."

A laugh bursts out of her like it surprises her.

"Is it too soon to know if it's a boy or a girl?" I ask wondering how in the world I'm so casually talking about *my* baby like this.

I feel her body still shaking with laughter. "Too soon. Are you wanting a little football player?"

I shake my head even though she can't see it. "Definitely not. Boys are terrible."

"Really?" She lifts to look at me in surprise. "I actually picture a boy when I think about it."

"Well, I'm still picturing a prune. I think I'm still in a bit of shock though." I feel one side of my mouth lift when a giggle escapes her.

"Are you hungry?" She asks. "I was going to make myself a grilled cheese and tomato soup, but I can see what I've got in there."

"I'll definitely take one... or two. I'm starving." She bounces up and walks to the kitchen. All that separates the two rooms is a bar, so I can still see and hear her.

I take this opportunity to pull out my phone and check in on the boys. A simple thumbs-up emoji allows me to return my attention where it's needed.

I don't even know where to start. What's the right thing to say... to do?

Do I have it in me to do right by everyone?

Is she still planning on leaving after a year, with our kid in tow?

I jump up to put a stop to my spiraling thoughts. I walk into the kitchen and lean against the refrigerator to watch her butter the bread.

She's got a clip in her hair that looks like it's fighting a losing battle. The majority of her hair is sticking out, spirals shooting in all different directions.

I drift my attention down the length of her, taking in the peek of back dimples flashing from her crop top rising with her movements. Her long legs peeking to her round...

I shake my head to put a stop to my line of thinking. "Do you need help with anything?"

She jumps around in surprise at the sound of my gruff voice.

"Jesus! You're like a freaking ninja!"

I glance down at myself and back up again. "A six-foot, two-hundred-pound ninja?"

Her face pinches together. "Ninjas come in all sizes." Then she goes right back to her task. "You can grab some cheese slices, though, while you're standing there."

I grab the cheese slices out of the fridge and get to work peeling off the plastic while she finishes the bread and heats up tomato soup on the stove.

"I swear I can do better than grilled cheese. It's just been a comfort food I can keep down."

"Morning sickness?" I ask, handing her the cheese slices and leaning an elbow on the counter beside her.

She adds four slices of buttered bread to a flat pan and starts to stack the rest of the sandwiches together. "Yeah, but I'm not sure why it's called that. Hits at any point of the day. It's not as bad anymore, though."

She twists to look at me, and suddenly we're only inches apart. Her eyes widen from the closeness, then drop to my mouth.

I can imagine exactly what she's thinking about right now because tasting that mouth of hers again has certainly crossed my mind multiple times since I'd first seen her after the game.

My mouth pulls up on one side, feeling a little cocky. "That's good."

Her gaze jumps to mine. "What's good?"

I chuckle. "Your morning sickness."

She quickly twists, giving her full attention to the stove. "Right. Much better now."

I grab two plates from the drying rack and set them up beside her before moving to a barstool.

"How long have you played?" She asks conversationally.

"Pretty much my whole life. You a fan?" Football conversations, I can do this all day.

"My dad was into the Browns, but I wouldn't call myself a fan or anything." She keeps her back turned to me, but the rhythm between us settles into something easy. "I can't tell you what play was ran, but I can follow the game easily enough."

"You should come to some more games. Homecoming's pretty insane." I say propping my elbows behind me on the bar.

"Oh yeah? When is that?" She flips the sandwich after a quick glance in my direction.

I stretch my feet out in front of me. "Second Saturday in October."

"That sounds fun. I'll see if I can tag along with Bex again."

I tilt my head to the side. "Wait, can it hurt the baby for there to be too much noise? It gets pretty loud at those games."

She's instantly alert. "I didn't even think about that." A hand shoots to her stomach.

I rush to squash any panic. "It probably doesn't even have ears yet. Here I'll check." I grab my phone and type in my search. While she maneuvers behind me to read over my shoulder. "Says here that the ears are starting to form, but noise isn't a huge concern until the third trimester."

I feel the release of her tension. "That's good." She says, turning back to the stove. "Geez, there are so many things to worry about. What can and can't I eat and drink? Am I taking the right vitamins? Just be thankful you have the penis and not the uterus."

I let out a full laugh. "I have to admit I'm pretty thankful right about now."

She lays down both of our plates and bowls of soup and takes the stool next to mine.

I'm not going to lie, I'm still pretty shook up about all of this. Not even sure if it's completely hit me yet.

But right now, I look over at the girl that moved mountains to be sitting beside me right now, and I'm thankful it's her.

I know there are harder days ahead, and we still have so much more we need to talk about, but if I'm going to go through this with anyone, I'm glad she's the one who's going to be by my side.

I can only hope I make her feel the same.

CHAPTER 14

Dylan

12 WEEKS

It's been a week since that first appointment. A part of me wasn't sure if I should count on him showing up, but when I got there, he was already waiting on me.

He stayed by my side the entire time, steady and a little nervous.

I'd hoped I'd be able to see it or at least get to hear the heartbeat, but the OB explained that they can't always pick it up this early and prefer to wait.

They took my blood for testing and told me it could be one to two weeks before we get the results in. When asked, I told them I absolutely wanted to know the sex.

So now it's a waiting game and my next appointment isn't until 16 weeks.

I've been on the hunt for a job that's even remotely related to my career, but so far it's felt like a series of doors shut in my face.

I'm doom-scrolling through Indeed over lunch at Creekside when a posting catches my eye: a part-time paid internship at CASA of Dry Creek County.

I read through the description of basic grunt work for a place that advocates for kids in foster care. It's not exactly what I'm looking for, but I shrug my shoulders and send in my resume.

I return to my cheeseburger with all the enthusiasm in the world, mostly because I know I can finally keep it down.

When I get down to my very last french fry, I'm surprised when I hear a tone that lets me know I have a notification from Indeed on there.

I quickly open the notification.

HI DYLAN,

THANK YOU FOR YOUR INTEREST IN THE PART-TIME PAID INTERNSHIP WITH CASA OF DRY CREEK COUNTY. WE'VE HAD A CHANCE TO REVIEW YOUR RÉSUMÉ AND WOULD LOVE TO TALK WITH YOU MORE ABOUT THE POSITION.
ARE YOU AVAILABLE TO COME INTO THE OFFICE SOMETIME THIS WEEK FOR A BRIEF INTERVIEW? PLEASE LET US KNOW WHAT YOUR SCHEDULE LOOKS LIKE, AND WE'LL DO OUR BEST TO ACCOMMODATE.

BEST REGARDS,
KATE COLLINS
PROGRAM COORDINATOR
CASA OF DRY CREEK COUNTY

What?! That was fast.

I decide to wait until after I get back home to reply so I don't look overeager.

After I finish the day's classes, I'm binge-watching Hart of Dixie when I remember to return my message.

> HI KATE,
>
> THANK YOU SO MUCH FOR GETTING BACK TO ME. I WOULD LOVE TO COME IN AND SPEAK WITH YOU ABOUT THE POSITION.
>
> I'M AVAILABLE MOST AFTERNOONS THIS WEEK AND CAN BE FLEXIBLE TO FIT YOUR SCHEDULE. PLEASE LET ME KNOW WHAT WORKS BEST FOR YOU.
>
> THANK YOU AGAIN FOR THE OPPORTUNITY.
>
> DYLAN WITLOCK

I'm staring at my phone still riding my giddy high when I hear a knock at the door.

Who the hell could that be?

I meander over to the peephole to get a look, but it's not someone I recognize. I unlock the door and peek through the small opening.

"Can I help you?"

There are two boys standing on the other side. The younger one has blond hair and familiar green eyes. The older one is taller, brown hair falling into mischievous brown eyes that assess me like I'm a puzzle.

He smirks. "You my brother's baby mama?"

The younger boy elbows the older one. "Really, bro?" He turns to me, wincing. "I'm sorry. I told him we shouldn't have come here." He says, his cheeks slightly pink.

It takes a moment for my brain to catch up, but I finally open the door all the way.

"As long as your brother is named Lane, then yes. I'm the baby mama." I pause, a corner of my mouth lifting as I take them both in. "If not, this is a crazy coincidence."

The older of the two looks bored by my answer, while the younger returns my smile and reaches out a hand. "My name is Blaze. Lane's baby brother."

I take his outstretched hand into mine. "I prefer to be called Dylan over baby mama."

A sideways smile that makes him look so much like his oldest brother shows on his face. "This is my other brother, Kohen."

Kohen gives me a cool-guy nod when his name is announced. I press my lips together to keep from outright giggling at their antics.

"Well," I say stepping back and sweeping my arm out. "You're welcome to come inside. Does your brother know you're here?"

They both try to enter at the same time and wrestle their way in when they can't both fit together.

Kohen heads straight to my remote and makes himself comfortable on the couch.

Blaze takes in the whole place before he moves his attention back my way. "Not exactly. He's at practice."

"Do your parents know you're here, then?" I ask, trying not to sound like I'm grilling him, but I also don't like the idea of Lane not knowing they're here.

Their gazes snap to each other. Blaze opens his mouth to reply but Kohen beats him to it.

"Dad's dead. Mom's not at home," he says flatly while his brother visibly cringes.

All at once, my chest aches for the three of them. I think to months back when I watched Lane look out over the lake with a weight to him I couldn't explain.

"I- I didn't know. I'm sorry."

"It was a while ago." Blaze says in explanation. He shoots Kohen a dirty look. "Excuse my rude-ass brother."

I smile warmly at the sweet boy. "Well I'll be texting Lane to let him know you two are here, but I can make you something to eat first if you want. I'm sure you have questions." Both perk at the suggestion of food.

"Whatcha got?" Kohen asks.

I shrug my shoulders. "I can make some spaghetti."

Blaze nods eagerly. "Hell yeah."

"Would you stop cussing? It doesn't make you sound cool, dude."

I chuckle at their arguing while I gather ingredients. "I don't have to worry about any more secret siblings showing up to my doorstep, do I?"

Their argument dies instantly and the room goes still.

"We had a little sister." Blaze says softly.

I turn to look at them each wearing their hurt differently and my heart drops. I squeeze my eyes shut for just a second.

When I open my eyes again, they're both staring anywhere but at me.

"I can make garlic bread too." I say through my emotions. "If you'd like."

"Yeah, that sounds good." Kohen huffs out before flopping back into the cushions again and running the TV.

I pause my cooking to send out a text to Lane… now that we've actually exchanged numbers. I figure since he's in practice, it could be a while until he gets it.

Suddenly, something occurs to me. "Did the two of you walk here?"

Kohen is the one to answer me, pulling keys out of his pocket and swinging them around his finger. "I'm about to be seventeen. I can drive."

"Oh" I bob my head. "Nice."

"So…" Blaze looks at me curiously still lingering close by. "You don't really look like you're having a baby."

"Thanks." I laugh. "I'm not that far along yet. I'm only a couple of months."

"Do you have pictures or anything?" Asks Kohen, and suddenly the surprise visit makes a lot more sense.

It's actually pretty sweet they're looking out for their big brother though, so I'm not offended.

"We won't get any pictures until the next appointment." I stab at the meat with my wooden spoon. "I can show you the test I took if you want."

Both of them look at me with wrinkled noses, and I bite back a giggle.

"No, thanks." They say in unison.

"I'm signed into my dad's stuff, and I'm pretty sure he has ESPN if you want sports." I try to win some brownie points, hoping their brother's love of football runs in the family.

Blaze lights up immediately while Kohen just nods and picks up the remote again.

My phone buzzes beside me.

> Shit. I'll be there as soon as I can. We're almost done with practice.

> It's no problem. They're actually pretty funny.

I see the message is read, but no reply comes through.

"Do either of you play football?" I eventually ask.

"Yep." Kohen deadpans, at the same time Blaze says, "I play baseball."

I throw noodles into the boiling water and add Ragu to my meat. "What positions?"

They both attempt to speak at the same time and end up shoving each other and throwing elbows. "Can we not break the furniture, please? It's new."

Kohen rolls his eyes, but lets Blaze go first. "Shortstop."

"No way. I played shortstop too!" I blurt out.

"You played baseball?" He quirks a brow.

"Softball," I correct. "But that was in high school." I cover the sauce with a lid and let it simmer. "Kohen? You play defense like your brother?" He's a bit slimmer than Lane, but just as tall.

He snorts. "Nah, I actually score sometimes. Tight end."

Shit. I have no clue what position that is. I file that away as something to research later. "Maybe I can catch some of your games sometime?" I say it casually, but I'm still bracing myself for their rejection.

"You want to come to our games?" Blaze asks.

"Not if you don't want me to." I say easily and shrug. "Just thought it might be fun."

"It would be pretty cool to have someone who appreciates the game there. These losers only care about football." Blaze gestures to Kohen. I smile at him and turn my questioning gaze to Kohen, who looks like he's searching for something from me.

Eventually he says, "Makes no difference to me." Before staring into the TV again.

I guess it wasn't a no.

None of us speak again as I finish cooking the spaghetti. The only sounds come from the football game that's on and the occasional cheer, or grunt of disapproval.

I bring them each a plate when I'm done and sit on my recliner.

"Who are we rooting for?" I ask.

Kohen looks at me like it's so obvious. "Cowboys, duh."

I laugh at his response, but hold my hand in surrender. "My bad. I keep forgetting I'm in Texas now."

"Lane said you were from Ohio. He told us how you changed schools and moved in next to Bex. Do you miss your family?" Blaze says all this around mouthfuls of spaghetti.

"Sometimes, but I'm used to not seeing my dad a lot, and I don't really talk to my mom anymore." I admit.

"Yeah, we don't really talk to our mom either."

Kohen smacks Blaze in the chest right after he says it.

What the hell is that supposed to mean?

Right then, there's a knock at the door.

"I bet that's your brother. I'll be right back."

I quickly move to open the door, and Lane rushes past me.

"Have you lost your mind?"

Blaze immediately throws Kohen under the bus, standing up and pointing at him. "I told him we shouldn't have come here."

Kohen looks completely unfazed. "Coach let us out early, and I was bored." He shrugs.

"That doesn't mean you drive to someone's house that you've never even met before!" He's not exactly yelling, but his voice is tight with restraint.

Kohen's gaze flicks to me, then back to his brother. "There was a truck in the driveway. Didn't want to go home."

I blink.

I look around at all of them, having their own silent conversation, and I realize there's definitely something strange going on here.

Suddenly the fight drains out of Lane, and I take this opportunity to say my piece.

"I really don't mind that they came over," Lane's attention shifts to me. "It was actually kind of nice to have some company."

He searches my face for the truth.

"Truly," I add. "They're welcome here whenever."

I'm not sure exactly what's going on, but clearly something's up, and I want him to know he can trust me to take care of his brothers.

He takes a second, but eventually nods. "Thanks."

I give him a small smile. "Spaghetti?"

He chuckles. "Is food your answer to every scenario?"

"It seems to work." I shrug, spinning to find my food again.

I tell him over my shoulder as I grab my plate. "It's on the stove. Help yourself." Then I fall back into the recliner.

I eventually hear him make his way to the kitchen and fix himself a plate before joining us in the living room to watch the game.

We don't talk much, but for the first time since moving in here, the apartment doesn't feel quite so empty.

CHAPTER 15

Lane

Even in September, the West Texas sun holds nothing back.

Nate and I are sitting on the tailgate of the pickup, guzzling water on our break. Not too long after we met, Nate introduced me to his dad and picked up some work for me on his ranch.

All morning we've been throwing bales of the last cutting of alfalfa into the bed of the truck.

"They're over there right now?" Nate asks like he's questioning my sanity.

"Not right now, they have school, but they're going after school." I shrug my shoulders. "They like going over there. Even Kohen seems to enjoy himself, and you know what a little shit he can be." I say after draining my bottle of water.

He jumps off the tailgate, lifting his ball cap to run a hand through his hair before putting it back in place.

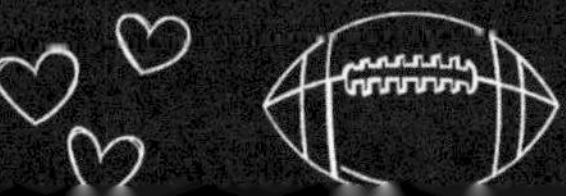

"You don't even know this chick." He turns to me, frustration written all over his face. "She just shows back up months after straight-up ghosting your ass claiming she's carrying your kid." He looks at me intently. "What if it's not even yours?"

"She's not like that." I grab a fresh bottle from the ice chest and reach to scoop some of the melted ice to run over my face.

"She fucked you that first night. How do you know she wasn't doing the same thing with someone else?"

If he weren't my best friend, he'd be on his ass right now.

I slam the bottle on the tailgate and take a step toward him, every ounce of warning on my face.

"That's enough."

He grabs hold of my shoulder, not backing down but realizing he crossed a line.

"I'm not saying this to be a dick, Lane." He sighs, his worry clear. "It just seems like a lot's happening all at once, and you're already carrying a lot."

The anger leaves me as quickly as it came. "Believe me, I'm freaking out about this plenty on my own." I step out of his reach and grab my gloves to slide on. "This isn't something I can walk away from, though."

"Obviously, because you're you." He rolls his eyes. "Just don't let her come in and take advantage. And remember, Bex and I will be here if you need anything."

This is why he's my best friend. Despite being an arrogant ass, he shows up when you need him.

"I know, man." I slide my fingers under the twine holding together the hay.

"You just gonna stand there all day or are you gonna help me finish all this?" I grunt out, throwing it into the bed.

He chuckles but gets back to work.

♡ ⚬⚬⚬ ♡

It took us most of the day, but we finally got everything done. Nate's driving me to Dylan's, since I left my truck with Kohen.

"You should come up and talk to her." I suggest.

Nate snorts. "What's wrong? Don't like when your best friend and baby mama are fighting?"

He's being a dick again, so I fire back. "Who said you were my best friend? Me and Jacob have gotten pretty close this season."

He looks at me like I slapped him. "You take that back, you son of a bitch."

I start laughing and refuse. "Yeah, we talked about getting tattoos together."

"Nice little butterfly tramp stamps, I bet." He grumbles.

He pulls into the parking lot still looking annoyed.

"I was going to drop in on Bex, I can stop by with you for a second. Maybe fuck with Kohen." He relents, throwing his truck in park.

"Thanks, bud."

"I think you meant to say, 'Thanks, *best friend*.'"

I chuckle and say mockingly. "Thanks, best friend."

While making our way down the sidewalk I hear Nate grumbling, "Jacob's not even that good."

I may need to keep an eye out for him at the next practice. Nate can be a little possessive.

I reach the door and rap my knuckles against it a couple of times before a loud, "You can come in. It's unlocked," carries through.

Nate shoots me an annoyed look. "Doesn't sound very safe leaving the door unlocked. But whatever."

"Be nice." I whisper-yell at him before walking through the entrance.

The scene I walk into slows me to a stop. They're sitting on the floor around the coffee table. Cards spread out in front of them and in their hands.

"Why the hell would you skip over me?" Kohen yells at Dylan and then gestures toward our baby brother. "He's winning right now. Logically, you should skip him."

I go to step in and tell him not to yell at her like that when Dylan snaps back. "Because you already phased, and I'll be damned if I have to play this round again because you go out." She sinks back into her cross-legged position. "Besides... he's nicer to me than you are."

"Nicer?!" Kohen scoffs and then slams his cards down on the table.

"You just have something to go out with. That's why you're mad, huh?" Dylan snaps smugly.

Blaze smirks and then picks up a card off the top of the biggest stack before laying out all of his with a cocky grin on his face. "I win."

Dylan and Kohen go off at the same time.

"How?!"

"I told you!"

Nate and I glance at each other and then back at the chaos unfolding in front of us.

I clear my throat, and they all finally look up from their game.

Blaze is the first to speak with a shit-eating grin on his face.

"Did you see me just kick their ass?"

"Watch your mouth." I say, amused.

"What the hell did I just watch?" Nate asks.

Kohen answers with his arms crossed. "You watched Dylan basically hand Blaze his last phase in Phase Ten."

She straightens defensively. "You're telling me you wouldn't have gone out if you weren't skipped"

Kohen lets a small grin slip. "I guess you'll never know. Maybe next time you'll skip logically."

She throws her head back, laughing. "You're such a sore loser."

I smile at their banter. It's not often I see the boys like this.

Even Nate is watching them with a hint of surprise.

"I hate to drop by and run, but Kohen has a home game tonight, so I should probably take him home to get ready." I say breaking up the moment.

"No problem," Dylan says as she gathers all the cards into a neat pile. "I'll see you later."

"Y'all coming tonight?" Kohen asks, pointing his question to Nate.

"I was just about to check and see if Bex wants to go." He probably wasn't even aware of the game until just now but his decision was made when Kohen asked.

Blaze turns to Dylan. "Are you coming?"

There's a beat of silence.

Dylan opens her mouth to answer.

"I'm sure she has better things to do." I say, trying to spare her from having to answer.

"I don't," she hesitates, looking at me with concern. "As long as it's okay with you."

"Of course." I rub the back of my neck. "I just didn't want you to feel like you had to."

I hate how awkward this feels. We're having a kid together, for fucks sake, we shouldn't be tiptoeing around each other.

Five seconds ago she was perfectly comfortable with my brothers. Why is she clamming up with me?

She smiles up at me. "I want to."

"Cool." Nate says dryly. "I'll go talk to Bex."

We watch him leave and the door clicks shut behind him.

Dylan stands to walk over and speak to me, voice low. "If it's too weird, I can stay home. It won't hurt my feelings."

Before I can answer, Kohen pipes up behind her. "Don't mind Nate. He gets jealous when anyone takes Lane's attention away from him."

He snatches the keys off the bar and calls out, "Blaze... Let's go."

Then it's just Dylan and me. Alone.

Fuck it.

"Look, I don't know what this is supposed to look like," I admit. "How we're supposed to be with each other."

She's bracing herself for me to shut this down. Her face is a mask of politeness, but her shoulders are tense and her hands are fists at her side.

"But I'd think being friends... hanging out... that makes sense." I grin and tease her with her own words. "It doesn't have to be weird."

Her entire demeanor relaxes, and she purses her lips to the side.

"Yeah. I'd like that."

She sticks a pinky out toward me like we're ten-year-old kids on a playground. "Friends?"

I make a face, but reach my pinky out to wrap around hers. "Friends it is."

Damn it. Did I just friend-zone myself?

The stadium lights, the band blasting, and sounds of helmets slapping together are home for me.

All of it comes together, putting me in the best mood.

I'm sitting between Nate and Blaze on the bleachers while the girls sit a row beneath us, chatting away.

I'm glad she found a friend when she moved. More so that it happened to be Bexley.

Dylan's rambling on—eyes big, hands waving—and I hear her say something about starting on Monday.

Blaze who's clearly also eavesdropping asks, "You got the job?"

She turns in her seat. "Yeah. I forgot to tell you that I got a call from them this morning. I start on Monday."

I frown at the fact that my brother is more up to date with the mother of my child than I am.

"Congratulations," I say, meaning it. "Where at?"

She moves her gaze to mine when she answers. "It's CASA of Dry Creek County. It's a place that advocates for foster children." She shifts her attention back to the whole group. "It's not exactly the hotshot internship I was originally after, but I'm actually kind of excited to work at a place like this."

Out the corner of my eye, I see Nate press his lips together and nod in reluctant approval.

"That's awesome. Sounds like a good place to work. Does it help with you being a lawyer?" Bexley asks her.

"I'll be around lawyers who go to court for the kids, so it'll look good on a resume. But experience-wise, not much. I'll probably end up getting coffee and doing a lot of grunt work."

"It's definitely a solid place to start." I encourage and she gives me a soft smile.

"I hope so. I didn't have any luck with any actual firms, unfortunately, but I think this should work just fine."

At the sound of the crowd's uproar, they all go back to watching the game.

I keep watching her, wondering if she's ever going to resent how much she's giving up or how much of her life she's turning upside down to be here.

Will she grow to hate me?

I think about what I know about her from our few interactions. She doesn't strike me as someone who lets herself get stuck somewhere she doesn't want to be.

"You're staring." Blaze whispers in my ear, jerking me from my thoughts.

I elbow him. "Watch the game, weirdo."

He laughs obnoxiously. "You too, creeper."

I roll my eyes at him but move my focus to the field.

Offense is heading out now, and I track down number eighty-seven on a jersey.

After the huddle, Kohen settles into position on the line. The quarterback hands off the ball, and Kohen seals his block perfectly, opening a clean hole up the middle.

I'm grinning like an idiot until Nate elbows me. "Yeah, yeah, big brother. He looks good out there."

"What can I say? He learned from the best." I rile him up.

"Psh," He slaps my leg with the back of his hand. "It's all the tips I've given him since I've been around."

He's so full of himself.

Kohen's team keeps a comfortable lead throughout their game.

We're all chatting and laughing between plays.

Everything feels... easy.

"I was hoping to get to see him make a touchdown tonight. Do they not give tight ends the football a lot in high school?"

"Not often," I tell her. "They mostly block at this level, but they'll sneak him one, eventually."

"I'm just impressed you knew what a tight end was," Nate says.

She shrugs. "I Googled it."

Nate lets out a deep laugh. "At least you're honest."

It didn't take long for Dylan to wear Nate down, not that she's trying. I'm not sure if he's completely sold on her yet, but there haven't been too many snarky comments from him.

I think it's the way she is with Bexley more than anything. Bex doesn't let too many people in so for her to have become such fast friends with her, you know Dylan's something special.

We finally get to the last quarter, and they basically have this game all tied up with a bow.

It's twenty-seven to fourteen with less than two minutes on the clock. Our offense just needs to get one more first down, and then we'll bleed the clock dry.

With the clock still running, Kohen sinks into his stance and slaps the side of his helmet... something I know he's seen me do a hundred times.

At the snap, he steps in to block but only holds for a beat before releasing upfield.

The quarterback fakes the handoff, then he tosses the ball to my brother.

Kohen pulls it into his chest after making the catch and tucks it tight before turning for the first down. The cornerback is already there, lining him up for the tackle.

Kohen drops his shoulder and drives through him for the final two yards.

My chest tightens with quiet pride.

The crowd erupts and doesn't settle again until after the final kneel ends the game.

When we meet up with him after the game the girls rush to him buzzing with excitement.

"You did so good."

"That catch was amazing."

Kohen rolls his eyes, but he's grinning. I know he's eating up every bit of attention they're giving him.

I walk up and slap a hand on his shoulder. "Y'all are looking good out there."

He turns his smirk my way. "Thanks."

Nate walks up and probably says something meant to piss him off, but I don't hear it...because I'm watching her.

She's looking at everyone, eyes crinkling in the corners... actually happy to be here.

When she catches me, I don't look away. I shoot her a quick wink and she doesn't shy away from it.

We stay locked like that while the conversation unfolds around us until Bex elbows her.

"We can watch it at my place if y'all want."

She breaks the connection first, turning to Bexley in question.

Bex lifts an amused brow and repeats. "Their game. We can watch tomorrow at my place."

Dylans cheeks are a little pink. "Yeah, that sounds good. I'll be there."

"Ya'll squeeze together. I want to take a picture of us." Bexley announces.

"You always make us take pictures." Nate complains but pulls Kohen beside him and Bex in front of him.

I throw an arm over Dylan and position her in the middle of the huddle by Blaze.

Bexley reaches as high as she can with her phone to fit us in the screen and snaps the shot.

After a few minutes of us chatting together, we start shuffling to the parking lot, everyone eventually drifting off toward their own vehicles while Kohen goes back to the locker room to get changed.

Dylan's car is parked by my truck, so Blaze and I walk with her, lingering there together while waiting for Kohen.

"Now that you showed up for one of Kohen's games, you better come to one of mine." Blaze says to her good-humoredly.

Her reply is instant. "Absolutely. I love watching baseball games." She leans in conspiratorially and tells him. "And I'll understand whats going on the whole time."

He shoots her a smile. "Keep hanging out with these losers and you'll know all the rules soon enough. I'm gonna go get shotgun before Kohen comes out."

She laughs at him before pulling him in for an easy hug. "Okay see you tomorrow."

When we hear the slam of the car door she turns to me. "I think Nate hates me a little less. The not-so-subtle jabs slowed by the end of the night."

I kick at the dirt, hands in my pockets. "He'll come around. It's not you."

"I think it most definitely is me." She bursts out. "I think he's more offended that I ran away from you than you ever were." She squeezes her eyes shut like she wishes she could take her words back.

"Since you brought it up, why did you run away that morning?" I ask her quietly.

"I guess I walked right into that." She lets out a rush of air making her lips puff out. "I don't know. It was supposed to be just a hookup. You were here. I was there. I didn't think it would bother you."

Something hot sparks in my chest. "I think we both know it was more than that. You could've given me your number. We could've texted. You could've at least said bye."

"And then what?" she asks, eyes sharp on mine "We would've got even closer. For what? It would've just been an even harder goodbye later." She brings up a finger to point at my chest. "You still would've been here. And I would've been there."

"Then I guess I was wrong. Because I wanted to at least try... Obviously, your mind was made up." I throw my hands up in front of me. "Should've picked up on that from the way you left."

"That's not fair..." She argues.

"No, it's fine. I didn't mean to start a fight." I can't look at her. I'm still too pissed—more at myself than at her.

"It was supposed to be one night. We live in completely different worlds. I didn't expect..." She hesitates. "We weren't supposed to mean anything to each other."

I hear a thud as she leans back on her car and I finally drag my gaze back to her.

"It took everything in me to walk away from you that morning." She admits quietly. "It's not supposed to feel like that."

Her confession hits me. She felt it too. She was just scared.

I take a step toward her.

She doesn't move, so I take another, until we're close enough that I can feel her breath on my face. I lift my hand and rest it at her neck, my thumb tracing along her jaw.

"You're here now." I murmur.

I feel her throat work against my palm.

"And I decided I don't want to be just friends." Her lips part.

I glance at her mouth, lean in just enough that she knows exactly what I'm thinking.

Her lashes flutter closed.

Fuck, it's so tempting to just close the distance.

"But I can wait," I whisper, our lips just barely brushing against each other. "Until you're ready."

Then I drop my hand and step back.

Her mouth drops all the way open as she brings her fingers to her lips.

I shouldn't, but I enjoy knowing I can still affect her like this.

She nods once, still speechless, then walks to her car.

I watch her drive away, knowing I crossed our unspoken line. But now that I know she felt the same spark I did, I'll be damned if I let her get away twice.

CHAPTER 17

Dylan

13 WEEKS

It took me a while to get to sleep last night, tossing and turning with my thoughts.

Now I'm lying here with the morning light peeking through the window reading and rereading the text I found when I woke.

Just got on the bus. Text you later.

Not that it's anything heart-stopping like the words he left me with last night.

I decided I don't want to be just friends.

It plays like a track in my head. On the one hand, everything in me wants to give in. Take the risk. Let ourselves dive in and shoot our shot at being a real family.

On the other... what if it all goes to shit?

What if we destroy the co-parenting rhythm we've slowly managed to build?

At the moment, we communicate easily enough as far as our baby goes. Thanks to the boys, I feel like I'm starting to really be a part of something.

Does a real relationship ruin that?

Because if we don't work out and it all goes down in flames? Sides will be chosen.

Our baby will get caught in the middle.

"Ughhhhh."

I throw my comforter off of me dramatically and drag myself out of the bed before making a beeline to the bathroom to pee.

I'd be lying if I said I haven't thought about it.

Watching him last night with his brothers, he seems more like a proud parent than a brother.

The thought of seeing him like that with our kid someday makes my insides go a little gooey.

I shuffle into the kitchen to fix myself a cup of coffee.

One cup is fine, the doctor assured me.

Thank the lord.

And geez… every time those penetrating eyes meet mine, it's like a fire igniting inside of me.

It took everything in me not to slam my mouth into his stupid, arrogant-ass grin last night. I think my shock held me frozen more than my self-control.

I take my first sip of the hot, french vanilla deliciousness and hum my happiness.

My toes curl at the thought of his mouth so close to mine. Close enough to feel the heat of him. Close enough to remember exactly what it felt like.

Maybe it was just the heat of the moment. I decide I'll just go on like it didn't happen and see how he reacts.

For now, I need to get dressed and ready to go to Bexley's.

♡ ﹏ ♡

I'm sitting between Wes and Bexley on the long part of the sectional with Blaze and Kohen sprawled out in the corner pieces.

Wes has been firing questions at me about the baby.

"Do you have any names picked out?"

"I actually don't." I tell him. "I'm like the worst girl ever. I mostly just compile lists of what I need and what I need to do. It's still so weird to think that there's actually a person in there."

"Blaze would sound really good as a middle name." Blaze chimes in teasingly.

I toss my head back in laughter. "I'll be sure to throw it in the ring."

"I've always liked Kinsley," Bexley chimes in. "If it's a girl."

"Just name it Boy or Girl like off that movie, call it a day." Kohen unhelpfully suggests, never taking his attention from the screen.

Bexley tosses a pillow at him, which he catches with ease and shoves behind his head.

Her eyes narrow at him before rolling them and bouncing back into the cushion.

I chuckle at her and return to the game that just came back from commercials.

The sports announcers ramble on in the background talking about stats and other sports matters I couldn't care less about.

The screen flashes across the guys standing on the sidelines, and I get a glimpse of Lane turning up one of those squirt bottles.

My teeth tug at my inner lip as my thoughts drift back to him.

What I'm going to say when he walks through my door later.

Am I more worried that he'll make another move... or that he won't?

I feel a hand lace with mine, and I look up to Wes watching me with a knowing smile.

My face soften as the tension leaves me. He gives my hand a little squeeze before letting go and turning back to the TV.

It really is crazy how fast this friend group just accepted my presence.

Back home... not counting Sierra, my friendships were more about networking and less about true connection.

Yet in the span of a month, I found people I genuinely want to spend time with.

Even Blaze and Kohen, though they're younger than me, are nice to have around. Almost more so, because they're the uncles to my baby, and I find myself hoping that they'll be really close since I have no aunts or uncles to give.

When the next commercial comes on, I scroll through my apps on my phone, checking for emails when I realize there's a notification bubble on my patient portal app. I click on it to see what it is and see that the results of the blood work are in.

Excitement bubbles through me at the prospect of knowing the gender, but my thumb hovers hesitantly over the screen.

I realize I don't want to have this moment with the people in this room. Not that I don't want to share it with them. I do.

I just want Lane to be the first person to know.

So instead of seeing the results for myself, I shoot him a text of my own even though I know he won't see it until after the game.

> Can you come over when you get back?
> I have something I want to tell you.

Then return my phone to my pocket to avoid temptation.

When the game ends—with an easy win—we all hang out together for a little while before I decide I should go home and study for my classes a bit.

Kohen drives a reluctant Blaze home, saying something about them getting their chores done.

I'm stretched out in my living room with my laptop open and the coffee table buried under flashcards and color-coded tabs as I try to drill this information for my Psychology class into my head when a text comes in.

> Yeah. I can get Nate to drop me off.
> We're about an hour out.

Every bit of my focus goes out the window.

I look around the apartment and jump up to panic-clean. When I get done washing dishes and picking up my study mess, it's only been about thirty minutes, so I decide to take a shower.

I get to the bathroom and pause in front of the mirror as I undress. I turn sideways to check the baby bump, and I'm surprised to see I can actually tell a difference.

To anyone else it probably isn't noticeable, but just below my navel is a slight firm swell. I run my hand over it and wonder at what it carries.

In just a short time, it'll no longer be an it, but a little boy or girl. A first hint to who this tiny person inside of me might turn into.

I take my time in the shower, letting the hot water wash away my nerves.

When I get out I do my face and hair routine, dragging it out to burn more time.

Once I'm done, I walk to the doorway of the second bedroom.

There's not much to it yet.

I wanted to wait until my second trimester and to find out the sex before I let myself do too much.

Still, I wonder what it'll look like a year from now.

I'd like a little glider to rock and read to them. Something to sit in for late night feedings.

The sudden knock at the door startles me from my imaginings, and I rush to unlock it.

He stands there with a look of worry... but that's not what I notice first.

He's in simple basketball shorts and a sleeveless shirt, muscles relaxed and on full display.

His ball cap is turned backwards, and that strangely does something to my insides.

"Come on in." It comes out a little more breathy than I intend.

When he walks and just stands there tight with tension, I go ahead and fill him in.

"I got the blood test results in." I exclaim.

The tension leaves him. "Oh. What did they say?"

"I don't know. I haven't looked at them yet." I go on a search for where I left my phone and I find the phone balanced on the arm of the recliner.

"Why not?" He asks, brows knit together.

I bring my phone back to where he's standing and flick through apps until I find the one I want.

"I thought we should find out together." I shrug nonchalantly, but fear that maybe he would've preferred this in text.

I add pausing over the results. "I could've just called. I'm sorry. I'm sure you're tired after your game."

"No," he rushes out. "I'm glad you asked me over for it. I just..." He pauses, trying to find his words. "I'm just happy you wanted to include me."

I look at him with a shy smile. "Of course. We're in this together, right?"

He gives me a lopsided grin and nods. "Right."

We linger in the moment until I can't take it anymore.

"Okay, I can't stand to wait another second. Are you ready?" I say just about ready to explode from the anticipation.

He lets out a chuckle and drapes an arm around my shoulders. "Yeah, let's see what we got here."

I try to act like I'm not melting under the weight of his arm.

I click on the message and slowly scroll through the results. "Everything says low risk." I let out a relieved breath.

"That's good." Lane's deep voice rumbles through me.

"And fetal sex is... female." The last part comes out in a squeal. I look at him emotions on full display. "We're having a girl!"

He smiles brightly at me. "Looks like I got my wish."

Then he pulls me in fully, both arms wrapping around me like the most natural thing in the world.

A little girl!

Who will she look like?

Will she have my curly hair that I'll have to teach her to tame?

Will she have Lane's bright green eyes? My hazel eyes?

I'm lost in visions of what our baby will look like when I realize I'm just hanging out on Lane's chest getting him all wet with my hair.

I pull back but don't let go, and neither does he.

"Penny for your thoughts?" I ask him.

"I'm thinking about all the things little girls want...bows, clothes, jewelry, toys. And I want her to have every bit of it."

I giggle and move from his grasp, but grab one hand with mine and drag him to sit beside me on the couch.

"Me too. I want to spoil her rotten." I say as I lean against the arm of the chair and swing my legs over his lap.

"But she's gonna be tough." He says. "I'm gonna teach her how to kick any little punks ass. Best right hook a girl can have." He jokes, slapping a hand on my lower thigh.

"Okay," I laugh, "maybe let's not encourage violence."

"Not violence," he counters, "just some self-defense." He tilts his head and asks, "What do you think she's going to look like?"

I shrug but answer. "I picture her with your hair color but my curls." And I really hope she gets your eyes. I love your eyes."

He raises his brows. "Oh yeah?" He leans into me, eyes wolfishly big.

I cackle, shoving at him. "Get off of me, you dork."

When he leans back into the cushion, I ask him. "How do you picture her?"

He looks at me for a moment with a serious look on his face. "I think I'd like her to mostly look like you, but with my brother and baby sister's brown eyes. She had the sweetest-looking eyes." He chuckles to himself. "Used them to her advantage too."

A little pang goes through me. His brothers must've told him that they let it slip the first time we met.

"How old was she?" I ask him softly.

He takes his hat off and tosses it onto the table, then runs a hand through his hair.

"Claire was three." He stares down at the hand on my thigh and starts to pull at lint balls in my fuzzy pajama bottoms. "My dad had just picked her up from daycare. Eighteen-wheeler at an intersection. They never even made it to the hospital."

"Oh my God. That's terrible." My chest tightens, and I gently lay my hand on his. "How old were you?"

He laces his fingers through mine. "I was sixteen." He lets out a heavy breath. "Mom never really got over it." He lifts his gaze to mine. "There's a lot I need to tell you about her. I just...don't want to get into it tonight."

I had a feeling there was something going on there. She's been strangely absent and never mentioned.

I pull our clasped hands around my shoulder again and lean into his side. "That must've been hard for you. Losing them." I give his hand a quick squeeze. "Taking care of the boys." I let it hang in the air. He doesn't respond, but he doesn't have to.

He hasn't said it, but you can tell in their dynamic and just knowing who he is as a person.

He stepped up when his mother couldn't.

From the moment he found out about the baby, he filled the role of responsibility like he was made for it.

I press closer, my voice no more than a breath. "I want you to know, I'm here for you too."

I close my eyes, hoping he hears the truth in it.

"Whenever you need anything," I add gently. "Even if it has nothing to do with our baby... I can help you."

After a moment of silence, I feel his arms tighten around me and he presses a chaste kiss to the top of my head.

"Okay."

CHAPTER 18

Dylan

14 WEEKS

I wake up wrapped in a comfortable heat, my head still drifting somewhere between awake and still asleep.

I hum and relax deeper into the solid warmth encasing me... and then it groans back.

My eyes snap open.

My mouth goes dry at the feel of his, uh, hardness pressing against my ass.

I glance around and realize I'm still on my couch, and the night rushes back to me.

The blood results. Us having a girl. Talking about anything and everything for hours before settling into a comfortable quiet that we must've slipped off to sleep in.

His hand that's holding me in place, fingers curled around my upper arm that's under my head, trails across my body to my hip.

He sucks in a deep breath through his nose and pulls me closer. Then he stills, jerking his head up to look around.

I close my eyes and pretend I'm still asleep.

He drops back down, laying his head where his mouth is resting at the curve of my neck.

I try to hold it back, but a shiver runs through me.

I feel his chest shake, and his voice comes out in a deep rumble. "Good morning." He says, his lips moving against my skin.

Caught, I pop my eyes back open and stretch, returning his good morning like nothing's amiss.

This feels like dangerous territory, but I also don't want to pop my happy bubble.

I choose to ignore the *very* obvious situation between us and grab for something safe. "I guess I fell asleep. Did you check on the boys to make sure they made it home yesterday?"

He pauses before answering. "I texted Kohen last night and made sure they were at home and good for the night."

"Oh shit." I push up on my elbow, suddenly more awake. "Kohen has the truck. I should've offered to drive you home or let you use my car."

He hums behind me, not bothered in the slightest. "It's fine. They're usually at home by themselves when I travel for games. They're used to it."

That eases my worry a little and I settle back onto his arm

that's being used as a makeshift pillow. "Still... Sorry I knocked out on you."

His arm moves in a shrug. "You look like you needed the sleep." He pauses then adds, "Or I guess I should say you *sounded* like you needed the sleep. You snore like a chainsaw."

"You're lying!" I say, twisting my body completely around in his hold.

I see his face lit up, all teasing. He pulls one of my legs between his.

"Oh yeah." He lifts a thumb to wipe underneath a corner of my lips. "Looks like there was some drooling too."

I narrow my eyes into slits.

He laughs out loud. "It's fine." His hand moves to the small of my back to rest there. "It does nothing to lessen my attraction to you, if that's what you're worried about."

He lifts a brow and looks down in gesture to his proof of attraction.

So I guess we're not just ignoring what he said the other night.

I blow out a breath in exasperation and lay my forehead against his chest tucked under his chin.

"Look, it's not that I haven't thought about it. I mean, I'm ridiculously attracted to you."

I feel his chest shake from my bluntness, and he replies, "But...?"

"But we have a kid, and I told you about my mom and dad and how all of that went down. I just don't want the same mess for my little girl." I say seriously.

He takes a hand and tips my chin up so I have to look at him. "*Our* little girl. And no matter what, I'm not ever going to let her feel like we aren't a team, with her best interests being the first priority. We'll be better than that."

He lets me sit with that, expressing with his eyes his sincerity. "I'm not saying we get a ring or grand announcements. I just don't think pretending this isn't here is doing either one of us any favors."

His gaze travels to my mouth and back again before reiterating, "I'll be here no matter what, though."

He makes no move, just holds me steady as I take in everything he's saying.

I'm not sure if I've made my decision or I've simply stopped fighting.

My eyes watch his as I lean in, closing the last inch between us until our lips meet.

It starts out slow, like he's letting me make sure this is what I want.

Then something in him gives.

His hands slide along the back of me, pulling me closer. And the kiss deepens, our mouths parting and tasting each other, unhurried but hungry.

Our bodies move against each other, chasing the friction we both crave. My free hand moves under his shirt, skimming over abs and a light sprinkle of hair before reaching around and clasping at his back.

One of his hands travels under my top, and I feel his thumb brush against the bottom of my bare breast.

He pulls back groaning, then puts his forehead against mine and goes completely still.

I catch my breath watching him rein himself in.

I smile and kiss the tip of his nose.

He chuckles, breath still uneven. "I gotta stop, or I won't be able to."

I roll my hips into his. "You sure?"

He groans loudly. "How about... coffee?."

"That sounds perfect. You making it?"

He moves to get up and grumbles. "Sure. I could use the distraction."

I giggle and pull the throw blanket back on me and over my stupid grin that won't go away.

I hear him shuffling around and opening cabinet doors then silence.

"How the hell do you work this stupid thing? I can only operate real coffee pots." Lane yells out.

I hop up to his rescue, squeezing between him and the Keurig when I reach the counter. He makes no move to give me space, letting my backside skim across his front.

I pop a pod in the top and close it shut, making sure the cup is center and press the required buttons.

I twist my top half to face him. "See not so hard."

His mouth quirks. "You gonna stay here and supervise, or was that a one-time lesson?"

I escape to sit on top of the bar. "Now, we see what you've learned."

When it's done, he replicates everything I just showed him with a second cup then turns and asks what I want in my cup.

He pours my creamer of choice and tosses a spoonful of sugar before stirring and carrying it over to me.

I grab the cup with both hands and take a sip. "Ahh. Perfect."

He takes a step between my swinging legs and lays his hands flat on either side of me. His lips touch mine, slow and lingering.

I can feel my heartbeat trying to jump out of my chest.

This kiss is quieter than before but somehow heavier. It's like a promise of all his intentions, and I can feel my fear starting to creep in.

The chime of the Keurig goes off, and he pulls away, eyes searching mine. "It's a little sweet."

It takes me a moment to realize he's talking about the coffee, and I let out a nervous laugh.

He walks over and adds a little milk to his cup and starts drinking. "I really don't want to, but I should probably leave here pretty soon. Get home and check on the boys."

"Yeah, of course. I can drive you there."

"I think Nate stayed at Bexley's last night, so I was just gonna grab a ride off him." He says between sips leaning back against the counter.

I try not to let the disappointment show in my voice. "Oh, okay."

"We can come back later," he rushes out. "The boys are wanting to watch the Cowboys games over here, anyway."

Oh crap. He doesn't think I'm going to be like super clingy or something, does he?

"No, it's not that." I say shaking my head. "I just realized I don't even know where you live."

He suppresses a grin. "It's nothing fancy. I'm not hiding it from you. Just..." His jaw tightens, and he runs a hand down the back of his neck. "Stuff with my mom." His hand falls to his side.

I feel a frown pull at my lips. I wish I knew what was going on but I don't want to push.

"Okay." I say softly. "I can wait." I give his words back to him.

The tension drains out of him, and he gives me a wink.

"And I already said they can come over whenever they want."

I hop off the counter and reach into a drawer. "Actually... I made some extra keys in case they wanted to hang out here when I'm gone." I pause, watching his face. "I just wanted to run it by you first."

He looks between me and the keys and I can't get a read on his expression.

I gulp and begin to ramble. "I don't want to overstep or anything. I just thought if they ever needed another place to go or got here before me after school because I'm at work, it would just be easier if they..."

He silences me in the best kind of way, and I melt into the kiss with a rush of relief.

"It's perfect," he murmurs against my lips.

I laugh in remembrance at what he once said to me.

"Hmm?" He hums in question.

"I was just remembering when you said I was the *almost* perfect girl."

He gives me a cocky grin. "Almost."

CHAPTER 19

Lane

After leaving Dylan's feeling a million times lighter, I cross the hall and knock on Bexley's door.

When the door finally opens, Bexley takes me in with a smirk before widening the door. "Come on in, stud."

I roll my eyes at her and walk up to Nate, who's stirring out of sleep in the corner of the sectional. "Any chance I could steal a ride?"

Perking up, he asks me, "Were you over there all night?"

Bexley shifts into view, eyes wide. "Did y'all...?"

"It wasn't like that. Nosy assholes." I soften the blow with a smirk and drop a little bomb on them. "She got the gender results in."

"What is it?!"

"Holy shit!"

They both say at the same time.

I grin and tell them. "I think she's gonna want to tell you, I shouldn't."

"What the fuck?"

"Are you serious?"

I hold my hands up in defense. "Sorry. Wouldn't want to piss off the pregnant lady."

"Screw this," Bexley says and walks out the door slamming it behind her. Shortly after, we hear a loud knock and a door open and shut.

"She has zero patience." Nate chuckles. "What is it?"

"A girl." I tell him, smile wide across my face.

"Well, you look happy about it. Congratulations, man." He stands up, slaps my hand in his before giving me the bro-hug. "Unless there's another reason you look like the cat that got..." he pauses, bouncing his eyebrows suggestively. "The cream."

I shake my head, amused. "You're an idiot. I'm just happy we're having a girl. That's what I told Dylan I wanted."

"If you don't want to tell me about fine. Unless my laid-ar is off."

I give him a look. "Laid-ar?"

"Yeah like radar. I've got laid-ar."

I shake my head at a loss. "Nate, I didn't get laid."

He tilts his head. "Blow job?"

"NO! Jesus, Nate. We kissed. That's it." I run a hand down my face.

"I knew it!" He points a finger at my face.

I roll my eyes at him because he knows nothing.

"She got keys made for the boys." I don't have to explain to him what that means to me.

His brows shoot up. "Damn." He lets out a low whistle. "Does she know about all the shit with your mom?"

"I haven't really told her anything, but she's smart. She knows something's up."

He nods, accepting my words. "You like her?"

I just give him a what-the-fuck-do-you-think look.

He laughs and claps a hand on my shoulder. "Well... I guess I'm gonna have to stop being a dick to her then."

"It would be nice. I'd hate to have to kick your ass." I say slapping him back on his shoulder.

"Like you even could..."

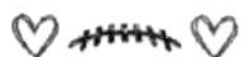

Nate drops me off and I make the trek to my house.

Despite not having a lot of money, it's actually a pretty nice place. We have some land, and it has two stories and four bedrooms. Not huge, but not small either.

It was paid off and left to my dad after my grandparents passed away, then to me and my brothers when my dad died.

When I step inside, the house is cleaned up for the most part... aside from a few of their drinks spread out on various tabletops.

I need to move some laundry around, fix supper and hopefully have enough time to do some studying before I catch up on some sleep.

"Where were you at all night?" Kohen asks from the table, never looking up from his phone.

"Dylan's." His fingers halt and he looks up. "She had baby stuff to tell me."

He sits back in his chair and waits for me to continue.

Am I crazy, or is he worried?

"We found out the gender."

Heavy footsteps thud down the stairs.

"What is it?" Blaze asks excitedly, swinging on the rail to face me. He must've been listening in after I walked in.

I pause just long enough to build it up and Blaze starts slapping his hands on the wall as a drum roll.

A grin tugs at my mouth. "It's a girl."

Blaze whoops. "Hell yeah."

Kohen's mouth twitches before he can stop it, pride flashing across his face just long enough for me to see it.

"Well, at least now we don't have to walk around calling her an it. Congrats."

"Thanks. I'm pretty excited." I tell them.

"You didn't want a boy?" Blaze asks.

"After dealing with you two all these years? No thanks."

"Blaze was the one you had to train to stop pissing all over the seat." Kohen snarks.

Blaze shoots right back at him. "At least I'm not an annoying asshole. We're just stuck with that."

"Solid burn." Kohen replies, voice dripping in sarcasm.

Just then, the door swings open with a *bang* against the wall. The easy warmth that filled the room just moments before gets sucked straight out, leaving the space tense and cold.

Mom bursts in, sloppy and loud. "Oh, my boys!" She squeals, throwing her hands in the air. "You're all here."

We all just watch her getting the door closed and then stumble her way to us, smiling like nothing's wrong. "Y'all look like y'all are having a little family meeting." She giggles at herself. "What are y'all talking about?"

Kohen immediately replies, "Lane was just telling us..."

I speak over him. "Jesus, Mom. It's not even noon." I let the accusation hang there. "Where the hell have you been for the last two weeks?"

"Can you at least just say hi to me before you start a fight?" Tears well in her eyes... tears that lost their impact a long time ago. "Why do you hate me so much?"

I notice Blaze pull something out of his pocket and stuff it in his ears before he shuffles back up the stairs to his room.

I hear the screech of the chair moving back before Kohen is at her side, doting and gentle. "Ease up, dude. She just walked through the door."

My jaw clenches as I swallow the words I know won't help.

She shows up. We fight. Nothing changes.

"At least one of my boys still loves me." She turns her swinging emotions to Kohen. Feeding him the attention I know he craves from her.

He wraps an arm around her protectively. "We all love you, Mom. We were just worried."

It pisses me off that only she gets to see this side of him. As soon as she walks through the door, all of his teenage anger and the mask he wears for the world just fall away.

He walks her to the master bedroom. "Let's get you to bed. I'll fix you some water."

I stand there listening to him try to coax back the version of our mom we used to have.

I don't know how to tell him to let go without sounding cruel.

Our mom died on the same day as Dad and Claire.

Only the grief of her hangs around to haunt us. It's destructive, with nowhere to go and no way to heal.

CHAPTER 20

Dylan

I've been sitting in the waiting room for twenty minutes now. I don't even realize my knee's bouncing and I'm picking at my nails until Lane reaches over, capturing one of my hands and resting our hands on my leg to still it.

"You're making *me* nervous," He says teasingly. "What's wrong with you?"

Over the last couple of weeks Lane and the boys have come over several times. And I've watched both of his games. Once with Bex and Wes. Another time Kohen and Blaze came over to watch it with me.

Lane and I have kept it pretty PG—mostly because we usually have an audience—but he always sits by me and holds my hand like he is now.

It's sweet how slow he's moving. Following my lead as I navigate through my feelings.

"I'm not nervous. I just really hope we get to see her today." I tell him.

He shoots me a grin. "Makes no difference to me. I can't ever tell what the hell is going on in those pictures, anyway. I was just gonna go off your reaction to see if there's actually a baby in there or some other sea creature."

My shoulders shake in silent laughter so I don't disturb the quiet office full of people.

"The app says there's an avocado in there. But it has bones and facial features now. And it moves... but I can't feel it yet."

"Hmm." He makes a face and nods. "I'll do my best to search for a bony avocado in the picture then."

"And I'll be on the lookout for any fins or antennas. Just in case."

A low laugh rumbles out of him.

"Whitlock." A nurse's voice cuts through the waiting room, drawing our attention.

I stand up quickly to follow the nurse.

We get through the routine nurse work: weight, questions, and the inevitable "the doctor will be in soon."

I sit on the little patient table and try not to rip the paper laid out underneath me because, for some reason, I don't want to mess it up.

I swing my feet off the side, waiting, and look up to find Lane with his hands in his front jean pockets... a Lane tell that he's a little uncomfortable. It's kind of cute when he's out of his element stripped of all his arrogance and confidence.

"Now you're making *me* nervous." I say lightly.

He looks around at the posters and diagrams lining the walls before he answers. "Just feels... surreal."

My lips puff out when I blow out a breath. "It almost feels like I'm playing pretend. I don't know how in a couple of months I'm going to walk out a hospital with a human I'm in charge of." I shake my head slightly. "I still feel like the kid who needs a grown-up half the time."

"I don't think anyone starts out knowing all the answers. We'll probably just have to learn on the job." A corner of his mouth tips up softly.

"What if I mess up?" I ask, half joking... half not.

"You just fix it." He says simply. "Kids can be pretty forgiving... when they know you're trying."

"You sound like you speak from experience." I accuse.

He rubs a hand down the back of his neck and chuckles. "Let's just say I burned quite a few meals before I figured it out."

I smile at him, but the questions that confession sparks sit heavy in the air.

A knock on the door breaks the charged silence, and the doctor steps in.

"Hello, I'm Dr. Mendez. How are you doing today?" She comes off professional but polite.

"I'm good. How are you?"

"Oh I'm doing just fine." She reaches into a drawer and pulls out a heart doppler, and I deflate a little.

"Aw man, I was really hoping to finally get to see her." I say, hedging.

She looks up at me. "You haven't received an ultrasound yet?"

"No ma'am. Not yet."

"Well," she says brightly. "It's too soon for your full anatomy scan, but I have a travel machine over here. We can take a sneak peek at her."

I try to contain my excitement, but a little squeak leaves me. "Yes, please."

They both laugh at my response.

I lie down and get into the assumed position while the doctor sets up the machine.

Lane moves closer, taking his place at my side, hand finding mine.

The doctor asks me a series of questions while she adjusts my shirt and pants out of the way.

"Alright, let's see what our girl's up to." She says warmly, before squirting gel on my belly.

She presses the probe in her hand firmly into my lower abdomen.

Ouch. Hope you're okay in there, tiny baby.

The screen in front of us begins to flicker as she finds what she's looking for.

At first, I kind of agree with Lane and have no clue what I'm looking at.

She settles into one spot and a shape forms.

She points to the screen. "This right here is baby's head. Her arms. Legs. Body."

I can see her little nose and hands, and—other than her body still looking a little stretched—she looks like a little baby.

My baby.

I feel my hand being squeezed, and I tilt my head up to see Lane's face taking both of us in.

Our baby. I mentally correct.

Her little arms are flailing and feet kicking.

"How is all of that happening inside of me and I can't feel it?"

"You can't feel that?" Lane asks surprised.

"Nothing." I confirm.

"That's normal. You should start to feel flutters soon, and then the kicks start," she says excitedly.

The doctor presses a few buttons, and a loud swooshing sound takes over the room.

"This is the baby's heart." She pauses to listen. "Sounds strong."

I nod my head, tears starting to form. She lets us sit in the sound a moment... the steady rush surrounding us. Then pauses the screen that has a cute little side-view of her, and the room goes silent.

"This is your first baby, I presume."

"Yes ma'am." Lane answers for me.

"And how's Daddy doing?" She asks Lane, letting me have a moment to compose myself.

He smiles and replies, "I'm just doing what I'm told so I don't get in trouble." He jokes conversationally with her, while rubbing a comforting thumb on my hand.

The doctor chuckles. "That's a good plan."

♡ ⚡ ♡

The doctor printed out two identical ultrasound pictures for us. Lane shoved his into the glass in front of his instrument panel, and I'm staring at mine.

"It feels a little more real now," I tell him as he drives me to my place.

"Definitely. I didn't expect her to already look like a baby. When I googled early ultrasound pictures, they all looked like tadpoles."

I look up, smirking at him. "I thought you couldn't tell what was going on?"

"That's why I had to do some research." He says easily. "Didn't trust you to warn me if it had been a sea creature."

I roll my eyes at him and continue memorizing every little shade of the picture I'm holding.

"I'm taking you home and not back to work, right?" He asks.

"Yeah. I asked for the afternoon off." I inform him.

"How's that going?"

"Really good." I lay the picture carefully on top of my phone. "Yesterday, one of the main lawyers told me he actually used something I suggested in a case."

"Wow. That sounds like a big deal." He glances over looking genuinely impressed.

"Well, I don't want to brag, but.. it's kind of a big deal." I say proudly.

"I'm glad things are working out for you here." He shifts and clears his throat. "You planning on sticking around for a while?"

I can tell his question is weighted, but it takes me a moment to figure out what he's actually asking.

"I'm not going anywhere either, Lane." I let that sink in before adding, "If something happens where that needs to change, we'll figure that out together."

His grip on the steering wheel loosens, and he nods.

I watch him to see if he's going to take me at my word. He just stares straight ahead and asks as if we never skipped a beat. "So, do you think you could see yourself working there after you finish school?"

"I don't know. I've always seen myself in a big law office, maybe as a partner, but I do love the work they do." I shrug my shoulders. "For once, I don't really have a plan. What about you?"

He glances at me, his brows knit together in confusion. "What do you mean?"

"Are you going to try for the draft?" I ask.

"Oh no. NFL was never my plan. I just used football for the scholarships to get me through school." He answers simply.

"But you're so good! And I can tell you love it. You don't want to even try?" It surprises me how final his answer sounds. It wouldn't bother me so much if I thought it had more to do with his decisions and less to do with whatever waits for him at home.

I see his jaw tighten. "Just not in the cards for me."

I squeeze my eyes shut and press into the seat. I know it's none of my business, but I really care about him and I'd hate it if he were sacrificing his dream.

Just keep your mouth shut, Dylan. This is clearly something he's not ready to talk about.

"I just think you deserve someone to worry about what you want, not just what everyone else needs."

I hadn't even realized we'd parked in the parking lot of my apartment building.

He doesn't say anything.

Just opens the door and grabs my book bag and papers from work from the back seat.

I gulp and get out of the car.

Fuck. I crossed a line.

He won't even look at me while we walk to my door.

I use my key to unlock it and walk through, feeling like I just ruined the whole dynamic we had.

It was going so good, too.

I throw my keys on the counter and kick off my flip-flops. I hear the sound of my door closing and my stuff falling briskly on the counter beside me.

I don't know what I'm going to say to fix this. I face him to try anyway...

But his hands grab my face, and the last thing I see is his bright green eyes looking into mine—hungry and intense—before his mouth crashes into mine.

My mouth opens for his instantly, and my arms wrap around him to hold myself steady. I stretch to push further into his kiss and body, heels lifting to stand on my toes.

One of his hands drops from my cheek to palm my ass as he lifts me with ease and gently sets me on the bar, never breaking our kiss.

My legs join my arms to wrap around him, my heels digging into his lower back. His hand slides to my lower back, clutching my shirt in a fist, like he's fighting to hold himself back.

He moves to kiss down my neck, and I tilt my head back to give him better access. I feel his lips graze over my collarbone before he groans and bites my shoulder.

Everywhere he touches me shoots straight to my core and makes me feel like I can never get enough of him.

"Tell me to stop," he says roughly. I can barely breathe, much less speak, so I just shake my head in answer.

He lifts and lays his head on mine, eyes closed. "If you don't tell me to stop, I'm going to do it."

"Do what?" It comes out in a whisper.

His green eyes pop open to look at mine intently. "Keep you."

You feel like something I'm not supposed to keep... but damn it if I don't want to.

It's almost poetic that the words that made me run from him in the first place are the ones that solidify my decision right now.

"Take what you want, Lane."

Not just in this moment, but in all the ones you've been denying yourself, I don't say.

I shrug my shoulders and tell him simply.

"I'm yours."

Dylan

I know I've already said it, but *fuck*, I love his crooked grin!

He pulls our mouths back together, less rushed than before but with just as much feeling.

He pulls me against him and starts walking. I don't even concern myself with where he's bringing me. I just wrap my arms around his neck and continue tasting him like he's the only air I need.

I feel the rush of the fall before my back lands on my couch cushions, softened slightly by Lane catching our weight with one hand.

I feel him kick off his shoes before his body shifts over mine and settles between my legs, that are still wrapped around his waist.

I press my body into his, needing to feel him everywhere I can.

Both of his hands move to take off my top, my shirt coming over my head the only pause in our mouths moving together.

His moves slow, open-mouthed kisses to my neck, and one hand travels up my side to cup a breast through my bra while the other slides under my ass and grips hard enough to bruise.

Goosebumps ripple across my skin everywhere he touches, and my nipples tighten in response.

My hand fists in the back of his hair as his wet kisses trail lower to the soft swells reaching for his attention. His tongue dips under the fabric of my bra. A tease that makes my body ache for more.

His fingers drag my bra down, baring me and pushing me up to his mouth.

The top of my head digs into the couch when his tongue finally makes contact with my begging nipples.

I claw at his hair and muscled shoulders, a loud moan tearing from me.

One of his hands creeps under the waistband of my yoga pants, until I feel a finger slide through my folds before dipping inside of me.

"Fuck, baby," he growls. "You're so fucking wet."

When his slick finger finds my clit, he starts to circle... slowly, making me writhe beneath him and drawing a whimper out of me.

It's almost too much to take. The slow torture of his middle finger, combined with the steady swirl of his tongue. My insides are burning, ready to explode.

I begin to move my hips, chasing the faster pace my body desires.

The rough, calloused finger presses more firmly and changes speed to a tighter, faster pace.

My hand clutching his shoulder slides to the middle of his back, squeezing him to me with all the pressure inside of me.

I cry out as my release finally hits me, belly coiling and warmth spreading all at once.

While I come back down from my high, he's peppering kisses back up my body, my arms hanging limp around his shoulders.

A light sheen of sweat coats my body, and my chest is heaving.

But I'm not finished with him yet.

"Clothes. Off," I demand, stirring to finish my undressing.

I toss my pants and bra behind me, shifting backward to let my head rest on the arm.

I watch him undress; watch every muscle tighten and release with his movements.

Until he's standing there completely naked, a hand stroking himself as he takes me in. "Fuck, you're so beautiful."

My heart squeezes inside of my chest.

"You're not so bad yourself," I reply with a huge, satisfied grin spread across my face.

"One orgasm and you think you're hot shit, huh?" he says, mouth tilting into a smirk.

I feign indifference. "It was a pretty good orgasm."

His laugh is low as he braces himself back over me, his body hovering over mine. "Pretty good? You saying there's room for improvement."

I flatten my hands on his pecs and watch as they glide over his shoulders and down his taut arms before looking back into his laughing eyes.

"I'm always here for you to practice on."

A deep chuckle rumbles out of his chest as he lowers himself with just his arms and drops his mouth to mine.

I need his skin on mine... need to close this distance between our bodies and feel him moving inside of me again.

I reach a hand between our bodies and I wrap it around his thick head.

He freezes instantly, the kiss breaking as he draws in a sharp breath.

I begin to move my hand up and down, squeezing slightly when I'm making my way back to the tip.

His head falls beside mine, mouth landing on my shoulder as he holds his body perfectly still, letting me explore.

I run my tongue up the side of his neck, letting it flick the bottom of his ear, and his whole body shivers.

My other hand slides over his ass cheek, feeling the muscle there flex under my palm with every slow stroke.

"You're killing me," he eventually groans into my skin.

I smile into his neck before using my hands to pull him closer. It does nothing to move him, but he understands the meaning and lowers his body until his cock is resting at my entrance.

One of his rough hands roams down the side of my body, tracing every curve until it slips beneath my thigh, hitching my leg higher.

I feel him stretch me, filling me, inch after tantalizing inch until he's fully seated inside of me.

Then he pulls all the way out.

And does it again.

Over and over, each drive a little faster, a little deeper, testing how much we both can take.

My hips rise to match his rhythm, meeting him thrust for thrust.

I bite his shoulder, needing an outlet from all the things he's making me feel right now.

His hand glides up my arm, lifting it above my head until his fingers thread through mine, pinning my hand to the couch.

Our movements are quick now, bodies greedily taking from each other.

My body tenses as another explosion of warmth settles in

the pit of my stomach, and Lane's hips stutter before slamming into me one final time.

He lets out a rough noise before collapsing on top of me.

We just lay there catching our breaths, spent... physically and emotionally.

After a few moments, he lifts his weight off of me. "Shit. I'm not hurting you, am I?"

"No," I say, pulling at his back with my free hand. "I like how heavy you feel on me."

He chuckles and settles back in, though I notice he's holding himself up a little more than before.

I let my fingernails scrape through his scalp, dropping light kisses on his neck.

"I think that feels better than the sex." He tells me, voice muffled.

I snicker. "Surely not."

He lifts his head to give me a boyish grin. "Definitely not, but don't stop." Then, he tucks his head back into my neck.

I keep scratching but inform him. "I won't, but I do think we should clean up soon."

He groans in annoyance even as he goes to get up. "I'll go get a towel."

I watch him walk to the bathroom... very appreciatively.

He pauses when he gets to the hallway entrance. "Wait." He turns back to me. "You're not gonna run off again, are ya?" He asks, mouth twisting into a mischievous grin.

"Ughh. Shut up."

I hear his laughter echo down the hallway.

He comes back in and hands me a towel before he goes to walk away.

"Where are you going?"

He fights off another grin. "Shower... if you want to join."

I'm already on my feet.

♡ ⊶ ♡

Later, we're lying in my bed, my arms and legs wrapped around him.

We're watching the Thursday night football game. I don't even know who's playing. I just enjoy watching him lose himself in the game.

I don't think I've ever seen Lane truly angry, but he probably woke up the neighbors when he *strongly* disagreed with a ref's call.

He's rubbing a hand down my arm while I run my fingers over his abs and through his bunny trail.

"How did you talk Kohen and Blaze out of coming over tonight? They're always trying to watch the games on the TV my dad got me."

"Well, for one, I have the truck, so they're stuck." He tells me.

"I forgot about that... You probably need to get home to them soon." I don't like that they're just sitting at home. Wait. "How did they get home from school?"

"Bexley picked them up and brought them home." He informs me.

"Oh. That was nice of her."

He's so on top of everything, making me feel a little inadequate. It's not a feeling I'm used to.

"What?" he asks.

"Nothing."

"Well, you stopped playing with my belly button hair, so I figured something was going on in that pretty little head of yours." I feel his hand squeeze my arm.

"Ew. I wasn't playing with your belly button."

He looks down at me, eyes expectant.

"You're just so good at all of this. I've always felt like I was one step ahead and always had a plan. Until all this happened..." I wave a hand at my belly in explanation. "And I watch you handle everything: your job, your school, the boys... me. It's humbling. You make it look so easy."

He huffs out a quiet laugh and shakes his head. "You're giving me way too much credit." His arm starts its slow circles on my arm again. "I'm just figuring it out as I go... same as you. I've just been doing it longer with the boys."

"Why?"

"Why, what?" He looks at me confused.

"Why have you been taking care of the boys?" I ask, a little hesitant.

We both know I know that all of this isn't normal. And after today, I don't really want to dance around it anymore.

He exhales out of his nose. "I guess because someone had to." He reaches up with the remote to mute the TV.

"After Dad and Claire died, Mom broke. It started out slow... just mostly drinking a lot at home, not getting out of bed."

He swallows. "We were all hurting, and back then I understood it. But at some point, you're supposed to get back up... start living again. If not for herself, then for her kids. Blaze was eight."

I watch his face as he relives his past, my heart breaking for the three boys I've already grown attached to.

"She didn't," he continues. "I mean, she got up... to go to bars. She'd leave and stay out all night. Shit was slipping. Teachers were starting to notice things. I was scared they were going to take us all away."

He shrugs his shoulders. "So I picked up the slack. The more I handled things, the less she showed up."

He pauses, and his voice goes low. "Last year, after I had to fight off a drug dealer that showed up at our house, I told her to get out. Kohen took it pretty hard."

He stares at the ceiling. "She was gone for about a month before she came back saying she was going to try to do better, but that only lasted a week."

I sit there in shock.

There's nothing I can say that wouldn't feel too small.

He continues, "She mostly stays gone now. It's better that way."

"Mostly?" I ask, my voice cracking.

"She likes to make the occasional appearance... sometimes to sleep it off... sometimes with promises that it's all going to get better." His hand laces through mine. "Those times are the worst."

"Gets all your hopes up?" I ask, trying to understand.

"Blaze just mostly avoids the whole thing. Goes to his room when she shows up. This is the way he mostly knows her. It's Kohen." He lets out a heavy sigh. "He still hopes we'll get back the mom we used to have."

I have to take a moment before I speak. Lane's telling me this because he trusts me to hear it, not because he wants my pity. So I shove down my emotions and ask him, "And what about you? How does it make you feel?"

"I feel like I lost my mom a long time ago. I've accepted that we won't get her back."

I nod my head against his chest, hating this woman for allowing this to happen.

"So that's why you're staying. That's why you won't chase your dream."

He doesn't hesitate. "They have no one if I leave."

And that's all it takes to understand.

They're his now, and they'll always be a priority.

CHAPTER 22

Dylan

"It's only been like a month, don't go turning us into a fairytale, Sierra."

I'm at the mall searching through this maternity store.

Other than old t-shirts, all of my cute tops are either crop tops or so tight they just make me look fat.

Not a cute baby bump... I look like I'm walking around with a beer belly.

"A month for you might as well have been a year. You're going to get married, have beautiful babies and live happily ever after." She gushes.

I roll my eyes, holding the phone to my ear with one hand and skimming through racks with the other. "You're ridiculous."

"Ughhh. Just don't freak out and push him away when he drops the L-word. I know your instincts will scream at you to run, but you can't this time." She says seriously.

"Calm your tits, we're nowhere near L-word. We're taking it slow; there's a lot at stake here." I move to a table to search through the neatly folded piles.

Sierra snorts. "Slow?! He's at your house almost every day, apparently having the greatest sex of your life, and you're having a kid together. That's the exact opposite of slow, my Dyl-usional best friend."

"Why do they have winter stuff out when it's freaking 90 outside?" I turn to find someone who works here. "Do you have any summer shirts? Shorts?"

She looks at me politely. "We just moved our winter supply in, but we should have some summer clothes in the back in the clearance section. I can show you if you need."

She already looks busy, so I reply, "Perfect! And that's okay. I can find it, thank you."

I twist the phone back to my mouth and head to the back of the store. "I realize that, but we're taking it slow. Emotionally, I guess." I find the clearance rack shoved in the back corner. "I told you I really like him. That should satisfy your love-thirsty brain."

"It does... for now."

I laugh, missing her so much right now.

"Speaking of that..." she trails off suspiciously.

"No!" I quietly yell into the phone. "Please tell me you didn't take him back."

"Of course not." She defends quickly. "He just texted me, and I may have texted him back."

Fuck. He's going to weasel his way back to her. He talks a good game but never comes through.

I don't want her to feel like I'm judging her, so I adjust my tone. "And?"

"Just saying he hated how we ended things and wanted to talk."

"Do you want to talk?" I ask her, concerned.

I hear her breathe heavy through the phone. "I don't know."

A reluctant snort escapes me. "We make quite the pair, don't we?"

She laughs easily. "That we do."

"Do you think a hot pink shirt that says 'eating for two' would look good on me?" I ask in faux seriousness.

"Oh yeah!" She plays along. "Go ahead and grab a 'Don't eat watermelon seeds' shirt while you're at it. But in black, really keep 'em guessing."

"I really miss having you around." I say, grabbing some denim shorts that have stretchy fabric replacing the button that's been failing me lately.

"I miss you, too." She says sadly.

I grab a couple of tops. Things that will look cute on me now and still work later when I finally look pregnant.

"I'm scared that my baby is too small." I admit. "Every time someone says, 'There's no way you're keeping a baby in there', or 'You look so small,' I feel like I'm failing her somehow."

"I'm sure it's fine. Your doctor would've said something if she looked too little." I hear her typing on her phone. "It says first-time moms usually take longer to show."

"Ughhh. Do you know how many things can go wrong during pregnancy? It's insane. And that's just when they're all safe and sound in their little bubble."

I find a cute little dress that's only eight dollars. Score.

"If anyone can get it all lined out, it's you." She says easily.

I snort, flipping through the rack. I don't share her confidence.

"You should see Lane with all the things he does. Puts me to shame."

"Oh wow, you went almost a whole ten minutes before bringing him up again." She giggles. "You're so in love."

"Oh my God. You're so annoying. I'm checking out, bye."

"Byyeee."

I check out with all of my new clothes and head to the exit. When I pass a store with a bunch of kids' clothes, it halts me in my tracks.

I hesitantly walk in, feeling like I don't belong here.

I drift to the back where the tiniest of the clothes are and don't stop until I'm surrounded by pink.

There's a small onesie that's completely pink with a bedazzled football in the middle. It comes with a tiny tutu and a matching beanie.

It feels like pure kismet.

I quickly bring it to the counter and make the purchase, buying it before I can overthink it.

Then, I leave the mall and go home.

I'm halfway home when I realize that I didn't even have to put my directions in this time.

I'm really starting to get the hang of this place.

I juggle my bags up to the door before unlocking it and swing it wide to fit everything through.

The noise is the first thing that throws me off.

I look around and find Blaze and Kohen sitting on my couch, feet propped on the coffee table, snacks in hand, and the TV on max volume.

I'm a little shocked at their presence but shout excitedly, "Hey! What are you two doing here?"

"We had to drop Lane off to leave for the night and figured we'd make sure our keys work." Blaze says with a boyish grin.

"Ah, makes sense. Kohen, you don't have a game tonight?" I ask over the TV.

Kohen takes the remote and turns it down to a respectable level, so we don't have to yell over. "Na. Not tonight. It's a bye week."

I throw all of my bags beside the recliner before falling into it. "When is your homecoming game?"

"It's October 20th," he supplies.

"You got a date for the dance?" I wiggle my eyebrows at him. "Wait, you do that here, right?"

He makes a face at me. "Yeah, pretty sure they have home-coming dances at every high school."

I choose to ignore the teenage animosity leaking out of him. "So...? Date?"

Blaze is the one who answers me, with a look of guilt. "He has to stay with me after the game."

"Why?" I ask, full of disappointment for Kohen.

Kohen answers me this time. "Lane has an away game that weekend."

"So. I can go watch your game, and Blaze can come hang out with me afterwards." I tell him like it's the most obvious thing in the world.

"Really? You don't mind babysitting?" Kohen asks, looking a little skeptical.

"I don't need a babysitter." Blaze complains at the same time I say, "I'm not *babysitting* him." Offended on Blaze's behalf.

Kohen stares at me a moment, jaw flexing, before he turns back to what he's watching. "Yeah. Sure. Whatever."

"Okay. It's settled then. As long as you're good with it, Blaze." My question implied when I look at him expectantly.

"Hell yeah."

"We can order some pizza and have a movie marathon." I suggest.

Blaze's smile is stretched across his face. "Sounds good to me."

I slap my hands down on each arm and push myself out of the seat. "Alright, I've got some stuff to do. Keep the TV down. I do have neighbors, losers."

I bring my new clothes and lay them out on my bed to inspect.

I look at myself in my standing mirror and pooch my belly out further, trying to picture what I'll look like when I'm big pregnant.

I walk back to the kitchen to grab a pair of scissors and my tool kit I bought for myself and head to the baby's room.

The giant box sitting there unopened feels like something I can't possibly accomplish.

But I take a deep breath and tear into it, laying out all of its pieces and directions in the big empty floor.

I apparently didn't need my little tool set, because it came with its own little wrench. I grab the instructions and start my puzzle.

I get the legs of the bed laid out and the bottom into position so I can screw them together when a voice makes me jump out of my skin.

"What the hell are you doing?" Kohen's deep voice rumbles out while he's leaning against the doorframe watching me.

"Shit! You scared the bejeezus out of me." I yell at him.

That makes him laugh, and he drifts towards my project, taking it all in. "Do you want some help?"

His question surprises me, but I try not to make a big deal out of it. "It's preferable to you sending me into early labor."

"Oh, don't be so dramatic." He grabs the instructions and gets to work instantly. "Hand me the screws that are labeled F."

I plop down and happily accept my role of handing out screws, letting him take over.

I watch his hands, sure and unhurried, slowly putting everything together, already taking shape as the bed it's meant to be.

"You're really good at this. Thank you, by the way." I say casually.

His mouth turns up on one side, reminding me of his brother. "I've built a lot of stuff like this. Blaze and I went through a wrestling phase... there was a lot of broken furniture before Lane threatened our lives."

My eyes bug out of my head. "I'm really glad I'm having a girl right now."

We hear Blaze yell, "DAMN IT! YOU CAMPING ASSHOLE."

Kohen lets out a huff of laughter when I look at him.

"Blaze must've slipped his PlayStation in the truck. Apparently, he just assumed I'd bring him over here." Kohen tells me, rolling his eyes.

"Oh please. I know you like hanging out with me too." I start batting my eyelashes at him comically.

He shoots me a look that's all skepticism and zero patience.

I start to tick off on my fingers. "I have an awesome snack selection. I let you win in all the games we play. And... I'm pretty damn funny."

Kohen never even looks up from what he's working on. "You don't *let* me win anything. And the only person who thinks you're funny is you."

"Blaze thinks I'm funny." I snap back.

"Blaze is in junior high... You're not helping your case."

I sit quietly, waiting for Kohen to look up. When he does, I use an imaginary dagger to stab myself in the heart and roll over into a heap on the floor.

He stares at me and deadpans, "This is what I'm talking about."

I lift up laughing at myself. "Well, maybe you can teach me the art of being cool. Since I'm clearly doing it wrong."

He tsks. "Not something that can be taught, I'm afraid."

I giggle, handing him the tool he's pointing at. "You were just born oozing sarcasm and unearned confidence... and here we are."

He looks up, surprising me with a full-faced smile. "Exactly."

When he gets done with the whole frame, I move it into place where I want it and go to grab the mattress that's leaned up against the wall.

"Jesus Christ. Let me fucking get it," Kohen says, moving in between me and the mattress.

He gets it in place, and we both stand there, hands on hips, looking at the finished product.

"The baby stuff is definitely your area of expertise, but isn't it supposed to look more like a cage?" Kohen asks with some of that oozing sarcasm I mentioned earlier.

"She'll sleep in my room at first, so I'll set up the *crib,*" I say to him pointedly before continuing, "in my room and let this be a guest bedroom for now."

"For all your friends that you don't have?" He gives me a teasing grin at first... then his face slowly dissolves when it clicks.

"Yeah. My friends." I reply lightly. "Short list it may be." I chuckle.

He takes me in a moment more, searching my face, before his head moves in the smallest of nods. "You got anything else that needs building?"

I twist my face to one side like I'm thinking about it. "We could take a crack at the cage in my bedroom."

His mouth twitches on one side. "Lead the way. Are you helping this time or just supervising?"

CHAPTER 23

Dylan

The next day, Bex, Blaze and I are squeezed together on my couch while Kohen lounges in my recliner. The boys ended up staying the night in my guest bedroom.

Well after staying up most of the night playing together on the Playstation. Maybe I should get one of my own so they don't have to drag one back and forth.

I know they're plenty old enough to take care of themselves, or at a minimum survive a couple of days alone, but it settled something in me knowing they were here instead of alone.

We had my coffee table decked out with game-day snacks and finger foods. Little One and I are most excited about the wings and are currently monopolizing that particular plate.

Bex leans over to me, eyeing me suspiciously. "You look like you were made to wear that jersey. Did he give it to you?"

I look down at the navy jersey with gold letters and number 21, I'd thrown on this morning on impulse. It does a good job of not clashing with my hair color and pale complexion. I paired it with some biker shorts that barely peek out beneath the hem since the practice jersey looks like a dress on me.

My cheeks feel a little warm when I answer, "He just left it here, and I thought I'd put it on for game-day spirit." I glance around at everyone. "Should I not be wearing it?"

Bex lifts a brow. "I'm sure he won't mind."

"He never lets me wear his practice jersey." Blaze complains.

"Yeah, but you don't do the stuff for him that she does." Kohen quips.

"Kohen!" Bex and I snap in unison.

Blaze rolls his eyes. "I'm not a baby." He drops his voice in a terrible imitation of his brother. "Oh, Dylan. You look so good in my jersey, I'm going to put my tongue in your mouth now. Mwah, mwah." We laugh at his dramatization of two people making out.

Kohen looks at him in disgust. "You're an idiot."

"It's weird that's kinda how I picture it going down too." Bex says dryly.

Blaze snorts, and they both break out in a fit of snickers.

"I'll just make sure it's washed before I give it back." I say, my face burning now.

We're down by three by the time the third quarter comes

around. We're super into the game, since we haven't had a loss yet.

We're sitting there in silence when my phone chirps out a notification for a text message. I pull my phone out expecting it to be Sierra but instead it reads:

Mom

I stare at it in shock.

My hand hovers over my phone trying to decide if I want to deal with this right now or not, but my curiosity gets the better of me.

I press on the notification and read. Then read it again.

> Hey honey. I'd really like it if you'd call
> and talk to me. I miss you.

"Everything okay?" Bexley's voice breaks me out of my spell.

"Yeah," my voice comes out in a croak, so I clear my throat. "It's just my mom. She just texted me asking if we could talk."

Both boys give me their full attention.

"Do you want to?" Bex asks softly.

I click off my phone and shove it back into my pocket. "I don't know. Let's just watch the game."

Bex gives me a concerned glance before turning her attention back to the TV. I still feel eyes on me though and look up to find Kohen's gaze locked on mine, burning with questions.

I give him a halfhearted smile, trying to relay that it's no big deal. He just shrugs like it was nothing and continues watching the game.

I can't get into the game quite like before. I'm wondering what she could want. Is she calling for information... just to judge me for it? Is she genuinely upset that we're living separate lives right now?

I continue down this road in my thoughts a bit before everyone's bursts of shock rattle me back into the game.

I'm watching a replay of Nate jumping up high to catch a long pass. Except when his feet come down for a landing he's hit at the same time, making his knee twist awkwardly on impact.

My stomach twists and my hands fly to my mouth.

I look at Bexley, who's staring at the screen in horror.

I grab her hand with one of mine and watch as he rolls on the ground, clutching at his knee.

The trainers sprint onto the field as the referees call a timeout.

The announcers speculate about a knee injury, their voices turning grim as the minutes stretch on. The longer the trainers stay down there, the more tension builds in the room.

Bexley's grip tightens around my hand.

They bring a cart out to help him off the field, and my stomach drops. Silent tears start sliding down Bexley's cheeks, but she never looks away.

They start to drive away, but not before Lane breaks onto the scene. He's running beside the cart, saying something we can't hear before he's grabbed by a shoulder pulling him back.

He shrugs free to finish what he's saying before he's stopped again, this time for good.

Lane stands there, frozen, watching his best friend disappear down the tunnel without him.

I turn to look at Bex, and she's just staring at the screen.

"Do you want to call someone?" I ask her softly.

She blinks out of the trance she's in and says. "That looked really bad, didn't it?"

I give her a pitying look. "It didn't look good." I gulp, then continue, "We'll just see what they say. Do you need me to drive you somewhere?"

She wipes at her tears. "I need to call my mom."

I nod quickly and grab her phone off the table before handing it to her.

Both of the boys are watching her now, stunned into silence.

Bexley's shaking hands fumble through her contact list before landing on one and pulling the phone to her ear.

I can't make out what's being said, but I can hear a deep rumble talking over the line.

The sound of the voice pushes her over the edge, and she asks, with a choked voice. "Is he okay?"

The steady voice responds to her before she asks, "Is he going to be able to play again?" Panic creeps into her voice, "Football means everything to him."

I have no idea what to do, so I just start to rub small circles on her back.

"Okay. I'll go get ready. I'll be waiting outside." She sniffles and says in a small voice. "I love you too, Dad."

She hangs up the phone and jumps up. "They're going to come pick me up, and we're going to meet up with him at the hospital they're bringing him to. My mom was booking flights when I called her phone and Dad answered."

"Is there anything you need me to do? I can help you pack."

She looks at me, eyes still brimming, and shakes her head. "I got it. I think I need a few minutes."

I nod quickly. "Of course. Just let me know if you need anything."

I want to hug her and tell her it's going to be okay, but don't want to keep her any longer, so I just open my door for her. I get to do it anyway when she pulls me to her.

"He's going to be okay." She tightens our hold briefly at my words before hustling back to her apartment.

I'm lying in the bathtub later that evening. The boys went home to grab showers and some clothes before they come back over here for us to all wait for some more information together.

Not knowing what else to do, we sat in silence and finished the game. They fought for it, but it just seemed like nothing could go right for our team. The final score was twenty-four to seventeen.

Our first loss of the season.

My phone starts to ring beside me, and I quickly answer it when I see it's Lane.

"Hello?"

"Hey." His deep voice rumbles down the line, making me close my eyes.

"Have you heard anything about Nate?" I ask quietly.

"That's actually why I'm calling. I didn't take the bus back earlier." He lets out a heavy breath. "After the game I came straight to the hospital and they're keeping him overnight. The MRI is scheduled for the morning. Do you think you can check on the boys for me at some point tomorrow? I just want to stay here tonight... at least until his family gets here."

"The boys have been over here since you left. They only went home a while ago to get some clothes and come back." I inform him. "I can text you when they get back, so you can focus on Nate."

"They've been there since yesterday?" He questions, momentarily taken back. "That's actually a load off my mind." He exhales, then his voice drops. "The doctors are saying what we're all thinking… they think it's an ACL tear. They have him on pain meds right now. They already did x-rays and ruled out any fractures."

"Will he be able to play again?" I ask him quietly.

"Not this year." He groans out, then I hear shuffling on the phone and the sharp sound of his palm hitting a wall.

"Fuck!" I hear him growl out.

I hear his voice coming closer to the phone again. "It's his third year. He wanted to go for the draft."

I swallow past the lump in my throat. "Shit. I'm so fucking sorry, Lane."

"Nothing to do but wait and see what they say, I guess."

"Yeah, keep us updated when you get the chance. The boys are worried about him."

I let my head dip beneath the water before pulling it up again.

"I will," he pauses. "What are you doing right now?"

"Taking a bath." I say, moving around in the water to lean closer to my phone.

He moans out. "I wish I was there right now."

"Liar." I call him on it instantly.

He gives me a half-hearted chuckle.

"Go take care of your best friend. Be there for Bex when she gets there too." I let out my own breath and sink back into the water. "She was pretty upset when she left here."

"Yeah, I can imagine watching your twin get hit like that would fuck you up."

My eyes snap open. "Twins?"

"Yeah, they're twins." He says like it's the most obvious thing in the world. "I guess I forget sometimes that you haven't been here all along. Figured it would've come up by now."

"Now that you say it, it seems obvious. They look exactly alike.. look the same age. I just never put it together on my own."

"Hey there are nurses going into his room." He rushes out.

I hurry to respond. "Okay, bye."

"I'll text you," is the last thing I hear before the click of the phone call ending.

♡ ⚡ ♡

We spend the next day mostly just waiting around. I attempt to do some studying and convince the boys to join me.

We all sprawl in my living room, each of us taking up different sections.

I'm actually impressed they even carried their bags around to be able to work on their homework.

It was about mid morning when I got the first text.

MRI confirmed the tear.

I relay the message and both Blaze and Kohen visibly cringe.

"Ask him how long recovery usually takes," Blaze tells me.

I shake my head. "I think we should just wait until he can tell us everything. We don't want to pull his attention away from anything important." I soften the blow by adding. "I can look it up and see if that tells us anything."

Kohen shakes his head. "You know what they say about the internet. We'll look it up and suddenly he has cancer." He tips his head in my direction before looking at Blaze. "She's right. We should just wait."

Blaze huffs out his frustration. "I'm just gonna go play the game."

Later, after we make ourselves some lunch, my phone buzzes again.

They're going to discharge him and transfer his case to a hospital at home. I'm trying to catch a flight home. Should be back by tonight.

After relaying the message, we all just settle in to wait on his return. I go back to my studying, while the boys play some shooting game together. Eventually it becomes dark and we make our way to our beds.

At some point, I fall asleep listening for a sound that doesn't come.

CHAPTER 24

Lane

19 WEEKS

I stir out of sleep when my Uber pulls to a stop in the parking lot I find myself ending up at more than my own lately.

"Thanks, man." I tell the driver before stepping out and making my way to the one place I want most right now.

I use one of the keys Dylan made for the boys that I claimed and walk inside before locking it back.

I get to the hallway and stare at the bathroom door, weighing between sleep and not smelling like a wet dog before climbing in bed with my girl.

I groan and move to take a quick shower, but I'm stopped by a throat clearing. I turn and find Kohen leaning on the doorframe of the baby's room.

"How's Nate?" Kohen asks me without preamble.

"He's upset, understandably. But he isn't letting it get him down. Says he'll be back out there next year, hell or high water." I say voice low, so I don't wake anybody up. It was

past one in the morning when I checked my phone on the way up here.

Kohen gives me a short nod. "We brought you a change of clothes back. I'll go get them real quick." He turns back into the dark room before shortly reappearing with a stack of clothes in hand. "Clothes for tomorrow and some shorts to sleep in." He tells me.

"Thanks. I really didn't want to put these same underwear on again." I tell him with a small grin.

Kohen gives me another sharp nod before turning to go back into the room.

"Why are y'all sleeping in here?" I stop him.

"Dylan put a bed in here. Blaze passed out on the couch, though." He says simply.

"She moved this bed in here?" I ask after looking into the space.

"Relax. I didn't let your do-gooder girlfriend hurt herself." He throws himself back on the bed. "I built it and threw the mattress on here."

I try to hide my smile at my brother's protectiveness— for Dylan, for the baby, maybe both. "Thanks, bro."

He just rolls his eyes and turns away from me, pulling his blanket over himself.

I get through my shower quickly and throw on my boxers, too exhausted for the shorts.

I crawl into bed behind Dylan, who's laying on her side cuddled up to a long, curving pillow.

Every bit of tension leaves me when I have her fully tucked into my chest, one hand under her head, the other resting gently on her slightly rounding belly.

I push my face into the side of her neck, weaving through the mass of curls before inhaling her scent deeply through my nose.

I place a soft kiss on the bare shoulder peeking out of the blanket before settling my head back on the pillow.

I hear her make a quiet humming noise while she wiggles her curves further into me.

"What time is it?" She mumbles sleepily.

"Probably close to two." I groan.

"How's Nate?" She laces her fingers through mine on her belly.

"I think he'll be okay." I tell her quietly.

"How are you?"

I lift a shoulder in a shrug. "Sleepy."

Her head moves in a nod. "Okay, we can talk about it tomorrow. Go to sleep."

I lift up and kiss the corner of her mouth. "Good night, baby."

I see a smile tug at the corner of her mouth. "Good night."

Then as I think about all of my people under one roof and safe for the night, I drift comfortably into the deepest sleep I've had in a long time.

I wake up groggily, reaching for something as my eyes slowly open, only to find I'm clutching a pillow.

I search around me and find myself in Dylan's room, but now there's a crib set up in the corner of her room.

I sit up quickly in bed when I realize the time from the alarm clock on the side table. I'm going to have to call the kids' school and let them know why they aren't at school. I don't have much time to get to my eleven o'clock Engineering Economics class.

I jump up and start throwing my clothes on and grabbing my hat and pulling it on backwards over my hair. I don't have time to mess with it.

I rush to the kitchen but slow to a stop when I see Dylan scraping some green stuff on some toast.

"Hey sorry to rush off. I need to get to my class. I already missed morning lifts with the team." I tell her quickly.

She jerks around at my voice, but she's already bobbing her head up and down. She puts the toast on a plate and grabs her cup of coffee and starts shoving them both my way. "Here, take mine. Eat on your way."

I mindlessly take the things she's handing me while I continue. "I'm going to need the truck, so I guess the boys will hang out here..."

She interrupts me to say. "I took them to school already, thought you might need the truck. I just didn't want to wake you up to ask." She presses her lips together to hide a smile. "Turns out I'm not the only one who snores."

"Oh." I stand there still trying to get my brain to catch up.

"I told them I'd pick them up, too." She continues. "So just go do whatever you do. I'll see you later." Then she walks back to the counter and starts making more toast and coffee.

I stare at her for a moment before I lay the to-go plate and cup on the bar beside me and go grab her from behind. She giggles when I nuzzle my face into her neck, then she twists in my arms and wraps her arms around my neck, pulling my mouth to hers with a smirk.

I smile into our kiss before I tell her, "Thank you."

She just nods and looks up at me. "I'm going to have to make a rule that you can't walk around with your hat backwards when you're rushing out the door." She taps at the brim hanging down by my neck.

A surge of confidence runs through me at her words. "You like that, do ya?" I wink at her before closing my lips on hers again.

She starts to push at my chest. "Get out of here, Casanova. You're going to be late."

I chuckle and grab the toast, shoving it into my mouth, then grab the cup, waving it at her in goodbye as she watches me leave.

"Too sweet." I tell her.

She looks offended. "You haven't even tried it yet."

"Wasn't talking about the coffee." I give her a cocky grin and walk out the door.

♡ ⚹⚹⚹⚹⚹ ♡

I make it to class with a couple of minutes to spare, which is late for me. I don't have my laptop, so I try to remember everything he tells us without taking notes.

Everything feels like chaos right now. I'm finding it hard to stay focused with my head spinning around in circles: Dylan, the baby, the boys, Nate.

It's like a NASCAR race up there, always changing which one is out in front.

I get through that class barely retaining anything. I go eat lunch and get to practice early so I can explain to Coach why I missed this morning.

I walk up to the office and knock on the door.

"Come in." Comes a gruff voice from the other side.

I step through the doorway. "Hey, Coach. Just wanted to come and explain why I wasn't there this morning."

"Ah, Kemp. No need to explain. I half expected you to still be at Maddox's side... the way y'all are tied at the hip." His thick grey brows are pulled together, betraying the concern he's trying to keep out of his voice.

"They sent him home, scheduled his surgery for a couple weeks out." I inform him.

"I hate it for the kid. He's a cocky little son of a bitch, but he earned it. I hope he still gets his chance."

A corner of my mouth turns up. "I don't think he'd let anything keep him from that field for long."

A harrumph escapes him before he says, "I suppose you're right about that."

I turn to grab the doorknob. "Alright, Coach. Thanks for understanding. I'll go get some weights in before practice starts."

"Hang on a minute. While I got you in here, sit down." He says, sitting up in his chair.

"What's up, Coach?" I ask sitting down in one of the chairs in front of his desk.

He lets out a heavy sigh. "I know it's a bit of bad timing. You have a lot going on with Maddox, your little baby you got on the way," he looks at me knowingly. "And everything else at home."

It's not something I've ever talked about with him, but this isn't the first time I've had to ask forgiveness for missing something for the team or asking to leave early.

He continues, "But we've had some scouts, quite a few asking about you personally." He puts his hands up to stop what I'm about to say. "I know your goal isn't the NFL. I just really hate to see a good player like you never reach his full potential. And you'd be lying out your ass if you told me you don't love the game."

He just looks at me, letting what he said settle between us.

I don't want to let him down... I just know there's no way I can make it work. I lift my cap to rake my fingers through my hair before setting it back in place.

"I just don't think it's where my future's headed, Coach."

He deflates back into his seat. "Alright son. Just so you know, I don't need an answer just yet. Sit on it for a while before you shut it down completely, alright?"

I give him one sharp nod and say, "Yes sir. I can do that."

He waves a hand at the door. "Alright, get out of here. Go and make up for this morning."

I stand up out of the chair. "Will do, Coach."

♡ ⚬⚬⚬⚬⚬ ♡

After practice, I make the drive a couple towns over to Nate's house. I text Dylan and the boys letting them know it would be a little later when I get there.

I pull up the long dirt driveway that leads to Nate's parents' house.

After greeting his parents at the door and walking the familiar route to his room, I step into his giant suite of a room and find him laid back, leg propped up, on his couch playing Madden on his PlayStation.

"Well this is a pitiful sight." I say as my way of greeting him.

Nate jerks his head in my direction before he pauses his game and responds, "Yeah. Pretty pathetic, huh?"

"How are you feeling?"

Nate slams the remote down on his side table.

"Not great, dude. And at the risk of sounding like an asshole, I'm about sick of answering that question." He rubs the heels of his palms on his temples. "It's just one season. I'll spend it getting better and be out there next year, better than ever. *I* still have a shot."

He crosses his arms over his chest and just stares at the screen, refusing to look at me.

"Absolutely!" I encourage. "We'll rehab, you'll come back strong, and next year when I'm not there to take your spotlight, scouts will be all over you." I say, trying to tease him out of his bad mood a little.

His gaze finds mine, not a hint of amusement on his face.

Okay. Maybe a little too soon.

"Not we. *I* will rehab. I'll be damned if you let me be one of your fucking excuses." The anger he's fuming at me makes no sense.

"What the fuck is that supposed to mean?" I ask my temper slipping a bit.

Instead of answering my question he informs me. "Coach called me today."

My tone softens a bit. "Y'all make a plan to get you back out there?"

"Yeah, we have a plan. Like I said, *I* still have another shot at this. *I'm* going to do something with it." Bitterness can be heard in every word he says.

"Look, if you have something to fucking say, get it out, or I'm just gonna go home. I'll come back when you're in a better mood." I hike a thumb towards the door.

"He told me what you talked about. How there are scouts asking about you specifically and you're pissing it all away." He shouts.

I exhale, closing my eyes. "Coach shouldn't have said anything to you about it..."

"I'm glad he did. You surely wouldn't have." He slams a fist into his cushion. "God damn it. I'd kill to take that one hit back just so I don't have to miss even one game. And you're just giving up."

"You know I don't have a choi—"

"Don't say it. Don't you fucking tell me you don't have any choices. I don't have a choice. Me. I have to sit out the season wondering if I'll ever come back the same." He says, voice cracking at the end.

I take in his leg propped and wrapped up, then look back at Nate not knowing what to say.

"And don't spout your bullshit responsibility line to me either. They aren't responsibilities, Lane. They're people. People that can take care of themselves when they need to. That can go wherever you go. You just refuse to ask them." Nate shrugs a shoulder and looks away, hurt written all over his expression.

The words land harder than the hit that took him out.

"You're giving up," he continues, his voice lower now. "So, yeah, you can leave because I'm not in the mood to hear about your lack of choices right now."

I sit there, mouth open to say something... anything. Defend myself, reassure him that he'll be okay.

But nothing comes out...and he refuses to look at me.

I nod, more to myself than to him. "Alright. I'll come back later."

All I hear when I go to leave is the sound of the PlayStation resuming right before I click the door shut.

CHAPTER 25

Dylan

Lane finally walks through the door later that evening while Kohen, Blaze, and I are finishing up our tacos. Monday night football is on the TV... feels like it's becoming a recurring theme in my life lately.

I look up at the sound of the door and yell, "Tacos are on the counter, if you want any."

He gives me a tired smile and goes to make himself a plate.

I watch him as he shuffles around the kitchen. He must be exhausted; he hasn't looked up to check out the game once.

He makes his way to the couch, feet dragging, and sits between me and Blaze.

"Well?" Blaze asks staring directly at Lane.

"Well, what?" He says around a mouthful of food.

Blaze's eyes lock on him expectantly. "What's the deal with Nate?"

I see Lane's jaw clench, but he releases it so fast I almost miss it. "He's at home now. They want to give him time for the swelling to go down, so they scheduled his surgery in a couple of weeks."

Kohen asks, his brows drawn together, "Is he going to be able to play again?"

"Can't know for sure, but knowing him, he'll be back out there before you know it. He's determined he'll be back out there, better than ever."

Kohen's head bobs while Blaze says, "Oh yeah. I know he can do it. There's no way Nate won't come back from this. He loves it too much."

Lane doesn't say anything, just continues to eat his food.

"How's Bexley?" I ask.

He turns to me, his demeanor softening slightly. "She's okay. Basically, his personal cheerleader at times, and a drill sergeant when he needs it."

I smile at his description, picturing my new friend filling those roles perfectly, and his eyes crinkle in response.

Are they going to stay here again? It's pretty late, so it would make sense.

I really like having all of them here, it's a little pathetic.

I imagine this being our life.

Busy days ending in all of us piled together, hanging out. Like a family.

Creepy, Dylan.

You can't just assume your place in his family.

We eat and sit in silence for the rest of the game, other than a few shouts of disapproval or excitement from the boys.

Not Lane, though. He stays quiet throughout the whole game.

I watch him from the corner of my eye, trying to decide if something's wrong... or if he's just exhausted.

Suddenly he moves to get up, but he just walks to the kitchen and starts to put food away.

"I can do all that if you need to get home. I'm sure you're worn out." I yell out over the TV noise.

"You cooked. I'll clean." He says simply.

It's like he's saying the right things, it just feels wrong somehow. I sit there trying to talk myself out of thinking I did something wrong.

Must just be worry for Nate.

I clear my mind and get up to help him.

"I'll put everything away if you want to do the dishes. And before you say anything, I'm giving you my most hated job in the world." I tell him while grabbing some Tupperware.

He chuckles and says, "Alright, deal." Then starts grabbing stray dishes.

When we get done cleaning everything up he calls to the boys telling them they're about to leave.

I try not to let my disappointment show.

I look up at Lane, smiling when they go to leave, and tell him, "I'll see you guys later."

He leans into me placing a quick chaste kiss on my mouth. I'm left wanting more of him, but don't want to keep him from his rest.

After they leave, I stand there in the kitchen looking around at the space that was just filled and is now wiped clean of any trace of the night.

Geez, I'm being such a girl!

Just because he had a few bad days doesn't mean he's already tired of our relationship. He's just exhausted.

I'm not going to be that girl that makes him feel like he has to choose me over everything in his life.

I decide to take a shower and make a pass around the place turning off lights as I go.

I'm lying in bed, trying to find a comfortable position when a text comes in.

> Sorry, I've been a little off tonight.
> Long day.

I stare at it for a bit, trying to weigh its truth. I decide I'm being crazy and reply.

> It's all good. I figured you were tired and ready to be in your own bed.

I see the typing bubble pop up and go away a few times.

> I think there's been some confusion.

I read the text multiple times in *complete* confusion. What's he talking about?

What do you mean?

I wait in the still silence for his answer, but it never comes.

I shove the phone under my pillow and groan out loud. He probably fell asleep and I'm going to wonder all night what the hell he was talking about.

Then I hear the shuffling and a deep voice coming from outside my room.

Did he drive all the way back over here?

Other voices join the mix. Oh my God. He brought them all back.

Kohen's never going to let me hear the end of this.

Lane walks in with a giant duffle bag.

"The boys told me y'all made plans for homecoming week." He searches my face for answers. "This week." He adds for emphasis. "You're supposed to help them get dressed up and do their makeup or something."

I slap my hand to my forehead. "That's this Friday?"

"We just went home to get some clothes. Blaze said something about it earlier, and you never said anything about it. We can go home. I know they've been here all weekend."

"No." I almost shout. "Of course, you guys can stay. I want you to stay." I rush out feeling a little distraught. "I just can't believe we missed crazy hat day. I had a really funny sombrero."

He gives me an amused grin. And sits down on the edge of the bed.

"I was nervous that you'd just got caught up in a moment being nice or something. I'd definitely understand if you expected us to go home tonight." He says to me sincerely.

"I've never really done all of this before. You're kind of the first relationship I've ever been in." I watch his face for his reaction but he's just waiting patiently for me to continue.

"So I'm just going to give it to you straight and hope I don't sound like the clingy girlfriend. I love when you guys are here. I don't have siblings and like having a version of that with your brothers." I hesitate because I'm starting to feel a little vulnerable. "I love having you here. I never get tired of you being around."

His mouth turns up lazily on one side. "I don't get tired of you being around either."

I laugh nervously, "I had a bit of a crazy girlfriend moment. I knew you were tired but you were... a little off tonight. I got nervous that you were just too tired to deal with me and needed to get away."

His brows draw together. "It wasn't like that..."

"It's completely understandable." I rush out. "I know it's been a rough couple of days. I just hope you don't think I'm someone you have to manage before doing whatever you need for yourself."

His face falls and he looks away like I hit a nerve.

"Fuck..." He drags a hand through his hair. "Is that just how I come off?" He stands up and starts to pace. "None of you are a burden to me." He gets a little louder, frustration rolling off of him. "I'm not some kind of fucking martyr or something."

I stare at him, eyes wide. Lane is normally so steady and calm. The sudden outburst knocks the words right out of me.

"See. This is why I should've left. Nate and I got in a fight and I'm pretty fucked up about it. I should've worked through it before bringing it to your doorstep."

It all comes together now, and suddenly I'm the frustrated one. I sit up on my knees in the bed and glare at him.

"*Or*. You could've just said something." My voice is raised, but not screaming. "Don't pretend with me. Don't pretend like everything's okay when it's not. *That's* the point I'm trying to make."

He stands there frozen in place, gaze locked on mine.

A cold trail running down my cheek tells me my anger is starting to spill over. "I can handle your distance if I know where it's coming from, but.. Damn it!" I swipe at the stupid tears on my face. "I thought you didn't want to deal with me... I thought you didn't want me." My voice drops. "And I thought I was being silly for thinking it, but something *was* wrong, and I knew it. All *you* had to do was tell me."

Fuck. These hormones are a son of a bitch.

Our eyes stay locked—mine blazing, his unreadable.

And then he laughs.

It slips out of him at first, short and breathless, like he's been holding something in too long. He scrubs a hand over his face, shaking his head, but it doesn't stop.

I sink down on to my heels, crossing my arms and say flatly. "I'm glad you think this is so funny."

He leans down, placing a hand on either side of me on the bed before planting a kiss on my unmoving mouth. His chest still shakes with laughter, only solidifying my anger.

He pulls back and takes in my look of aggravation. "I'm sorry. It's not funny." Another chuckle. "You just made it sound so simple."

I throw my hands up and give him a duh look.

"I'm sorry if I made you feel that way." He lifts a hand to my cheek, thumb resting at the corner of my mouth. "I just didn't want to make you feel like there was another problem you had to solve for me, and honestly, I don't even know if I want to talk about it yet."

My anger leaves me all at once, and I nod my acceptance. "Okay."

He brings his lips to mine again, and I immediately respond this time. My mouth opens for his, and I bring my arms around his body, falling into him.

Then we hear a throat being cleared. "You about done fighting, Mom and Dad? I seriously have to pee," Blaze yells from around the corner of my door that was left wide open.

"Yeah, y'all could at least shut the damn door." Kohen shouts from the room down the hall.

I groan and throw myself back on the bed absolutely morti-fied that they both just heard my meltdown.

I see Blaze peek around the corner with a boyish grin, then he points towards the bathroom past my doorway. "I'm just gonna go."

Lane swoops a hand in the direction of the bathroom still leaning over me. "Hurry up, you nosy assholes."

He walks over to the door and yells out, "And go to bed."

I hear Blaze say mockingly, "So you can kiss and make up?" He snorts out his laughter.

Lane shouts, "And close the damn door. There's a girl around, you little shit."

This only encourages Blaze's laughter, but it's muffled when Lane closes the door to my bedroom.

"Well, that was embarrassing... I kind of forgot about them being here." I glare at the ceiling like it offended me.

Lane falls on his back beside me and lays his arm out in a silent invitation. I take it, inching closer until my head rests on his shoulder and my arm's draped over his chest.

"Don't pay them any mind," he says easily. "I'm honestly surprised they didn't come running in here to gang up on me. They'd never forgive me if I did something stupid enough to run you off."

I don't know how true it is, but I smile at the thought of them wanting me to stick around.

We lay there in silence, other than the steady rhythm of his deep breaths moving in time with his chest.

Something pulls my attention away from the moment.

A flutter, low and unfamiliar, skims across my belly.

"Lane!" I whisper shout like my voice could scare the movement away.

"Yeah?" He whispers back with a smirk on his face.

"Very slowly, give me your hand."

With exaggerated slowness he lifts his hand from his side, so I grab it mid air and pull it to my belly where I'm feeling the flutter.

"Do you feel that?" I ask him still whispering.

His face draws in concentration, patiently waiting to feel something.

"I don't." His deep voice fills the room at the same time the flutter turns into a bump.

His face lifts to mine in surprise.

"I felt her." He says before looking back down at the hand resting on my belly.

Then a quick succession of bumps breaks out and stops again.

"Holy shit." He breathes. "She's really in there."

He drops to his knees beside the bed so that his face hovers over where his hand's resting.

"Did you have doubts?" I ask sarcastically, and at the sound of my voice the thumps take off again.

Completely ignoring me he demands, "Say something."

I chuckle at his excitement and try to think of something to say when he exclaims, "It worked when you laughed too!"

"Now I'm starting to feel like a toy." I say eyes squinted, but I can't stop smiling.

He glances up with a brow quirked for just a second to say, "Not right now you're not." Then returns his full attention to the little thumper inside of me.

"Say something again." He orders me.

"Hello, baby girl. Can you hear me in there?" I singsong, feeling a little silly especially when nothing happens.

"Maybe she likes my voice better."

My chest tightens when the little traitor inside of me starts bumping into his palms again.

"I feel betrayed!" I say in faux horror.

He chuckles. "I'm not sure if kicking me means she likes me. But I'm gonna take the win."

We take turns playing our game of seeing who she'll kick for until I can't feel her moving anymore.

We drift off later wrapped around each other, Lane's hand resting protectively over the small rise of my belly housing our little girl.

CHAPTER 26

Dylan

I'm pulling into my job on Monday, holding a stack of coffees in place in my passenger seat.

All the guys went back home last night after a week of crazy dress-up days leading up to Kohen's homecoming game. Lane had another away game to get to so it was just Blaze and me cheering Kohen on from the bleachers.

Lane got home late Saturday night, and we had one hell of a welcome-home night before we had to jump back into the monotony of the week.

They all packed up after we ate together and watched all of the Sunday games together. I'm actually starting to understand it more and find myself getting just as heated when things don't go our team's way.

I grab the stack of coffees and files that I need to bring back in, and walk in the direction of the building with CASA of Dry Creek stamped on the doors.

The building itself is nothing special. Sand-colored bricks, sun-faded and chipped, hold the one-story structure together like it's been standing there longer than anyone remembers.

Walking through the doors feels like stepping into a time machine set permanently to the eighties. Mismatched patterns on the waiting-room chairs. A bulletin board crowded with announcements no one ever reads. Cubicles wedged between the actual offices like an afterthought.

But it's busy. Phones ring nonstop. People move with purpose, files tucked under arms, voices low and urgent.

I'm making my rounds of dropping off cups to their appropriate people, and I wait to bring Rebecca hers last so we can chat.

She's obviously above me in the food chain but she's not too much older than me, and talking to her never feels like work.

She slams a pen down and tosses back her sleek, straight blonde hair. "Oh, thank God! I desperately needed this."

I slump into one of her chairs placed in front of her desk, its surface littered with papers. "Rough morning?"

Rebecca takes a sip of her coffee and groans in satisfaction. "More like a rough weekend."

"Oh no. I hope everything's okay." I sit up straighter in the seat.

"Everything with me is fine, but there's this case I have that's been bugging me." She starts shuffling through the papers on her desk. "I have a parent that's been working so hard to get her kids back. She's done everything by the book. Until," she taps a page. "She skipped this Saturday's visitation that was set up for her."

"You think she's giving up?" I ask wondering why someone who wanted their kids back would skip the visitation of all things when there are much more difficult requirements throughout the process.

She presses her lips together and sighs. "She's saying that she was never informed about it. But it was clearly in the system. And there's an email logged saying she needs to be there this Saturday."

I lean over her desk to take a peek at the papers she'd pointed to. "Hmm, do you believe her?"

Rebecca throws herself back in her chair. "I don't know. I mean she had a pretty rough history. I really thought she'd finally got it all together. Clean drug tests. She's just really shown up lately, and I wanted it to work out for their family."

I'm searching through the paperwork like it's a puzzle that I can solve. I'd just hate for a misunderstanding to fail these kids and a parent that's actually trying.

"I don't have all day to look into it, though. I'm working on four other cases and I just don't have anything here at the moment that can help her." Red manicured nails gather the papers in a neat pile before sliding them into a manila folder.

"Can I look over it?" Her gaze jerks to mine. "I doubt I'll be able to find out anything more than you did, but I have a little time on my hands and if I look busy, maybe Jerry won't find any more things for me to clean."

She smiles with a conspiratorial grin. "Go for it! I hope you find something I missed."

♡ ⚡ ♡

Turns out I didn't have some extra time after all.

Apparently, a big storm is rolling in next week, and court dates are getting canceled left and right. All of the rescheduling chaos landed squarely on my desk.

I spent the next couple of hours calling parents, foster families, caseworkers, and attorneys, juggling calendars and court availability, making sure no one falls through the cracks.

At the end of my very long day, I walk through the doors of my home straight into Monday Night Football chaos.

None of them except for Lane, even look up at my entrance. To my surprise, the bar is already covered in a full meal.

Porkchops, mac-n-cheese, broccoli, and baked beans.

My mouth is already watering.

I toss my things on the counter and toss off my heels.

I grab myself a plate and make my way to the couch, ruffling Kohen's perfectly gelled hair on my way past my recliner that he's claimed for himself.

He scoffs at me, which only makes me grin before I drop down beside Lane.

Lane pulls me to his side, kissing the top of my head, and asks, "How was your day?"

"Busy." I say between bites. "Apparently judges melt in the rain or something, because they're all canceling court dates from the storm coming in. Yours?"

He shrugs eyes never straying from the game. "The usual, I guess."

How informative.

"What about you two? Girls still drooling from redneck day? I'm sure the bubba teeth really did a number on them."

Kohen replies dryly, "I never wore the teeth."

At the same time Blaze says, "I got them taken away today for wearing them in class again."

I laugh at his junior high shenanigans.

I end my line of questioning when the pork chop I take a bite out of hits the freaking spot and it has my full attention.

When I get done with my second helping, I bring my plate to the sink.

I pause when I see the case file that I got from Rebecca and drag it with me back to my spot.

I'm turned sideways on the couch, back leaning against Lane and trying to find something that could prove the woman's explanation.

The visitation is clearly set up, and in the system well before it comes to pass. So I take another look at the email that's logged, and the date's clearly stated inside of the email that it was sent out in plenty of time.

It's bothering me that the date is written in the body of the email instead of an automated time stamp.

I wouldn't think that someone's out there just lying to cause problems, but maybe someone was covering their ass or there was a glitch in the system and it never sent.

"Hey Blaze, can you hand me my laptop off of that side table?" I ask, saccharine sweet.

He rolls his eyes at me, but grabs it and passes it over.

I quickly turn it on and log into the automated email system.

I search the date that it should've been sent out and can't find an email relayed to the client that day.

So I go to the next day. And then the next.

I repeat this process all the way until the date of the visitation and see that the email was actually sent Saturday evening *after* the actual visitation was assigned.

I squeal out loud, making everyone in the room jump and turn to me.

"She didn't skip the visitation!" Pure delight bursts out of me.

"Oh-kay," Lane drawls, stretching out the word into two syllables.

"Never mind. I need my phone." I rush out, reaching for my phone on the table and walking out of the room to call Rebecca.

Both of the boys follow me with their eyes as I pass, brows arched in amusement.

"Hey," I chirp holding back my excitement when she answers the phone.

"Dylan?"

"Yes, sorry. I just couldn't wait to tell you. Are you near your computer?" I see Lane walk into the hallway to listen in on my conversation.

"I'm actually on it right now. I still haven't escaped the office yet. What's up?" The clacking of her keyboard pauses in the background.

"Okay. Sign in to the automated email system and look up the date of the visitation." I inform her.

I hear her sharp intake of breath. "Did you find something?"

I'm nodding even though she can't see me. "I think so. I just wanted to run it by you and make sure it all makes sense." I look at Lane and do a little bounce of excitement, and his shoulders shake in amusement.

Her typing in the background resumes and then a click. Then another click.

"It was sent out after the visitation!" She exclaims. "The date in the email was wrong!"

"So that's it, right?" I asked hope creeping in my voice. "That's the proof she needs?"

Her laugh comes over the phone, light and musical. "This is perfect, Dylan. I can't believe you caught that. I knew she wasn't lying." I hear the sound of her chair creaking. "Okay, I'm going to go deal with this. Thank you."

"No problem. I don't have work tomorrow, but I'll drop by and give you the files back before classes."

"Perfect. See you then." Then I hear the click of the line going dead.

I can't hold back the satisfaction blooming in my chest anymore, and I run straight into Lane's waiting arms.

"Oh my God. I can't believe I actually found something for her. It's like a freaking adrenaline rush!"

A deep laugh rumbles through him. "You did awesome, baby. Now explain what happened?"

I rush out the summary of what went down. "...And I'm not completely sure I should've told you all that... client confidentiality and all that."

He holds out a pinky. "I'll never tell a soul."

I giggle before locking our pinkies together and kissing my fist.

When he kisses his, a loud knock sounds from the kitchen.

A look of confusion crosses both of our faces.

I shrug my shoulders. "Maybe Bex needs something."

Another knock echoes through the apartment.

"I'm coming." I shout.

I walk to the door with Lane following me to listen to me still raving about how Rebecca reacted to my find, and open the door without checking.

"...so I'm going to wake up early to make sure she gets that case file." I turn and the person standing at my door halts me in place.

"I'm glad you're still pursuing your career, at least."

Seeing her standing there meticulously put together, it's like she stepped out of another life.

"Mom?"

CHAPTER 27

Dylan

She looks around at the strangers (to her) in my apartment before her gaze lands on me again and checks over me head to toe, pausing on my slightly rounded stomach.

Her eyes start to fill with unshed tears, though I'm not sure of the meaning behind them.

She takes a second to compose herself before she says, "It looks like you've settled in nicely here."

I'm still frozen, hand holding the door open. "What are you doing here?"

My mom glances around at the boys settled in the living room then travels to Lane standing directly behind me. She's taking in his hand on my shoulder that's tense like he might drag me behind him in a moment's notice. Then she returns her gaze to mine again.

"You never answered my text," she answers, letting a little hurt show in her voice. "Can I please come inside?"

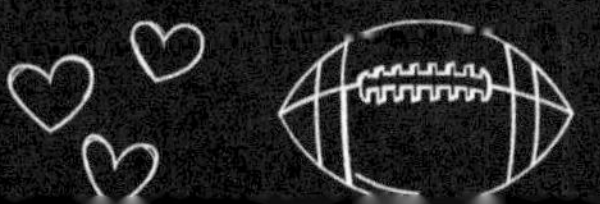

I turn sideways to make room for her to walk past before closing the door behind her.

I hear Lane clear his throat before asking close to my ear. "I can get out of here if you want to be alone." His hand slides to my arm and squeezes, letting me know it's okay—whatever I decide.

I jerk my head sideways to look at him. "No. Stay."

He nods his head once and turns his head to Blaze and Kohen. "You two go finish the game in the guest room."

Blaze looks a little worried, but hops right up. Kohen does a slow walk-by, eyes darting between all of us, assessing before he finally follows Blaze down the hall.

My chest loosens just a little. I'm not sure where this conversation will lead, but I know I don't want it spilling over onto them.

"How did you find me?" I try to keep the hostility out of my voice, wanting to keep this civil.

"Your father. He said that we should try to mend things." Her voice wavers when she continues quietly. "He told me you're having a little girl."

I rub a protective hand over my stomach, still not sure if she came here for a fight. "We are."

"Jesus," she exhales. "Could you please just talk to me? I'm your mother, not your enemy." Her composure slips further as she unfolds her hands that had been clasped together in front of herself.

"Then why are you here?" I ask, the hurt bleeding into my

voice despite my best effort. "I thought you refused to watch me *'destroy my life.'*"

I feel Lane shift behind me.

Her eyes shut at the sting of my words. She slowly opens them, tears shining in her eyes. "I came here to tell you I was wrong." She lifts her chin, shoulders straight, like she's bracing herself to say what she came to say. "You're a much stronger person than I ever was. I'd like to think I had something to do with that, but you were born with that hard-headed determination."

It sounds a bit rehearsed like maybe she'd planned what she was going to say on her way here, but I wanted to believe her.

I wanted to, but what if this is just another manipulation tactic.

Is there something she's wanting from me?

"I'm not going back, Mom." I say softly, but with finality, feeling the fingers on my arm tighten, just slightly. "I have a life here now." I pause to look at her intently. "One that finally feels like mine."

I'm a little shocked at my words. I hadn't even realized until I said the words how true they are.

It's like I was meant to be here, even if there wasn't a baby involved.

I have my own real friendships; my own job that I got by myself. One that honestly makes me feel like I'm doing something that really makes a difference in the world, even at the level I'm at.

And even if I didn't have Little One, I'd still want to be right where I'm at.

My mom lifts her hands in surrender. "I'm not asking you to. I swear."

Something cracks inside of her and she steps towards me until she can grab one of my hands with both of hers. "Whether I was right or wrong," her voice cracks. "I know I can't do this. I can't go months without seeing you or talking to you ever again."

A tear slips free before I can stop it. "I don't either, but you have to accept my decisions, Mom. All of them."

I hesitate, then add the thing I know can really test her. "Even if I decide to stay home with the baby," I don't see myself making this decision, but I need to know. "You have to let me."

In her defense, she just squeezes her eyes shut, jaw tightening as she swallows the opinion I *know* she has. When she opens them again she simply says, "Okay."

It wasn't exactly enthusiastic, but it feels like a step in the right direction. And for now, I'll take it.

I smile at her, a bit timidly, before embracing her, her arms wrapping around me in a tight hug. Her body melts into mine, the tension easing from her and the room.

I pull back and tell her, "This is Lane, by the way." I say with a small huff of laughter.

She pulls back with a smile that's polite and forced and reaches out a hand. "Victoria Whitlock. You must be the reason we're all here today."

"Mom!" I warn.

Lane only chuckles and shakes the hand she's extending.

"I believe the reason we're here rests in your daughter's belly. If it had been up to me, she would've stayed with me from the second I found her."

I feel my cheeks grow warm in response to his claiming to want to keep me from the very beginning.

Mom straightens and looks to me, brow arched. "Well, I can see the appeal." At my groan, she continues. "You two lingering around the corner... You can come out now. I won't bite. I promise."

I feel Lane stiffen beside me when both boys step into view, Blaze looking a little nervous while Kohen wears a familiar smirk.

"As I'm sure you just heard," she says smoothly. "My name is Victoria. And you are?"

Lane answers for them. "These are my brothers."

Blaze lifts a hand in a small wave.

"Blaze." He says a little nervously.

My mom smiles warmly at him. "Nice to meet you. And you?"

I can already tell Kohen has a smart-ass remark up his sleeve by the evil turn his grin takes. "Kohen. You must be the mom that kicked her pregnant daughter out."

The room goes silent at his calling her out.

Then my mother bursts out laughing. "It seems you *do* bite. Nice to meet you too, Kohen."

The moment reminds me of when he first showed up at my doorstep, guns blazing, trying to feel me out for his brother —and I'm unexpectedly touched that he'd do the same for me.

I hear Lane release the air from his chest. "Kohen. Really?"

He just shrugs his shoulders. "She doesn't seem mad."

Mom replies to Lane. "*She* had an ornery teen at one point, if I can handle Dylan going through puberty, I can certainly take a few deserved hits from this one."

Blaze starts cracking up, breaking up the tension completely. "I've seen her lose at Phase Ten. She can get pretty mean."

"Hey!" I say in faux offense.

Mom laughs. "Oh yeah, she's such a sore loser. She thinks she has to be the best at everything."

We eventually ease into the living room carrying on a mostly easy conversation between all of us, until eventually all of my guys are satisfied enough to leave me alone with her and go home to get some sleep.

"So... how long are you staying?" I ask when the silence settles after their departure.

"My plane leaves tomorrow night. I wasn't sure how this was going to go." She explains. "How are you feeling honey? Is everything going good with the baby?"

"Everything's good." I hesitate. "I have an anatomy scan tomorrow after classes if you want to come with me. Lane's friend is having surgery tomorrow, and I told him he should be there with him.

She brings her hands to her mouth, nodding her head in excitement. "I'd love to."

I smile brightly. "Okay. It's at three."

"Does Lane usually go to the appointments with you?" She asks, attempting casualness.

"He's been to every one since I told him." I tell her.

She gives me a knowing look. "You really like him."

It's a statement, not a question so I don't reply.

She throws her hands up. "Okay fine. I get it. I haven't earned back the gossip part yet." At my eye roll she continues. "I'll wait patiently for you to tell me all about it."

I groan in submission. "Yes mom. We're together. And I really like him. You happy now?"

She tries to repress a smirk. "A little. Just be careful." At my look of contempt, she continues, "Your father was wonderful at first. Until he wasn't. And I've never seen you in a relationship, much less falling in love. I'm just scared for you. No ultimatums. Just a worried mom scared of history repeating."

"I can say one thing about Lane for sure. Even if we don't work out, he'll do the right thing by everybody. No matter what it takes." I shrug my shoulders like I have no concern with our outcome. "And that's enough for me to take the risk."

She takes me in, weighing my truth with hers, brows drawn.

She looks away and nods. "You must have some reason for believing all of this. Does it have anything to do with the way those boys listen to him like he's a parent and not like an older brother?"

My mouth drops open at how my mother had already clocked their dynamic.

I close my mouth and draw a line. "I don't know what you're talking about."

"Sure." She gives me a skeptical look. "Don't worry, I won't push. I just needed to know you weren't walking in blind."

I let out a heavy sigh. "There's a lot I want to tell you, but some of it isn't mine to tell, and to be honest, I'm just not there yet." I soften the blow by adding. "I'm really happy you're here, though." I start to tear up a little. "I really missed you. You've always been my biggest cheerleader all along. I still want that." I choke through a sob now that my emotions are completely betraying me. "I need my mom to help me learn how to be one."

"That's all I want, honey. I'm not saying I'll always be good at it, it's like I've always told you: This is my first time, too. But I want to be a part of it."

I look at the hand my mom claimed and look at the one resting on Little One. I think about all of the mistakes I'm bound to make as a mom and silently pray that she'll give me grace when I fall short.

I lift my gaze back up to my own mother, who didn't promise perfection, just honesty, commitment, and her love.

And for now, I decide to give her some of that grace.

CHAPTER 28

Lane

20 WEEKS

As I slowly drift out of my dreamless state, sounds start to take shape around me… a shower running somewhere, footsteps thudding up and down the stairs.

I reach for Dylan, only to find cold, empty sheets on her side of the bed.

I lift my head, scanning around my room, barely lit by early morning light. And then let it fall back down into the pillow.

I slept terribly last night. I want nothing more than to ignore all the things I need to do today and just sleep the day away.

Groaning, I force myself out of bed and go to get dressed.

Once we're all up and moving, I drive the boys to their schools, drop them off, then head to the gym for a light lift and a short run. Just enough to burn off the restless energy sitting in my chest. After that, I point my truck toward the hospital where Nate's having surgery.

I don't really want to show up uninvited, but I also know I'd regret not being there. We may be pissed at each other right now, but he's my best friend.

I'm going to be there.

I even skipped the anatomy scan appointment that I was really looking forward to.

I'm glad Dylan has her mom. I just hope her mom was serious about what she said.

I know not every mother is like mine, but I've seen how a parent's influence can pressure their children.

Not that I think Dylan would just ditch me, I mean she chose to be here before there was even an us.

I was ready to step in when she called my brothers out of the hallway. I wanted to be respectful, but *they're* mine.

Turns out, I didn't need to. She was actually kind to them —in her own way.

I pull into the parking garage grabbing my ticket at the entrance. I park and text Bex for the room information. I run through the maze of the huge hospital and finally find his room.

A chorus of voices tells me to come in at my knock and I ease the door open.

I walk in and return all of their greetings before taking in Nate stuck in his hospital bed, leg propped up and gown already on.

He isn't wearing his usual cocky grin, and that's my first

sign that he's actually more nervous about this than he'll ever say out loud.

"You showed." He deadpans.

I arch a brow at him. "Obviously."

"Bex said you had some baby stuff to do today, you didn't have to come. I get it."

"I know." His shoulder drops just the slightest bit as he nods his acknowledgment. "I'll be here when you get out, and the doctors tell us everything went perfectly."

The sound of gagging draws our attention away.

Bexley is making a face and pretending to hold back vomit. "Would you two get over yourselves? Your testosterone-flavored make-up sesh is making me sick."

We're all laughing at her when nurses start pouring in saying it's time to prep Nate and we need to go to the waiting room.

I give him a fist bump, leaving the room first to leave him with his family and make myself comfortable in a chair.

I text Dylan letting her know he's going back and ask her how everything's going. But I think she's still in class because I don't get an answer for about an hour.

> Just got out of class. Grabbing a late
> lunch with Mom before the appointment.
> I'll send pics. Everything going good on
> your end?

I jump at the sound of Bexley's voice so close.

"Her mom?"

"Jesus, Bex. You ever heard of privacy?" I whisper-shout at her.

She laughs, leaning back into her own chair. "I prefer to call it being overly observant." I shake my head at her. "When did her mom get here? I thought they weren't speaking?"

"She got here last night, said she was sorry... kinda." I shake my head again, this time in refusal to say anything else, even if I don't think she'd mind me telling her. "Just talk to her about it."

She rolls her eyes but accepts what I've given here. "Boys are terrible gossips. I'll talk to her later." She glances down then back up at me a serious look on her face.

"You're going to help him, aren't you? I know he was kind of a dick the last time y'all talked to each other, but he needs to get this back. I think it'll break him if he loses football."

I pull her to my side. This girl who comes off like nothing could touch her, cares more fiercely about her people than anyone would ever believe.

"He's going to be okay." I know she doesn't want to hear the pretty positives, so I give it to her straight. "He won't break if he can't play again. It'll hurt like hell for a while, but he has you there to kick his ass until he dusts himself off and realizes he didn't lose everything. He has all of us at his back."

Her head moves up and down against my shoulder. "And I'll be there whenever I can to help him." I assure her.

We sit like that for a little bit, mirroring her parents as Susan cries heavily into her husband's shoulder.

Tom whispers in her ear before she nods and sniffles, before turning to us to say they're going to get some coffee.

Bex straightens in her chair, wiping away her tears. "How are you and Dylan?"

A smile breaks out on my face. "We're really good. I'm sure she already told you but we can feel her moving now. Pretty crazy actually."

She returns my smile. "Look at you, proud daddy."

"It might be weird to say, but I'm already in love with her."

Bex looks at me conspiratorially. "Are we talking about your daughter or Dylan?"

I huff out a laugh at her digging. "I was talking about my daughter, but...I think I loved Dylan from the moment she fell into that bed with me."

Her eyes spring wide open. "That good, huh?"

Oh shit. "Not like that, we just met-"

She laughs out loud, interrupting me. "I know she told me." When she composes herself, she asks, "Have you told her?"

"Definitely not." I chuckle nervously. "Too scared she'll run out on me again."

"Hey." She says a little offensively for her friend. "This isn't the same as that. She really likes you."

"I know she won't outright leave again, but I can feel it sometimes. She clams up or starts joking when things get too serious, like she's scared to let it get too deep. If it hadn't been for the baby, I'd have never seen her again." I let out a heavy sigh.

Bexley looks at me like she's coming to a decision before she tells me, "She looked for you too."

"Well yeah-" I start before she interrupts.

"*Before* she found out about the baby. She told me. And I swear to God, if you tell her I told you, I'll kill you! But she wanted to find you too."

My brows shoot up, and I sit back in my chair as pieces in my brain quietly rearrange themselves.

I'm so wrapped up in my own thoughts that I never notice when Nate's parents walk back in. I'm startled to find a doctor that joined the room at some point is addressing our small group.

"...only two at a time can come back for now. But everything went perfectly on our end, and he should wake up soon." The doctor finishes up with a polite smile then turns around and walks out.

Bex wraps her arms around my forearms and squeezes. "He's okay." I hear her whisper to herself. Then louder to her parents. "You two can go in there first. I'll wait with Lane but come get us soon after he wakes up, please."

Susan and Tom take off to Nate's room hand in hand, drawing strength from each other.

♡ ⚡ ♡

Nate was pretty out of it with his pain meds so I didn't hang around too long.

I'm leaving the hospital when a cluster of pictures come in from Dylan. I'm dying to look, but wait until I pick up the boys and get back to the house before I look at them.

I'm sitting at our dining room table, swiping through my phone, looking at black and white ultrasound photos. Pictures of a little foot, a little side profile, one of just her face and one of her whole tiny body, her little butt and legs with an arrow and bold text that says 'it's a girl'.

Then the last few are not black and white. They're a slightly yellow, bubble-looking pictures of an actual baby.

I can see her little plump lips sucking on her thumb. A little wide, upturned nose. Chubby cheeks. It's insanely detailed.

That's my little girl's face.

My voice cracks when I yell, "Y'all come see my kid."

I can't tear my eyes away as I hear the thud of footsteps.

Kohen's voice cuts in, dry as ever. "Isn't it a little early?"

Blaze, who must've ran, is leaning over my shoulder. "Aww. That's definitely your fat nose."

Kohen smacks him as he steps up. "Your fat nose too, dumbass." He leans over and takes in the shapes for a moment. I'm expecting some smart-ass bullshit to come out of his mouth. "She looks cute," is all he says.

I look up at the soft smile on his face, then it shifts into his signature smirk.

"Bet she comes out looking most like her Uncle Kohen."

There it is.

I hand them my phone to look through all of the photos and they take turns making comments.

"Alright, give it back to me." I yank my phone back. "Y'all good staying here by yourselves tonight?"

They roll their eyes.

"Yeah, we're good." Kohen says, already heading back upstairs.

"I'll leave you the truck just in case." He flicks two fingers behind his head never looking back as he disappears around the corner.

I use my phone to order my Uber, wondering if Victoria has already left or if she'll still be there when I get to Dylan's place.

I wouldn't mind a little more time around her. Not to start anything—just to let her see that I'm not going anywhere. That I plan on taking care of her daughter, whether she believes it yet or not.

I'm waiting outside when a girl pulls up asking if I ordered an Uber.

I slide into the backseat, buckle up and pull my phone back

out to look over all the pictures again, as if I might have missed something.

"My name's Cassie," she says politely enough as she makes the turn off my road.

I quickly glance up and tell her, "Lane."

"Where are you headed tonight?" She asks, giggling.

I quickly shut down any notions that might be going through her head. "My girlfriend's."

"Oh."

I think that will be the end of this, but she rallies.

"Wait...Aren't you Gavin? From the football team, Gavin?"

I keep my tone even though my patience is thinning. "Yeah, that's me. I just go by Lane."

"Oh my God. I love football. It sucks that Nate got hurt. He was so good."

"Yeah." I deadpan, getting a little more pissed off about her talking like he died. "That sucked."

"I actually hooked up with Nate one time." Of course she did. "So you can get my number from him if things don't work out with your girlfriend."

Fuck she can't read a room.

I look up at her eyes in the mirror trying to eat me alive with her heated stare.

"Not a chance." I say flatly. "And keep your eyes on the road."

Her face immediately falls, but she keeps her attention to the trip and doesn't speak again until we pull up.

"Here we are." She mutters.

I get out as soon as she puts it in park and slam the door mid-sentence.

When I step into Dylan's space, the day's weight falls off of me all at once... like just being around her is all the peace I need.

I slip off my boots at the door and walk back to her room. I hear the shower running and groan out loud at finding her exactly how I wanted to.

I open the door to the bathroom, steam pouring out when I do.

"Lane, is that you?" She shouts over the rush of the water.

Instead of answering I strip out of my clothes in record time before stepping into the boiling hot water with her.

She does a little excited shriek at my quick entrance.

"You asshole. You scared me."

"Jesus what do you have this set to? The depths of hell?" I reach around her and turn the hot water all the way down. "Can't be good for the baby."

I smirk when she slams me into the wall to get away from the icy spray.

The look she gives me could mean my end. "You're so dead!"

I glance down at all of her wet curves pressed deliciously against me and let one corner of my mouth lift.

"I may have already gone to heaven." I run a hand down her back ending by cupping one of her cheeks, drawing her closer.

Despite her anger, a little smile peeks through. "That was awfully cheesy."

I lean down to take her mouth but she bites my lip.

"Ouch."

She has a brow arched. "Heat first."

I grin big and decide she needs a little more cold water for that temper. I use my body to pin us both under the stream.

"No!" She screeches and tries to pull herself away from the tight hold I have on her.

Slowly, I twist the hot water into a more reasonable temperature.

I let go when she stops fighting, the water warmed back up, but she's fuming. She turns around dismissing me.

Alright let the games begin.

CHAPTER 29

Dylan

20 WEEKS

I turn around because even though I'm genuinely angry —I hate cold water—I'm buzzing with excitement from the battle of wills we're having right now.

I can't see him, but the air is charged while I wait for his next power move.

I'm surprised to only feel his lips at my neck, kissing me so sweetly.

Well, it wasn't the battle I was wanting, but I'll accept his submission all the same. I stand completely still, making him work for it a little.

Rough fingertips trail up and down my sides, sending shivers through my body like the cold water never could.

I want to reach behind me and pull at his hair, but I ball my fists and keep them at my sides.

He hums into my skin. "My girl's going to make me fight for it, huh?"

One of his hands stops their torturous movements and clasps one of my tits roughly, pulling it up and then dropping it letting his palm graze over my puckered nipple on the way back down to repeat the motion.

Achingly slowly, his other hand skims down my side, my hips, my thighs, until it circles my leg to my inner thigh to make its way back up.

Up.

Up.

Until it pauses at the apex of my legs, hovering, never quite landing where I want it most.

The hand that's punishing my nipple moves to the other breast to give it attention, while his fingers tease my folds brushing my wet seam without quite giving me what I want.

Okay, maybe this *is* a power play.

"Come on, baby. I need a little something in return." He rumbles in my ear, only adding to the heat building inside of me.

I clearly don't want him to stop, so I close the distance he left between our bodies and let my head fall to the side so he has easier access to undo me with that mouth of his.

I suck in a sharp breath when I feel his hardness pressing into me from behind. Our skin is sliding against each other in time with the movements his hands are making.

My hands are shaking now, but I keep them firmly in place at my sides.

"That's a little better." He says nipping at the tight line of my neck.

Heat sparks through me when his finger finally slide through my wetness, just enough to catch the tip of my clit with his circling fingertips.

A whimper escapes me.

He chuckles darkly, teeth nibbling at my earlobe now.

"Come on, Dylan. You have to give a little to get a little." He rumbles into my ear.

I think about standing my ground and keep trying to hold back my reactions, but then decide, I don't actually win in that scenario, so I give a little more.

I release my hands from their metaphorical chains, clasping one behind his head while the other reaches blindly back, finding skin to anchor myself to.

I moan when his restraint loosens further. The hand at my breast moves to wrap around my throat, tilting my chin up and pulling my mouth to his.

His kiss is hungry and a bit feral.

I soak up every second of it, letting my body thrust into his fingers to get the harder pressure I need.

My stomach tightens, nearing the point of release when he pulls away and every inch of his skin disappears from mine, leaving me cold.

I turn to see if this was his plan all along, half expecting to see victory shining in his face.

But his eyes are burning into mine with an intensity I wasn't expecting. It's like this means more to him than the game we're playing.

Without breaking our gaze he shuts off the water behind me, leaving me even colder than before.

He looks away to reach around the shower curtain to grab the towel hanging on the rack on the wall.

His expression never shifts back to the playful mood this started with. His green eyes penetrate mine like they're trying to see into my deepest thoughts.

He reaches around me, holding opposite ends of the towel, and dries me off. Roughly in some places and super delicate in others before using the same towel to run it over himself.

He flings the shower curtain open and steps out, extending a hand for me to take.

I'm not sure what turn we took or if it's something he was feeling all along that I never picked up on.

I take his hand, and he leads me to the bedroom.

When we're standing in front of the bed, I take a step around him to face him.

He searches my face while I search his, both of us waiting for the other to move.

He stands perfectly still while I get on my tiptoes to place a kiss on his mouth.

Apparently, it's his turn to let me fight for him.

And if I didn't feel like this was something he needed, I might have let our games play out, let him chase me a little more. But something in his eyes is begging me to fight for this.

For us?

I get on my toes again to start peppering kisses at his throat that gulps under my lips. I slowly make my way down his chest until my heels meet the floor again.

His arms go around me, hands making fists at my back, as he kisses the top of my head.

My legs start to fold underneath me as I let my mouth trail lower.

And lower.

His muscles tighten under my tongue as I close in on my destination.

His hands are dragged into my hair as I land on my knees, and I grasp his length with one hand at his base.

I watch him watching me as I pull his tip to my lips, tongue peeking out to taste.

His eyes close briefly before popping back open to take in everything I'm doing.

I widen the opening of my lips and put as much of him as I can fit into my mouth.

He sucks in a sharp breath.

I close my lips around him and suck as I draw him back out.

He groans loudly and throws his head back.

I lose myself in the sound as it sends a strange rush of pride through my chest.

I quicken my pace, moving my hand in time with my mouth and bring my hand up to cup his balls. My fingertips curl under the soft skin.

His hips start moving with me, pushing his cock deeper with each thrust until I can't even breathe.

I feel his fist in my hair tighten, pulling me away from him. He chuckles when our eyes meet.

"You're going to make me embarrass myself." He says hoarsely.

I smirk confidently at him, feeling a bit more at ease now that I've taken some control back.

I lift myself back onto my feet smirk intact.

"Plum giddy with yourself, aren't you?" He asks playful tone back in place.

My smile widens, and I nod.

He quickly lifts me up from the back of my thighs and drops me down on the bed, following me but catching himself before his weight falls on me.

He wastes no time returning his attentions to my body.

His mouth trails down me, trading between sweet kisses and the scrape of his teeth.

When he gets to my swelling stomach he doesn't rush past it like I expect. He just slows his hunger, leaving sweet lingering kisses.

Then he kneels down at the foot of my bed pulling my legs over his thick shoulders.

When I feel his warm breath hitting my wetness, I could scream from all of my pent-up anticipation.

Finally the tip of his tongue slides up me, tasting.

"Oh God." I groan in satisfaction at feeling him there again.

My hand fists in his hair, while my other one rubs at my nipples trying desperately to get the release I'm dying for.

He plunges a finger inside of me in one swift motion while he sucks at my clit.

He gives me a few deep thrusts, curling his finger to hit that perfect spot inside of me, before pulling it out slowly and sliding to my back entrance.

"Fuck!" I yell out as he rubs, pressing into the untouched part of me.

The pressure's building inside of me again, making my toes curl as I lift in the bed, before he pulls back. Tearing himself away from me completely again.

"Why?" I scream in frustration, slamming my fist down onto the mattress.

He gives me my favorite crooked grin with a darker edge to it.

"Because I want you begging."

My eyes narrow to slits in challenge.

He grabs me from underneath and flips my body until I'm on my hands and knees. His hands are kneading my ass cheeks when suddenly he spreads them.

That's when the flat of his tongue tastes all of me, from my clit all the way to my tight ring.

This time two of his fingers slide into my wetness. His tongue drawing delicious circles, while his fingers pump in and out of me in time.

His movements start out slow and languid, but eventually build into a faster pace.

I'm screaming and moaning, pushing into his fingers in desperation. I'm almost there, core tightening when he stops again.

"Oh my God." I shout, letting my front half fall onto the bed in defeat.

"Please," I cry. "Don't stop."

The mattress creaks when he crawls on the bed to position himself behind me.

"That wasn't so hard, was it?" His hands travel up my back and down my sides before settling on my hips.

I'm bracing myself to lift up and give him a dirty look, but he slams inside of me unexpectedly, filling me all at once.

I turn my head sideways, still pressed to the comforter, to catch a glimpse of him staring at where our bodies meet. Watching as he pulls himself out a millimeter at a time before slamming back into me again.

A small cry escapes me, and I push back into him, letting him know that I need this... now.

His fingers at my hips tighten until I'm pretty sure they'll leave a bruise, holding me in place so he can repeat his motion a few more times.

Then—finally—he switches gears. He thrusts into me faster and faster until the pressure that's been building since he first touched me in the shower, rips out of me in agonizing perfection.

His movements falter a little when I finish, but he pushes through, wringing out every drop of pleasure from my body, before I slump even further into the bed, drained.

He pulls our still-joined bodies to our sides, cradling me into him while we catch our breaths.

"Has anyone ever told you," I ask him between heavy breaths, "...that you're an asshole?"

His chest shakes behind me in silent laughter. "The best kind, though."

"Mm hmm." I hum sarcastically.

He presses a kiss to my shoulder and holds me a little tighter.

I let my eyes fall shut, warm, spent, and exactly where I'm meant to be.

CHAPTER 30

Dylan

"No, Mom. Lane and I talked about it, and we'll decide the name after we have her."

"But I want to buy her things with her name on them before she gets here." She complains over the line.

I smile, shaking my head at her persistence. "You can use Kemp, or Kemp girl, or whatever. I like to call her Little One. That would be cute."

She exhales dramatically. "Fine. I'll see what I can do with that."

"I know you can make it work." I chuckle. "I have to go, Mom. I'm going to be late for work."

"Alright honey. I love you."

"I love you too."

When the line disconnects, I run inside. I'm brimming with nervous energy. I have so much planned for today, and I'm so excited about it.

Today is November 21st—Kohen's birthday—and I've planned a surprise party with Bex that I'm hoping he won't hate me for.

Lane and Kohen both have their own home games this weekend, so we have a whole ass weekend planned and everyone's going to be here for it.

I'm ready to get through this workday and get it started. Bex has the apartment handled, and we've been texting all afternoon while I count down the hours.

I just need to grab the cake and something to put the gifts in before heading home.

I don't know why this has me so on edge. I mean, I know he isn't going to squeal in delight, but I hope that under that guarded teenage attitude he feels seen. Knows he matters.

I hate how he keeps everyone who loves him at arm's length.

According to the few things Lane's told me, it's their mother who hurts him the most.

I try not to think about her at all. It's easier that way.

Still, I can't stop the flicker of anger that comes with knowing someone could walk away and leave their kids to figure it out on their own.

I dread the day we cross paths. I wonder what she even had to say when she found out her firstborn was having a child of his own. Did she even care?

Did it even register to her, or does she just show up long enough to be able to function and leave them all over again.

"Dylan," Jerry's nasally voice interrupts my thoughts.

I straighten in my chair and pause filing the paperwork. "Yes?"

"Could you please empty out all of the trash cans before you leave? Mine is almost spilling over."

I hold back my look of disdain and offer him a tight smile.

"Will do."

He shuffles back to his office, not even looking back when I answer.

I quickly finish putting paperwork in their corresponding files. I grab a roll of trash bags and start half an hour's worth of work with only twenty minutes left.

I rush out the door five minutes late. Kohen only has a small window between school and heading back to the field.

Luckily the cookie cake store and the personalized gift store are on the way home.

When I finally make it back everybody's already there except Kohen and Blaze. Nate's propped up in my recliner that's been turned around to face the dining room.

Lane's finishing up the smash burgers while Bex runs around busily behind him. I set my gift on the table and ask Bex where she wants the cake before giving my chef a quick kiss.

"Jerry," I say, rolling my eyes at Bexley. "Decided I had to do trash duty before I left, so I almost didn't make it in time."

"He's such a dick." She grins, feeding me lines for my pettiness.

I scoff in agreement. "I can't wait to be his boss one day and throw my trash can at him."

Bexley is laughing when Nate asks, "Is that where you think you're going to end up? I thought you were about to be the next Legally Blonde or something?"

I raise my eyebrows and smirk at him referencing a girl movie.

He rolls his eyes, "Twin sister. Remember?"

"Sure. Whatever you say." I chuckle, but answer him seriously. "I actually decided that this is exactly what I want to do." I glance to Lane, who sends me a quick wink. "Maybe not that office specifically, but I want to work somewhere like that."

I pinch my nose at Nate. "Besides, I'm neither blonde nor that into pink."

"I don't know." He gives me a grin. "Have you seen the shit you've bought for y'all's kid? It's almost exclusively pink."

"Okay, fine." I throw my hands up in defense. "I like pink. Clashes with my hair, though, so until she has opinions of her own, she gets to commit for both of us."

We all get a laugh out of that before we hear the jiggle of the doorknob.

Blaze walks in first, hiding his grin, then jumps around to shout at Kohen with us.

"SURPRISE!"

Kohen waves his hands around with a very fake look of shock. "Oh my God, I'm so surprised."

"Who told you?" I hear Bex ask behind me.

He laughs. "You should've never told Blaze. He can't keep a secret to save his life."

"You said you weren't going to tell." Blaze crosses his arms and huffs, "Last time I tell you anything."

"Yeah, Yeah. We'll see." He turns his attention back to everyone else with a small grin. "Thanks, guys."

Lane steps forward. "Let's eat first. We don't have a lot of time, and I want you to get some food in you before you have to go back."

Kohen rubs his hands together. "Sounds good. I'm starving."

"You're always starving." I laugh, heading to make myself a plate.

Kohen hands me one, brow quirked. "Look who's talking." He waves a hand in front of himself, for me to go first.

"Shut up. I have two appetites right now." I use the probably-over used excuse.

"Mmm hmm." He grins. "I'm sure that's it."

"I remember that first time we ate at the diner for lunch together. Your burger looked like something off of *Scooby-Doo*." Bex reaches between us to grab two plates.

I hear Nate and Lane lose it in the living room.

"Hey! You're supposed to be on my side. Girl power and all that."

"I am. Eat whatever you want, I got your back." She pumps a fist in the air by her head. "Girl power."

We all meet in the living room, plates in hand. After twisting Nate around in the recliner to face us, Lane settles on the floor in front of the couch, his back resting easily between my legs. Blaze sits between me and Bex, while Kohen sprawls out in the LoveSac I just bought.

I smile happily, eating my food while everyone carries on around me. Laughing at each other, talking about their days. Nate tells us how his rehab is going.

It's nothing special, but everything to me all at once.

Lane wraps a hand around my calf and squeezes before smacking a quick kiss to my inner leg. I think he feels it too. All of his people together in one room, just living.

Bex jumps up. "We need to do presents. We don't have a lot of time left."

"We don't have to." Kohen groans out, not wanting to be the center of attention again.

Bex grabs all of them in one trip and sets them beside him where he sits. "Just open them, grumpy."

"Wait," Blaze shouts, getting up and reaching into his pocket. "Mine first." He stops in front of Kohen and pulls an empty hand out and holds it up. "It's a crisp high-five. All I could afford with no job and all. Want it now or later?"

We all crack up at Blaze's dumb joke.

Kohen kicks at him. "Go sit down, you idiot."

Blaze cackles at himself, making his way back to the spot he was sitting.

Kohen pulls up the first present that's just a Lids shopping bag.

"That's from me." Nate holds up a hand.

"I wonder what it could be." He chuckles, pulling the black cap out of the bag. He pulls off the dingy one he'd been wearing and replaces it. "Thanks, man. It's nice."

"Looks almost as good on you as it would on me," Nate tells him with a cocky grin.

"Psh. You wish you looked this good." He reaches for the next one.

"That's mine." I perk up.

He pulls out the two onesies sitting on top. "These aren't exactly my size." He laughs, holding them up.

"Okay, those aren't exactly for you. Just read them." He starts to read them, and I explain. "I saw them in the personalization store I got your present and had to get them."

He rolls his eyes and holds up the one that reads, "I get my attitude from my uncle."

We're laughing while he reads the other one that says "That's my uncle" on the front and has KEMP and his jersey number on the back.

"Aww. I love that." Bex gushes.

He pushes his mouth to one side. "That's cute."

Lane twists around. "It's my kid. Shouldn't she have my jersey number?"

Blaze shouts, "What about me?"

I purse my lips at them both. "I have ones for you two in my room. Now hush, it's not about you right now."

"Well now, it doesn't feel that special," Kohen teases.

"Kinda feels like I should get one too." Nate grumbles not so quietly from his seat.

I roll my eyes. "Sure. I'll look into onesies for a dad's best friend. I'll see what I can find." Bex's gaze snaps to mine. "I already got you a little something, too." I wink at her, and she's satisfied.

"So I'm the only one who doesn't have a onesie?" Nate looks at me a little more hurt than I expected.

I can feel Lane's silent laughter at my expense before he says, "Maybe you shouldn't have been such an asshole to her at first."

"That's not why-" Nate cuts me off.

"I wasn't an asshole. I was protecting my best friend, which is why I think I should get one too."

"Nate!" I shout. When I have his attention, I continue, "I'll get one for you, I swear. Kohen's birthday remember?"

"Okay. I'll be keeping my number next year," He shrugs his shoulders and settles back into the cushions, mollified. "In case you're wondering."

I press my lips together to hide my smile. "Noted."

"Now that we're done with that," Bex laughs at her brother. "Still on a time crunch here."

I snap my attention to Kohen. "Right. There's something in there for you too. You just have to dig under the tissue paper for it."

He digs further into the bag and drags out a pair of football gloves. "Nice," he comments, before taking a closer look.

KEMP is embroidered into the wrist, and the corners of his mouth lift slightly. "Thank you. I really like them."

I hold back my squeal of delight. "I'm glad."

He pulls out the next present.

"That's from me and Blaze," Lane rumbles out.

Blaze chirps up. "Totally helped pick it out."

Kohen pulls out a new PlayStation remote and then some really nice bluetooth headphones. "Sweet. These are the new Turtle Beaches."

"They're the best!" Blaze says staring directly at Nate like he's baiting him.

Nate falls prey when he snaps back. "That's weird I didn't hear him say Hyper X."

Must be a recurring argument because they all throw a few hits at each other over it for a few minutes before Bex interrupts them.

"Would you please open mine!"

Kohen chuckles darkly at her like maybe he waited to do

hers last on purpose, then picks up her perfectly wrapped present.

He surprisingly opens it delicately, pulling the tape off and unfolding it carefully instead of ripping into like I would.

When he gets it all unwrapped he pulls out a scrapbook.

He starts flipping through it, taking in every page before he turns it.

"Where did you get all of these?" Kohen asks never looking up.

Bex pulls her feet up on the couch and wraps her arms around her knees. "Lane brought me some old usb's and some off of Facebook," she shrugs. "Some of the newer ones I took. You know how I'm always taking pictures."

"I didn't even know some of these pictures existed." Kohen clears his throat and looks up at her.

"Must've taken a lot of work." His thumb drags down one of the pages before he looks up at her. "Thank you."

Bex waves a hand at him. "Oh it's nothing. You know I love an excuse to do stuff like this."

He gives her a soft smile and a curt nod.

Bex jumps up. "Okay, now we have to go get ready. I'm going to go get dressed real quick."

Everyone else jumps up to get ready too, except for Nate, he slowly gets up and hobbles around in his brace, refusing any more help.

I sit there until Lane gets up to help me out of the couch. I'm not that helpless, but I do enjoy his hand in mine, and I definitely don't mind the extra help. Little One is really getting big in there.

We all get dressed, needing a little more clothes on us now that the fall weather is starting to actually feel like fall.

We spend the evening watching Kohen kick ass with his team, laughing and cheering him on together from our spot on the bleachers.

I rub slow circles over my belly and smile. Little One's going to have this world waiting for her when she gets here, and nothing's ever felt more right.

CHAPTER 31

Lane

We're lying in Dylan's bed under the covers. She's tucked beneath one arm while my hand rests on her very rounded belly.

Little One is going wild tonight. Like she can feel the left-over excitement from the day too.

"I swear she always gets more active the second I lic down," Dylan mumbles into my chest, never even opening her eyes.

I smile, shifting my hand when another sharp kick lands against my palm, "Feels like she's doing cartwheels in there. How do you ever sleep?"

"Not much," she murmurs. "Between her and my bladder."

Her belly shakes with a quiet laugh, and right on cue, Little One kicks again, like she's got something to say about it.

"Could be all the cookie cake getting to her." I suggest.

After Kohen's team blew out the other team, we came

home and celebrated by eating his birthday cake we never got to earlier.

Dylan groans. "I gave our baby a sugar rush."

I kiss the top of her head, fighting against the urge to itch my face where her curls attack me. "I'm sure she'll be fine."

"Kohen played really good tonight. It's like it runs in your blood. Did your dad play?" She asks, flipping around in my arms to get more comfortable.

I start kneading at her back and she relaxes into it. "Yeah, he played safety. His team won state when he played. But he says it had nothing to do with him. Swore he was the worst player on the team." I smile remembering the time he told us about him tripping over his own feet and falling on his ass in the middle of the field one time. "Everyone always told us how good he was though so I think he was just being humble."

"Sounds like someone else I know. Did he play in college like you?" She grunts out in between my thumb pressing into the muscles along her spine.

"Nope. He graduated and started working pipelines. Hard work, decent money, until he worked his way up." I tell her.

"Is that why you went to school for engineering? Same type of work he did?"

I shrug my shoulders. "I'm good with numbers, know the work and it pays pretty good. Seemed as good a job as any."

She twists around to her back to look at me. "But is it what you want?"

Air bursts through my lips. Should've seen that one coming.

"Is that what you and Nate fought about?" She asks, letting me know for sure exactly where this conversation is heading.

I run a hand through my hair before letting it fall on the bed beside me. "Basically. He said I'm giving up because I won't ask everyone around me to completely rearrange their lives so I can play a game."

She stays quiet, grabbing the hand of the arm still under her and watching her fingers trace over my skin.

"Do you want to keep playing the game?" She finally asks.

"I mean, yeah. I love the game, obviously. But it's a bit of a long shot anyway, so it really doesn't matter." I tell her enjoying the slide of her finger over my skin.

Her gaze shoots to mine. "So where's the harm in trying? Sign up for the draft, if nothing comes of it," she shrugs. "Then, oh well. It was a good run."

"And if something does?" I hedge.

Her face turns teasing. "Mmm, I like when you're cocky." She laughs when I roll my eyes at her but she settles and looks at me intently. "Then we figure out."

Fuck, she's perfect.

"It's going to be an even longer shot if we don't win tomorrow's game. No more games if we lose."

She shrugs again, like this is all simple to her. "So don't lose."

She lifts up onto her knees and holds out her pinky. "Win tomorrow's game, you sign up. Deal?"

I see the joy shining in her eyes. Joy for me. For what *I* want.

And even though a hundred things crash through my head, all of them warning me this is a bad idea, I lock my pinky with hers.

A bright smile breaks across her face, and I don't think there's a single thing in this world I could deny her.

She kisses her fist. Then I kiss mine—locking in our deal.

♡ 〜 ♡

I'm standing by Nate in the tunnel, and by the sound of it, we have a massive crowd out there today.

"You hurting?" I ask Nate.

He makes a face and shakes his head. "Not so much. I'll definitely be glad to get this brace off, though."

I nod and look back at the field waiting on our cue. I'm going to walk out with Nate instead of running out on the field.

"I heard there are scouts out there watching." Nate informs me.

"Better give them a show then." I tell him with a cocky smile.

His brows shoot up as he walks beside me, doing his best to hide his limp.

"Oh yeah? Have a change of heart?" He asks me excitedly.

"Between you and Dylan, I guess I finally realized I can at least try." I shrug my shoulders. "Who knows, maybe something will come of it."

Nate's eyebrows go up. "Dylan talked you into it?"

"Yeah," I chuckle. "She made me pinky promise her last night that if we won this game, I would sign up for the draft."

He lets out a low whistle. "Who knew all it took to get you to sign up was some good—"

I cut him off with a menacing look.

Nate laughs out loud and throws his hands up in defense in front of himself. "I'm just kidding. I'm really happy you got her back, man. She's a good one."

I'm astonished at his confession, and it must show on my face.

"Yeah, yeah." He waves a hand at me. "She grew on me, I guess."

"I'm glad." I nudge him with my elbow and throw his words back at him from when he first met her. "Wouldn't want my baby mama and best friend fighting."

The quarterback starts running, letting me know it's time to go. Whatever response he makes is drowned out by the crowd that I'm searching. Dylan said she got everyone good seats close to the field.

When my eyes finally land on her wild red curls shining like a beacon in the crowd, my heart damn near skips a beat.

She's wearing a long navy jersey as a dress, and in bright gold sequins, 31 shows starkly on the front. I love how my baby in her belly makes it stand out even more, like it's showing the world they both belong to me.

Her cheeks are a little rosy from the cool air, and her smile is wide across her face as she yells with my people around her. My brothers. Bexley. I guess our people now.

I point at her with a huge grin on my face, and she shoots me a wink.

Nate and I are the last to settle into the sidelines, then we wait for the coin toss.

Heads. We win.

Things are looking good.

It's not looking good.

Our offense just isn't the same without Nate.

It's 14-10 in the fourth quarter.

They've scored on us twice to our one touchdown. A field goal got us close, but it's not enough. If we could score on this drive, we have a chance.

We inch down the field a few yards at a time. Our playbook has shrunk down to run after run, with Nate being out.

Our other guy we pass to, Zack, is constantly getting double-covered.

We're in the red zone now, but our run game is getting us nowhere.

"Fuck!" Nate yells out beside me when our runner only gets a few yards on the third down. "We need to go for it. We can't win this with a field goal."

"It looks like they are. Hopefully, they can fucking do something with it." I shout back slamming my helmet on the bench.

At the snap, the quarterback fakes a handoff and then sets up for the pass.

Once again Zack has two players on him, but Nate's backup, Alex, is wide open.

Our quarterback takes the shot with a perfect spiral to the corner of the end zone. A defender clocks it and goes to make the tackle.

When Alex jumps up to make the catch over him, he gets hit while he's in the air. Alex cradles the ball to his chest and stretches his legs to stay in bounds.

We celebrate when he keeps hold of the ball while he lands.

The stadium erupts into a chorus of boos, crashing over our excitement like a tidal wave.

Of course, the refs call it back. His feet crossed the line when he came down.

"Damn it!" I scream, slamming my helmet on my head again.

I don't think there's enough time for us to hold them and for our offense to go back out there and score without a Hail Mary pass out of this world.

But it isn't over until the whistle blows.

Nate slaps the side of my helmet and grabs on to the cage of my mask. "Go out there and work your fucking magic. Shut their asses down right now. It's the only chance we have."

I give him a sharp nod and head out onto the field.

They're lined up at their eight-yard line, best case scenario would be a safety.

Odds are they're going to mostly run. Nobody's going to want to risk an interception when all they need to do is run the clock.

Just like I predicted, they run the ball on the first two plays, for six yards total. And kind of killing our chance for a safety.

This could be a shot for an interception if they decide to pass and hold the ball a little longer.

They don't take it though, and their runner just juked out of the middle of the line... right towards me.

I shove through my block and I hit him as hard as I can to keep him from getting those last few yards for a down.

As he goes down, the ball slips free, bouncing loose right in front of me.

My heart is hammering as I scoop it up and run with everything I have in me.

Fifteen yard mark.

Don't look around. Just run straight and fast.

Ten yard mark.

I can hear someone coming up behind me, but he gets hit by one of my teammates.

Five yard mark.

There's another guy coming up beside me about to make the tackle.

I push harder. Then I feel him hit me in the side.

I reach out with the ball in both hands, doing everything I can to get this ball past that line before I go down.

The crowd explodes and the ref's arms shoot into the air.

Touchdown.

Holy shit, I did it! I slam the ball into the ground before getting up with a smile that feels like it's splitting my face.

The boys jump up around me and I crash my helmet into theirs before running with the ball right in front of my girl.

She's holding her hands around her mouth, screaming her cheers for me until I'm standing right in front of where she is in the stands.

Without missing a beat and a proud smile never leaving her face, she holds up her pinky at me.

I hold mine back up to her and kiss my fist. I wink at her when she kisses hers, making the crowd around us go even wilder.

I break contact with her and start running to Nate with the ball.

He's ready and waiting to celebrate with me when I get to him.

"You think that'll get the scouts' attention?" I ask handing him the ball.

He throws his head back laughing, slapping me on the shoulder. "That ought to do it."

CHAPTER 32

Dylan

"I watched the whole game. I'm not going to lie, I didn't think your team was going to be able to pull it off. That damn scoop of yours was pure magic."

"Dad, I called to tell you Happy Thanksgiving. Not for you to moon over my boyfriend." I smile teasingly at my dad over the FaceTime.

Lane shoves a hand over my mouth. "Moon away, sir."

My dad's smiling face shines over my phone. "Baby, I'm so happy for you. I'm glad everything's working out so perfectly down there. I hate missing everything." He looks at me, already getting all mushy. "But we have a lot to be thankful for this year. Huh?"

Dad instantly loved Lane. I think the moment I told him we were together, he was relieved—amazed, even—that I'd found someone I liked enough to claim. That alone was enough to make him happy for me.

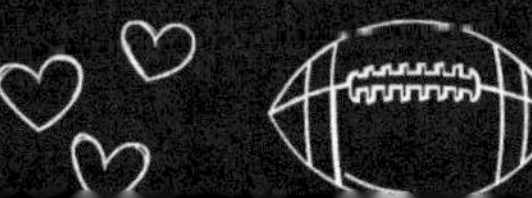

He trusted my judgment of Lane, and that was enough for him.

Lane replies to him. "I'm sure we'll make a trip up there after Little One is born. The boys and I are dying to go up there to escape the summer heat we have here."

My dad chuckles. "I can imagine. Sounds like a plan to me. You're always welcome to bring the whole crew here. Plenty of room for everyone."

"Sounds good, Dad." I smile, laying my head on Lane's shoulder.

Dad lights up at my words. "Alright. Well, I won't keep you. Happy Thanksgiving. Love you, kiddo."

"Happy Thanksgiving." We chime back together before ending the call.

We already had our Thanksgiving lunch. It wasn't much but we had a turkey and some sides. We were happy enough with it.

For once, we were at their house, and it felt a little strange—being let into his world when he usually works so hard to keep everything separate.

I shift and stretch my legs out across the loveseat we're sharing.

"Is your dad like really rich?" Blaze chirps up.

"Jesus. You can't just ask that." Kohen shouts at him across the room.

I shrug my shoulders. "He isn't like billionaire-rich, but, yeah—I was definitely spoiled growing up."

Lane laughs. "You *can* be a brat sometimes."

I throw my head back to look at him. "You like it."

He leans down to kiss me and growls low so only I can hear. "I like dealing with it later."

"Mmm. And that's why I'll keep being a brat." I hum back.

"Go away."

"Y'all are so annoying."

The boys groan out together.

His lips stretch into a smile on mine. "I'll be right back."

I pout. "Okay, fine."

"Brat."

I stretch all the way out when he leaves his spot and go back to watching the Cowboys game.

When the quarterback throws one wide, the boys yell out their profanities, making me laugh.

"It's not looking good for your boys. I can go get the Kleenex if you need me to." I taunt.

Kohen jerks around eyes blazing—the exact reaction I was shooting for. "Get out of here with your negativity."

"Yeah, whose team are you on?" Blaze yells at me from his spot on the floor.

I crack up at their twin looks of rage. I point at the screen and shout, "Oh shit, was that a sack?"

They both turn at the same time to see their quarterback

throwing a long pass, and it's caught, getting them the first down and more.

"I hate you." Kohen deadpans.

I laugh again. "You make it too easy, grumps."

"Want to go somewhere with me?" Lane startles me by saying in my ear.

"Freaking ninja," I mumble under my breath. "Where are we going?" I ask, looking down at my leggings and maternity undershirt.

He drops a sweater on top of my head, blocking my vision.

"Put that on. It's a surprise. And don't worry, it's unlikely that anyone will see you looking less than perfectly dressed up."

Satisfied, I shift to stand, pulling the sweater over my head and inhaling the familiar scent of him.

"You do realize you're not getting this back." I say standing in front of him.

Without even looking down he tells me, "Looks good on you." Then he kisses the tip of my nose.

"We'll be back later. Call if you need anything." He says loudly to the boys.

"Good, get her hater-ass out of here." Blaze teases.

"Watch your mouth." Lane says more out of habit than the expectation of it ever happening.

I look at Blaze and stick my tongue out at him.

He rolls his eyes. "See y'all later."

When we get in his truck, I notice bags and a blanket propped up on the seat between us

I look at his smiling face in question.

"It's a surprise." Is all he says.

A few minutes later, we pull up to a familiar spot. He grabs everything he packed, tells me to stay put, then jogs around the front of the truck to open my door.

"Oh, wow. You're really going all out. Is this a surprise *date*?" I don't hide the excitement in my voice.

He gives me a confident grin. "Yep."

I look around at the familiar lake and can see his spot through the thinning trees. I grab the hand he's holding out for me and lean in to ask, "We aren't going fishing, are we?"

He tosses his head back in laughter. "No, I'm not putting you through that yet." He pauses to look at me seriously. "It's coming, though. Be prepared."

I giggle, giddy about this whole setup. "Well then, lead the way."

He walks me to his spot and spreads out a blanket in front of the log we sat on last time. He gestures for me to sit, and I comply, making myself comfortable, leaning back on the log.

He lays out some containers filled with fruit and hands me my favorite brand of water before relaxing beside me.

"I'm sure it looks nothing like the falling leaves you have at your spot, but when the wind picks up our ugly brown ones will go all over the place. Thought it would be close, at least."

I'm staring at him in awe. "You remember me telling you that?"

One side of his mouth lifts. "I remember everything about that night."

My chest tightens, and I swallow past the lump in my throat. I grab his hand with mine and lay my head on his shoulder.

He kisses the top of my head before resting his cheek there. We watch silently, waiting for a heavy gust of wind.

When it finally does, dead brown leaves fill the space in front of us; falling diagonally but twisting in circles in places before settling in the water.

"It's perfect." I whisper, not fully trusting my voice, yet.

I clear my throat when the world around us settles again. "What brought all of this on?"

"Am I giving it to you straight or keeping things light?" He asks seriously.

I squeeze his hand, preparing myself for some huge confession I'm not sure I'm ready for. "Give it to me straight."

"I guess I just wanted to go back to the beginning. I don't want to skip over any of the steps because of our situation. I want to make sure everything's done right. I-" he hesitates. "I don't want to mess this up."

I smile and squeeze my eyes tight. How did I manage to find the most perfect human being on a whim of a trip.

"Give it to you straight?" I repeat back to him.

"Always," he answers without hesitation.

I let out a heavy breath. "I'm glad you said that. A tiny part of me is always wondering if you're only with me because of the baby."

He lets out a huff of laughter. "It's not tiny on my end."

I lift my head to meet his gaze. "What does that mean?"

"I constantly wonder the same thing. If I hadn't gotten you pregnant, would you even be here? Would you choose this? Choose us?"

My brows draw together in concern. Can't he tell how crazy I am about him?

He lets out a self-deprecating laugh. "I looked for you. I went to the front desk. I went back to the house where the party had been. I asked around like an idiot about a mystery girl who was only in town for a couple of nights. But you... you left." He's not accusing me, just stating the facts as he sees them.

It stings anyway, leaving me hurt and feeling a little guilty.

I sit up and shift to face him.

"Before any of this happened, I always had a set plan. Graduate. Go to college. Go to law school. Be the best. Have my own law firm that rivals my father's. I wanted to do it all on my own. Nobody else. No feelings. Nothing to distract me from my plan."

He leans in, resting his elbows on his bent knees, and I watch my fingers pick at something on the blanket. "In one night, you had me questioning all of that to see if I could fit you into that plan. It scared me. I ran from it, thinking that if I put distance between what happened between us, I'd be able to forget about it. Didn't think it would matter to you that much."

I take a deep breath, meeting his watchful eyes.

"I looked for you too. Maybe not as intensely as when I found out I was pregnant, but I searched every social media well before that plus sign showed up."

I let out a sigh. "So I don't know where we'd be if I weren't pregnant. But I can tell you, I'd at least be wondering about you and if I made a mistake leaving that morning. Because I did. For over a month."

He nods his head, taking in everything I just said. "And now?"

I give him a small smile. "Now I can't imagine a life without you in it."

His eyes bounce between mine for a second.

"That's good because I'm not going anywhere," A slow smile stretches across his face. "And I'm pretty sure I'm in love with you."

My eyes widen, and he chuckles. I'm frozen in shock, no words are registering in my brain other than his last ones.

"Don't worry, I don't expect you to say it back... I don't even *want* you to. Just," He tilts his head to me, watching me with amusement. "...giving it to you straight."

He leans back into the log, grabbing a container and tossing a grape in his mouth before holding them out to me. "Want one?"

And like nothing had ever happened, I lean into him, grabbing some for myself. We go back to our usual banter, finishing out our date like he hadn't just scrambled my brain.

♡ ⚡ ♡

When we get back the boys are sitting exactly where we left them like they were just on pause until we walked back through the doors.

"About time. Y'all have been gone forever. Where did you go?" Blaze speaks up immediately.

Kohen answers for us. "Who cares? Did you bring back any food?"

Lane scoffs. "There are plenty of leftovers in there. Why would we get more food?"

"We were a little light on desserts." Blaze complains.

"That's what I said." I tell him. "So I talked him into finding me a red velvet cake from the store."

"Sweet!"

I lay the cake out on the table and go to get me a plate.

Lane yells out behind me. "She's not going to make it for you. Get up and fix your own."

I shrug, "I don't mind."

But I can hear both of them shuffling into the kitchen.

I pause when I hear what sounds like keys rattling in the doorknob. "Are you expecting someone?"

All of them look to the door with different expressions.

When the door finally opens, a woman's hoarse voice shouts into the space. "Happy Thanksgiving, my..."

Her voice cuts off when our eyes meet, and she looks at me in confusion.

Lane takes a small step in front of me laying a hand on my belly protectively.

All it does is draw her attention there though and her eyes go wide in shock before they slowly start tearing up.

I'm not sure what I pictured this woman looking like? But she has Lane's eyes. Blonde hair that probably once matched Blaze's, looks frail and thin. She's terribly skinny and the soft skin under her eyes are intensely dark.

I forget all the things that made me hate her before this. The woman standing in front of me isn't evil... she's just broken.

She drags her gaze to Lane's, tears starting to spill over. It does nothing to him. His face stays hard as steel.

"Is it yours?" Her voice cracks.

Kohen's taking everything in before anger takes hold and he aims it directly at the man standing in front of me.

"Fuck Lane. You didn't tell her you're having a baby?"

CHAPTER 33

Dylan

I feel a tug at my hand and find Blaze tilting his head in the direction of the stairs. I assess the room around me and give him a quick shake of my head, not wanting to leave Lane in this moment.

Blaze just pulls out ear buds and sticks them in, and jogs up the stairs to his room.

"It's not like she's around much for me to tell her or coherent when she is." Lane says to Kohen but it lands on his intended target because I see her physically flinch at his words.

I feel like I should say something to defuse the situation, but I remember the way Lane stayed silent and let me decide how to handle my mom, so I do the same for him.

Kohen is fuming on behalf of his mother. "It's her grand-child. You find time."

Their mother just stands there, staring into space while the tears run steady down her face.

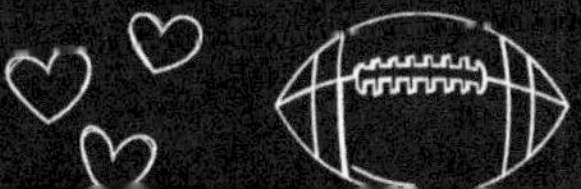

Lane takes a step towards Kohen, putting me further behind him.

"Come on Kohen. Can you really blame me for not wanting to tell her? I don't trust her with y'all, much less my daughter."

This pulls her attention back to Lane, with a sharp inhale.

"A little girl?" She chokes out.

Lane never even acknowledges her, just keeps trying to explain himself to Kohen.

Her eyes flick to my stomach before finding my face. I glance to the back of Lane's head, but he's still talking to Kohen so I meet her gaze and nod my head the smallest bit in confirmation.

She gives me a small, sad smile before her face pinches together in anguish.

A part of me wants to hold the woman who lost so much.

Some unfairly. Some from her own actions.

"Jesus," Kohen is screaming at him now. "You can stop guarding her. She's not going to fucking hurt her. Why are you like this?"

I take Lane's hand in mine and step around him to his side, showing Kohen I'm not afraid of his mom or the situation.

And truly, I'm not.

My heart cracks in my chest when Kohen's eyes meet mine, like he's begging me to see his side.

I open my mouth, not really sure what's about to come out, just desperately wanting to say something to help these two people I care about so much.

"He's right."

We all turn to the small woman standing a little straighter now, looking right at Kohen. She steps closer and cups his face, her touch feather-light.

"I'm a mess, honey. He did what he felt he needed to do for his family. Please don't get mad at each other."

"Mom," Kohen croaks out.

"I'll do better. Okay? I can do it." She declares to him, and Lane stiffens beside me.

Kohen looks attentively into her eyes and nods.

Their mother turns and walks a little more hesitantly to me. Lane's grip on my hand tightens and pulls slightly, like he wants to shield us again but I stand perfectly still—waiting.

She lifts a hand tentatively and lays it on the one I didn't realize was spread out over my abdomen.

"My son seems very protective of you. You must mean a lot to him." She isn't asking, so I don't answer. "This is a miracle. I'm so happy for y'all."

I smile softly at her. "Dylan." I clear my throat and look up at Lane. "My name's Dylan. And your son means a lot to me too."

"It's nice to meet you, Dylan. I'm Morgan."

I feel her hand drop, and she shifts her body to face Lane, fresh tears running down her cheeks. "I know you don't believe me, and I don't blame you." Her voice cuts out as she faces the son who did her job when she couldn't—but when she continues, it's full of determination. "I *will* be better. I owe you that much."

I watch his jaw clench and unclench several times before he looks up at Kohen's pleading face.

He looks down at me, and I'm not sure what he sees there, but his body wilts a little, like holding himself together just got heavier.

"We'll see."

Morgan nods her head in acceptance of his answer.

"I'm going to go shower and go to bed. But can we all talk in the morning?" She turns to me, eyes still bloodshot. "I'm not sure what you've been told, but I hope you'll give me a chance to prove myself."

The hand holding mine tightens.

"I'll support Lane. However he needs me to." Is the only answer I can give her.

I want this for them desperately and certainly don't want to discourage her, but I'll stand by Lane with his decision.

She nods her head and shuffles to her room.

Kohen walks up to Lane and tells him quietly, "Don't be an asshole to her. Maybe this will be the push she needs, but if you don't give her a chance, it's never going to work."

"I'm not being an asshole, Kohen. I want her to get better, and I'd love to think that maybe my baby was something that meant enough to snap her out of this." He swallows.

"But... I don't want you to get your hopes up again. I've watched it crush you too many times."

Kohen stiffens. "I'll be fine. Just don't do anything to fuck this up."

I mentally flinch at the hardness in his tone.

"I won't say anything to her," Lane replies.

"You have to *help* her." Kohen amends, his voice lower but no less firm.

Lane's jaw clenches again, and he gives him a sharp nod.

You can physically see the fight Kohen was about to have for his mom leave him all at once. "Thank you."

Then he walks to the fridge, grabs a bottle of water, and digs through the cabinet for medicine before disappearing into the room his mom just went into.

"Do you want me to go?" I ask Lane when we're alone in the room.

"I don't want you to, but I'd definitely understand if you wanted to get the hell out of dodge." He says running a hand down his face.

I feel like I don't even need to answer that because unless he wanted me to, there's no way I can leave him right now.

"Is she going to be okay in there?"

He scoffs. "Yeah, she'll be fine. She'll get some sleep, talk to us in the morning, and then it's just a waiting game until she leaves again."

I'm sure my concern shows on my face, but I don't try to push back and offer him hope. "Why don't you show me to your room then? I think we could all use some sleep."

A funny look crosses his face. "It's weird that you haven't seen it."

We start shuffling up the stairs, him behind me, a hand on my back like I might not be able to handle the stairs on my own.

"Never made it further than the bottom floor, and most of that was today."

"Sorry. Just seemed easier to keep the worlds separate. Didn't want to scare you away." He mumbles.

We get to the top of the stairs, and I twist to face him while he's still a step below, leaving us face to face.

"Do I look scared to you?" I grab his face with my hands and his go to my sides.

"You don't look scared," he says quietly. "But I'd really like to know what's going on in that head of yours right now."

I bring my lips to his, letting them brush together when I tell him. "All you have to do is ask." His mouth slips open slightly, tongue slipping out to taste my bottom lip before we pull apart.

He leads me to the door at the end of the hallway. "Where's Blaze?" I ask on our way.

He points to the door closest to his. "Is he okay? He just left."

Lane shrugs. "I'm not sure if it's the best way of coping... he just avoids everything. I'm scared it's my fault." He opens his door, letting me in first. "I always sent him to his room —TV, games, whatever—anytime I thought something might be too much for him. And now it's just... what he does."

"You're all just doing the best you can." I say sincerely to him before taking in the room.

It's simple. A desk. A dresser. A bed with a plain navy-blue comforter.

There are some personal things thrown around the room: trophies, pictures, he has some school work laid out on his desk and football stuff here and there.

"Not much, but here it is." His arms sweep the room before falling to his side with a slap.

"Not much of a decorator, are you? Don't worry, are you I'll always be there to fancy up our room."

He chuckles. "Oh yeah, when you planning on moving in?"

My face goes hot when I realize what I implied. "I didn't.. I mean.."

He laughs even harder. "Careful. I could get used to the idea."

I push at him for his teasing. "Oh yeah. Me, you, your mom, your brothers all in one house. That'll be fun."

"Maybe we'll live at your place then."

I give him a knowing look. "You aren't leaving your brothers."

He smiles and pulls me to him. "Okay, so we kick my mom out of the master and take over the whole downstairs."

I purse my lips. "Making your mom take a smaller room in her own house is pretty fucked up."

He starts rubbing up and down my back. "Not her house. It's mine."

That surprises me. "Yours?"

"Mine and my brothers'," he corrects quietly. "It was left to us when Dad died. I'm just the only one old enough to hold it right now."

I'm not sure what to do with that information, so I just table it in my mind. I lean into his embrace, laying my head on his chest.

"Well, what are we doing in here then? Let's swap with her right now." I say trying to lighten the mood and I feel his chest shake.

"You really don't think she can do it? She looked so determined. Maybe if we help her. Or get her some help." I press.

Lane takes a deep breath before releasing it. "I'd be lying if I said a small part of me doesn't hope. I've tried to get her to go to rehab before; she refuses. I just don't think she can do it. I think she wants to but her demons won't let her."

I hate that he doesn't sound angry... just certain.

"It was supposed to be her. She was supposed to pick Claire up that day, but she talked Dad into it because she had a long day at work. I don't think she can ever forgive herself for it, even if nobody else holds it against her."

My eyes squeeze shut to the tears his revelation brings.

"It's so unfair. All of it." I choke out, wrapping my arms around him like I could shield him from all the hurt he's had to face.

A rough hand threads through my hair pulling at the back of my head and I let it fall back, accepting his silent demand.

"I learned a long time ago that life doesn't play fair." His lips ghost over mine. "So when it tosses me something good, I protect it with all I've got."

♡ ⚬⚬⚬⚬⚬ ♡

I wake up early the next morning to make me some coffee before I have to go to work. When my alarm on my phone goes off, I groan loudly reaching blindly for it to turn it off.

Lane moans pulling me tighter to him. "No."

I giggle. "You're going to squish Little One." His hold on me loosens, slightly.

I run a hand down the side of his face, the rough growth of his facial hair catching as I do. I use my thumb to brush over it while I watch him, his face still mostly asleep and relaxed.

It's unfair to all women that there's only one of him. Even unshaven and rocking some serious bedhead, he's one of the most handsome men I've ever seen.

I lean over to suck his plump bottom lip into my mouth between teeth, biting into it just a little.

Bright green eyes pop open.

I laugh and push off him. I go to find my clothes that I brought with me, taking Lane's shirt off that I'm wearing and tossing it over his watching gaze.

"You could just call in. Stay in bed with me all day." He suggests pulling the shirt off his head with a huge grin on his face.

"I can't. I have to save time off for after the baby's here." I remind.

I pull on my slacks over my belly and tuck in my shirt. There's not much hope for my hair, so I pull it into a bun on top of my head, pulling down the small hairs by my ears.

I know girls don't do that anymore, but it's something that's stuck with me from high school.

I grab my blazer and walk to his side of the bed to give him a kiss. "Get yourself some more sleep. You need it while you have some time off."

He grabs my wrist when I go to leave. "One more."

I smile and lean down to lay a good one on him.

He's already rolling over on his stomach when I'm walking out the door.

When I make it down the stairs, I pause when I see Morgan sitting at the table, cup of coffee in hand.

"I made a pot. Help yourself." She gestures to the coffee pot on the counter.

"Thank you." I say politely as I walk past her to make me a cup.

I take my first sip, and it's a little strong, but it does the job.

"Do you have a minute before you have to leave?" Her hoarse voice asks behind me.

I got dressed in record time, so I'm not in a huge rush. I sit down beside her at the table and brace for what she has to say.

"Where do you work at?" She asks, lifting her cup to her mouth with a shaky hand.

"It's a nonprofit child advocacy office in town. I'm studying to go to law school." I tell her.

"Law school and a baby? That's very impressive."

I scan her face for any skepticism, but she's smiling softly at me.

"Thank you. But you know what they say. It takes a village, and definitely plan on using mine. I'm putting those boys of yours to work."

"You're funny." She laughs. "I can see why he likes you. Not only are you beautiful, you're smart." She gives me a meaningful look. "And kind."

"It's Lane that's the good one. I'd probably be one hot mess without him."

She looks down at her hands. "Lane's the best. A lot like his father. That man would do anything for us, if it meant we were happy."

Her weary eyes meet mine, a sheen of sweat lining her fore-head. "I'm embarrassed to meet you like this. I know what you probably think of me, and you're not wrong. But I mean it this time. I just hate that it took my son hiding something so important to him from me. I'll do everything I can to help fix what I broke with them."

My brows draw together. I don't know what the right thing to say is, and I'm not sure if I believe her after everything Lane's told me—but I really want to.

I take a deep breath, hoping I'm not about to cross a line. "I don't really know you, only what you've been through. I certainly can't speak for the boys, but maybe healing from that is the best place to start."

She blinks hard, a tear slipping free. "I think you're right."

CHAPTER 34

Lane

26 WEEKS

It's been almost a week and Mom's still hanging in there... for now.

The first couple of days she mostly stayed in her room, probably getting through the worst of the detox symptoms. Luckily, I had a bye week, so I was here the whole weekend.

She got out to watch football with us on Sunday. I kept my word to Kohen. I never said one thing to her.

I didn't really say much to her at all, but the entire day she went on pretending like everything was normal. I never once called her on it.

She surprised me on Monday when she woke up in the morning with us and told me she's going to look for a job. I was nervous that was her way to get out of the house and sneak a drink, but when I'd get home in the evening, her car would be in its spot and her eyes were clear and coherent.

I do notice her spacing out every now and then. The boys could be in the middle of talking to her, and it's like her

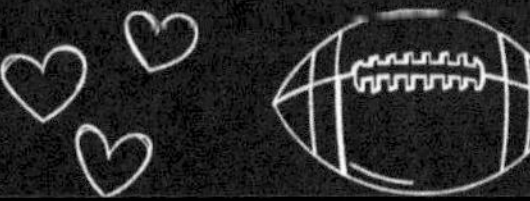

mask slips—lost inside her head a moment—before she remembers to look happy again.

She had supper waiting for us last night and invited Dylan to join us.

Which was nice, but I want a night with just me and Dylan again. Kohen won't leave Mom, though, and I won't leave them with just her.

I sent Dylan a text earlier asking if she'd meet me at lunch between our classes.

I'm sitting at the table now, waiting for Dylan and our orders.

A terrible part of me is ready for Mom to fail—to get the fuck out of our lives again. We have a normal without her. A normal that already stretches me thin, but trying to make sure she isn't alone with the boys has me running on fumes.

And then there's the other part of me. The one that wants to believe her. Wants her to pull a full 180 and be the mom I used to depend on. For Blaze. For Kohen. Hell... even for me.

Being stuck in this limbo—waiting for her to prove herself one way or the other—is killing me.

The doorbell rings, announcing my girl's arrival. She's wearing tall brown boots over jeans with a matching brown shirt underneath an oversized flannel.

Actually—yeah. That's my flannel.

She's wearing a beanie with two braids and giant hoop earrings sticking out from underneath it.

Her face, flushed from the cold, scans the room and brightens when she finds me.

Dylan slides into the booth across from me. "I was really hoping the food would already be out. I'm starving!"

"Shouldn't be long." I appease.

She grabs her sweet tea and drags in one long gulp before answering. "I had that glucose test thing this morning and went from that straight to class so I haven't had a single thing to eat all day. I might die."

"We can't have that." I say with a grin. "It should be out soon. How did the test go?"

"Good, results came back fine. I was nervous about it. I heard a lot of horror stories about the drink they give you, but I was so hungry I was just glad to put something in my stomach and chugged the whole thing."

"Does it taste that bad?" I ask, my lip pulled up in disgust.

"Meh. It wasn't great, but wasn't as terrible as the mom groups made me believe."

Her look of moderate distaste quickly changes into over the top excitement when the waitress lays her burger and onion rings in front of her.

"Oh my gosh. You're a saint. Thank you." Without even waiting for a response, she starts digging in.

"Excuse this weirdo, she's delirious from hunger." I tell her as she lays my plate down.

The waitress chuckles. "It's always nice to get some proper

appreciation." She smiles big at us. "Y'all are so cute. When's your baby due?"

I look at Dylan, cheeks puffed out from food, and figured I'd better answer for her. "March 18th."

"Well, that's exciting." The waitress' attention gets pulled to another table, but she hurries to say, "Let me know if I can get you anything else."

I pick up a fry and toss it in my mouth. In not even three months, I'll have my own baby out in the world. It's so hard to wrap my head around sometimes.

I know we were joking the other night, but I don't want to be away from my baby after she's born. I don't want to leave my brothers alone with Mom, and I'm not sure how all of us in one house would work out either.

Maybe I'm being a pessimist, but I don't expect Mom to be around long. She's always going to come back around, though. How can I raise a baby like that?

I may have to start a war with Kohen, but maybe this time he'll see she can't be helped and we can't keep letting her back into our lives.

"Hey." Dylan draws me from my thoughts. "Where'd you go?"

She has a worried look on her face as she drops her last onion ring.

"Yeah, I'm fine. Just thinking about all this shit with my mom." I take a bite of my burger.

"Has something happened? Everything seemed fine last night, other than you not talking... at all."

"You know what they say about having nothing nice to say." I shrug.

She sinks into the booth, brows drawn together. "She seems like she's really trying." Dylan says carefully.

"Yeah, and I'm trying really hard to give her a real chance. I just don't feel it. History isn't on her side." My burger drops from my hands.

"She knows you aren't going to trust her right away, but she's made it almost a week. That's...something."

"I don't know the right thing to do here. If she keeps going, what's the timeline where I decide it's okay to trust her with everything?" I let my forehead fall into my hand. "And if she doesn't, how do I explain to Kohen I can't keep letting her come around. Our daughter will not grow up watching all of that."

Her small fingers wrap around my wrist, pulling it to the table before laying her hand in mine. "I think you're jumping ahead. We just have to take this one step at a time."

"In two and a half months, our baby will be here." I say quietly. "I want to focus on that. Not on how to manage my life around an addict." Her face scrunches together, and she nods her understanding. "I want to be with you after the baby's born. If we're at your house, my brothers are with her. If we're at my house, y'all are around her, and I don't want that either. With her in the picture, I'm just... stuck."

"And you've spent too much time already rearranging your life because of her." She exhales sadly. "It's easier for you when she's not there." She says what I feel too guilty to say out loud, understanding without any judgement.

"It's shitty, I know." I feel her hand squeeze mine.

"You're not shitty," she says immediately. "This is her mess. You didn't make it, and you can't fix it."

My jaw tightens, but she keeps going.

"It's her fight. Whether she beats this or not, that's on her. Not you."

She lifts my hand to her face and presses a soft kiss into my palm.

"Do what you need to do for you. Kohen and Blaze might not like it at first, but they trust you. They always have." She gives me a small shrug. "And so do I."

All this girl ever does is try to get me to put myself first. I really don't know how I made it so long without her. Someone that sees me. The good. The bad.

And here she is, right in the middle of the mess that's my life. Calm and steady and by my side.

I don't know what the right move is yet.

But I know this... I'm not dealing with it alone.

CHAPTER 35

Lane

I walk into my house at the end of my long day that still isn't over. I still have finals to study for and a weekend to plan for, since I leave tomorrow night for an away game.

The boys are in the living room playing a zombie game together. I make my way to the kitchen and pull out the defrosted meat that's in the fridge.

"Where's Mom?" I yell over the gun noises.

"Still isn't home." Blaze shouts back.

I quiet the questions running through my head and focus on cooking. It's not my problem. Wherever she is, whatever she's doing.

Not. My. Fucking. Concern.

It only takes me a few minutes to finish the sloppy joes I decided to make, and I call the boys to supper.

When Kohen walks in behind Blaze, I ask them, "What are y'all's plans this weekend? I have to leave Friday night to go

to a game and probably won't be back until late Saturday night."

"My playoff game is Friday." Kohen states.

"Yeah," I say with an exhale. "Unfortunately, I won't be able to watch it from the stands, but I figured out how to stream it on the bus." I look over to Blaze. "Dylan said she'd drive you there if you wanted to go."

I'm trying to casually get them to stay the weekend with her without making it seem like I'm forcing them to.

Blaze is grabbing the bread out of the cabinet, slightly turning his head to tell me, "Yeah, sounds good to me."

"She said y'all could hang out with her until I get back." I suggest cooly.

Kohen catches on instantly. "You mean she can run interference on Mom while you're not here to do it."

I sink into the chair at the table. "Kohen I really don't want to fight about it."

He takes a deep breath, trying to contain his anger. "I don't either. But she's been doing fine."

"It's been a week, Kohen." His jaw tightens. "I'm not saying that she's going to mess up, I'm just taking precautions."

"You know I'm not your kid. You don't need to take care of me. You may not notice," he shoves a thumb in his chest. "But I do my fair share of shit around here too. I know you think you're the only one around here making sacrifices and taking care of everything, but you're not, and you're not our Dad."

I'm stunned because this isn't the argument I was prepared for. "I don't think that."

"You do."

I look over to Blaze, whose eyes are bouncing back and forth between us. When he starts to reach into his pocket for the familiar headphones, I stop him.

"Come sit down, please, and just talk to us." I look at Kohen intentionally. "We won't start screaming at each other."

Blaze hesitates but sits down, followed by Kohen.

I take in the two of them waiting on me to continue. "I'm not trying to run y'all like I'm your parent. That's not what this is."

"Then what is it? I get you don't trust Mom. Fine. But don't act like you can't trust us either."

I run a hand through my hair, exhausted. "I just want to protect you from having to be the adult when she can't."

Kohen huffs. "I'm not a kid, though. And I don't need you to protect me anymore. Who do you think holds shit down when you're gone all weekend for games."

"I know you do," I say gently. "I see it. I also see how much all of this has already taken from both of you. Maybe because of her. Maybe because of me. I don't know."

Kohen's arms tighten across his chest.

"But that's exactly what I'm trying to stop. I can't stand watching you get hurt every time she goes off the rails again or Blaze completely shutting down anytime she's even around."

Blaze clears his throat. "I think what he's saying is that we get it. We appreciate everything you've done for us, but you're our brother. And maybe instead of trying to protect us all the time, we should figure everything out together. It doesn't have to be all on you."

I stare at my little brother. The one that I had to let sleep in my bed with me for two years after the accident because he had nightmares about it. The one who's always the first to try and lighten any situation because he doesn't like the conflict he's had to witness.

He shrugs and looks down at the untouched food in front of him. "None of us had a choice. Life hit us, and hit us hard. We all had to grow up fast. And I feel like we all just fell into roles to get us through it."

I swallow the lump in my throat and take both of them in. Maybe he's right. Maybe trying to protect them, I just silenced their own pain. My head falls in my hands.

Fuck. Am I just making everything worse?

I lift my head and take them both in. Blaze still staring at his plate and Kohen with his brows drawn staring at Blaze.

"Okay. You're right. So where do we go from here?" I look to Kohen, trying to see him as an equal and not someone to shield. "You can't expect me to just let her back in with no pushback."

Kohen jaw tics. "I'm not saying you have to let her in completely, but I think you should let her try."

I look at Blaze and he nods. "I think we have to let her try."

I reluctantly agree. "Okay. We're giving her a chance."

"A *real* one." Kohen declares.

The tension in the room eases a little, but I'm about to ruin that with my next words. "If she can't do it?"

"We shouldn't be thinking like that yet," Kohen says.

"We have to." I look at him, trying to make him understand my predicament. "Kohen, in less than three months my daughter will be here. And I want Dylan and the baby with me. With us."

"That makes sense. We have plenty of room." Blaze chirps, not seeing the issue.

I keep staring directly at Kohen's face. "I can't let my daughter grow up seeing that." I draw my line, but hope he can see where I'm coming from.

He tears his gaze away from mine, staring at the wall like it might have the answers he's searching for. Eventually, he returns his gaze to mine looking conflicted but he nods his head sharply.

Blaze asks quietly. "You mean if she doesn't get better, then we don't let her come back?"

"Yeah," Kohen answers for me, voice dry. "That's what he means."

The room feels heavy.

I lean forward, bracing my forearms on the table. "I'm not saying we don't help her. If she ever truly wants it, I'll do whatever it takes to get her real help." I swallow. "But not under the same roof as my kid."

Silence.

"I'm not trying to tell y'all how it's going to go. I'm asking you to understand that this is something I need."

Blaze slowly nods his head. "We have to do what's right for Little One."

Kohen loosens his arms and lets them fall to his knees. "I get what you're saying. I just don't like the idea of kicking Mom to the curb if she slips." His hands rub up and down the denim on his thighs, contemplating. "Lane, you have to give her a real chance. You don't get to half-ass it and call it fair. It's like you walk around here just waiting for it to be done already."

He's not wrong.

"I know." I let out a long breath. "I'll try harder. I promise."

And I mean it. If this really is the last time, and I actually have them on board, then I owe it to them.

"Okay." Is all Kohen says, but I can see what it cost him.

"Okay." I echo

"Okay." Blaze seals it.

Just then the door opens and we hear our mom burst out. "Guess what!"

"What?" I ask.

She looks surprised that I'm the one who answers. I'm relieved to find her eyes clear and present.

"I have a job interview on Friday." She squeals, looking around for all our approval.

The boys are smiling at her, then they look at me expectantly.

"That's great, Mom." I tell her. "What's the job?"

They both relax, satisfied that I'm following through with our deal.

She goes on to tell us all about her day and the waitress position she thinks she's found.

I let myself fall a little deeper in the hope that maybe... just maybe this time could be different.

CHAPTER 36

Dylan

26 WEEKS

"**F**uck! I feel like I haven't seen you in days."

I'm propped up against Lane's headboard, fingers scratching lightly at his scalp. His head is tucked against my side, body stretched along mine, carefully curved around the undeniable swell of my belly. One arm's wrapped around me, the other tucked under his head.

"We ate lunch together yesterday." I giggle.

"Doesn't count." Is his muffled reply.

I roll my eyes while also grinning like an idiot because I get it. I didn't realize what a routine we'd fallen into. All of us.

I got used to having them around me all the time, and coming home last night to an empty house was disappointing.

"Well I'm here now. And no work tomorrow. We should probably be studying, but I'm worn smooth out."

Lane turns his head a little so that he can be heard. "How did that go today? Do I need to go up there and punch Jerry in the face?"

I smile at him. "I think I can handle him for now, but I'll let you know if I have a change of heart."

I look at his face, dark lashes resting on his pushed-up cheeks and a small smile forming on his lips.

"I actually wanted to tell you something about all of that." I say a little hesitantly.

"Hit me." He mumbles, never opening his eyes.

"I don't think I'm going to go to law school." His eyes snap open, and he lifts his head, making my hands fall to his shoulders.

"Why not?"

"I think I'm going to switch my major after this semester. I want to do what Rebecca does. I want to work *with* the families, not for them. Does that make sense?" He looks at me as if he's trying to understand, so I keep going.

"I've done my research. Most of the classes I've already taken will count towards my new major. I'd just shift my upper-level courses toward social services or advocacy. I can graduate at the end of my four years. I wouldn't need law school."

"Are you sure that's what you want? You've been pretty adamant that finishing law school is important to you. I guess I just assumed when you said you wanted to work at a place like CASA, you'd just be a lawyer for the families."

"Me too. But the more I work there, the more I can see the difference in the attorneys and the advocates. The advocates get to be with them, work with them, know them." My fingers trail to the nape of his neck. "I think I wanted to prove I could be the best. That I could compete with Dad. But that's not what I want anymore."

His brows are still drawn together, and a small insecurity tells me that he thinks I'm shrinking myself, that I'm giving up.

"This isn't because everything going on is it?" He looks down for a moment before glancing back up. "It's not because of me?"

A breath I didn't realize I'd been holding escapes me, and I lose tension in my shoulders. He wasn't judging me, just fighting his own insecurities.

I give him a confident smile. "Absolutely not. I've been wanting this for a while...maybe before I even met you. I just hadn't figured it out yet. I needed to be sure before I said it out loud.

His mouth turns up on one side, making my heart kick into overdrive. "Alright then, sounds like something you'd kick ass at."

My smile takes over my face as I press my head into his. "You're damn right I will." Then I smack a kiss on him before leaning back against the headboard.

Pride flashes in his eyes as he pushes himself into a seated position. "Okay, I'm in. What do you need from me?"

"Mostly I just need you as arm candy. But the occasional back or foot rub would be nice." I stretch out, extending my belly, and slide my feet up and down the bed. "Especially these next couple of months."

"Geez. You get a girl pregnant one time…" He scoffs, but there's a grin fighting its way onto his face.

"I better be the only girl." I narrow my eyes at him and cross my arms, completely irrational.

His brows lift in surprise, but a cocky smile tugs at his mouth. "Is my girl jealous?"

I arch a brow at him. "I don't share my toys."

"A toy, huh?"

His hand slides up my thigh before he drags me underneath him, bracing himself on top of me. I let out a squeal at how fast he moves.

"Good," he says, brushing his nose along mine. "Because I don't share what's mine either."

I fight a shiver at his words and decide to keep pushing him. "Who said I was yours?"

He pulls back to take in my smug face. He presses his lips together, but the smirk wins.

Without either of us breaking eye contact, he lifts his body completely off of mine, and reaches over to his side table to grab something.

I'm surprised to find him standing over me with a football in hand.

"Take your clothes off." His voice is rough but unyielding.

I narrow my eyes at him, but intrigued enough to comply.

When I'm lying beside him completely bare, nerves creep in. My body's not what it used to be. Other than the obvious giant belly sticking up, I'm getting stretch marks on my thighs, stomach, and boobs.

He doesn't look disappointed, though. He takes every inch of me in, jaw clenched like he's holding back, working to control himself...

My confidence rushes back.

When his gaze finds mine again, I make sure he sees it.

I lift my arms, arching my back to push out my chest before tucking my hands behind my head.

"You got a point to prove," I challenge, "or are you just going to stand there staring at me all day?"

Still, he doesn't say a word..

He lowers the tip of the football and lightly presses it to the tips of my toes. I keep watching him even when I feel the bumpy leather begin its slow climb up my leg.

He doesn't break eye contact once. Not when it glides over my knee. Not when it drags along the inside of my thigh. Not when it skims around my nipples.

When he moves it back down, his eyes finally follow the path it takes, watching every inch like he's memorizing it.

He never touches exactly where I expect him to. Just barely skimming. Circling. Teasing the edges of the places that make my breath catch.

Over and over.

Up my body. Down my sides. Along every curve.

The leather is cool, and the rough seams catch just enough to make me shiver.

I'm a trembling mess of goosebumps, trying my best to stay perfectly still.

He stays in complete control. If it weren't for the serious tent he's pitching right now, I'd think he was unaffected.

He uses the ball to spread my legs, pressing hard into each of my inner thighs, and I let them fall open.

He lays the ball flat on my thigh, letting the seams dig into my skin while he drags it up. Then he does it to the other one before tilting the tip to my middle.

A whimper leaves me when a seam catches me just right.

My hands, still at the back of my head, clench. I close my eyes and throw my head back when he starts to move faster.

He stops suddenly, and my eyes snap open furiously. Not this again. Not tonight.

"Eyes on me, baby." He demands in a hoarse voice.

I don't even have the fight in me anymore. I just need him to finish.

I do as he says, eyes pleading with him to keep going, and he chuckles darkly before continuing.

I can't hold back my moans when he hones his circles on my clit. I release my arms from their hold to rub my breasts, needing to feel the touch he won't give me.

He leans over me and lets his lips ghost up my neck until they stop just beside my ear. "I don't even have to touch you to have you coming undone." He moves quicker, making the crescendo inside of me build to the point of losing it. "You're mine, baby. Say it."

"I'm yours." I yell out with no hesitation.

"That's what I thought. Now come for me." He commands, and my body shatters beneath him.

After the waves of pleasure have run their course, I go boneless on the bed. Eyes closed and breathing hard, I hear a shuffling beside me.

It doesn't take long before I feel warm, rough hands traveling up my sides. His mouth lands on my collarbone, but leaves a wet trail as he rushes to taste as much of my skin as he can before he twists my lower half to one side.

He holds one of my legs up with one arm, straddling my other. His other hand wraps around the back of my neck holding my head, pinning me in place with his hand and gaze when he slowly enters me.

When he's fully seated inside of me his expression slackens and his eyes grow heavy.

"Na ah." I laugh breathily. "Eyes on me, baby."

"Fuck. You don't even know what you do to me." He drawls out low and wrecked.

Then he snaps his hips forward, hitting a spot that instantly has me squirming.

I suck in a deep breath when he starts driving into me at a relentless pace.

The hand holding my leg up slides up to rub my swollen

nub. I bring a fist to my mouth to smother the sounds I can't hold back.

It only takes a few more pumps to have me coming completely undone again. He keeps going, his hips and hand moving in time through the entire orgasm.

When I'm done, his hand goes back to my thigh, gripping tightly as he pumps into me one last time, eyes hooded but they never leave mine.

His head falls to my shoulder and bites it before he drops behind me with a satisfied groan.

His arm slumps around me, drawing me closer to him.

We lay there a while catching our breaths until he gets up and grabs a towel to clean us up with.

When he's done, we both slip under the covers, limbs tangling together.

I have my head on his chest, listening to the steady beat of his heart. Strong and dependable as he is, lulling me into a comfort and peace I didn't even realize existed.

His hand swipes down the side of my head, pulling my hair back and tilting my face to his. He looks down at me with a look that could only be described as adoring, and it steals the breath out of my lungs.

I really don't know what I'd do without him.

I love him so much. The truth of it settles over me, heavy and undeniable.

I open my mouth to tell him, but the words lodge in my

throat. So I swallow them down and bring my mouth to his... the only way I can tell him right now.

I kiss him with the desperation I feel to keep him, and he matches me, hands clinging to my still bare skin.

When I can't take anymore, I tuck my head under his chin, squeezing my eyes against the emotion threatening to spill over.

I will *not* be freaking crying right now.

He cradles me into him further and kisses the top of my head.

"I know, baby." He whispers into my hair. "I know."

I relax into him, nodding my head. I'm not sure if he's talking about the words I can't say or if he's just feeling the same rush of emotions I am.

Either way it anchors me... drawing me back to safer waters.

We fall asleep like that, wrapped around each other, breathing in the steady comfort of us until the world finally slips away.

CHAPTER 37

Dylan

26 WEEKS

I'm currently wondering why in the hell I offered to drive Blaze and Morgan to this game. This has got to be the most awkward of all awkward silences.

And there's still... Yeah, forty-five minutes left in the drive.

Blaze is supposed to be my talking buffer, but he brought those stupid fucking headphones and he's playing on his cell phone.

Morgan sits in my passenger seat, hands folded neatly in her lap, and staring out the window.

She clears her throat. "Thank you again. For driving us."

"Oh, no problem. Anytime. I don't mind at all." Son of a bitch. Pick one answer.

Another silence.

Fuck.

"Oh." She jumps slightly when I break it. "How did your interview go?"

Her fingers twist together in her lap. She doesn't look at me.

"I, um..." She swallows. "I won't know anything until Monday."

There's a beat.

"That's good though, right?" I try. "At least they didn't say no."

She gives a small smile. It doesn't quite reach her eyes. "Yeah. That's... good."

"Are you okay?" I ask softly, checking the mirror to make sure Blaze isn't listening.

She lets out a nervous laugh and stills her hands. "I think I'm just nervous about going to Kohen's game." She looks a little embarrassed. "Sounds silly, doesn't it?"

"Not at all." I reassure. "Kohen can be a little intimidating sometimes I still can't tell if he likes me or not."

She looks at me in surprise. "Kohen? He's my sweetheart. Always so attentive. It's Lane that's intimidating."

I tilt my head in confusion. "Lane?"

She gives me a soft, almost wistful smile. "Well, I'm sure *you* don't think so, but Lane's always been... solid." She searches for the words. "What's right is right and what's wrong is wrong."

Her gaze drifts back out the window.

"And when you've spent years doing nothing but wrong..." Her voice fades off.

I purse my lips, trying to see him through her eyes.

She lets out a soft laugh. "I remember when he was little. Blaze was a newborn and such a fussy baby. I was exhausted. Everyone kept telling me to just let him cry it out. Said he was too attached."

Her fingers twist together in her lap.

"So I laid him down and went to my room. I told myself ten minutes. I'd wait ten minutes."

She smiles faintly. "After a while he stopped crying. I thought—see? It worked. Then I let my self take a nap."

Her voice grows quieter.

"When I woke up and it was still silent, I panicked. I ran to Blaze's room."

She swallows.

"I found Lane in the rocking chair. Holding him. He'd been in there the whole time. He couldn't stand listening to him cry. He had him fed, changed and rocked back to sleep."

Her gaze lifts to mine.

"Even then, he'd do whatever he could for the people he loves. I think that's why it hurts so much that he's given up on me. It feels like confirmation that I'm a lost cause."

"That's not true." I rush out. "He wants you to get better. He told me."

She studies me like she's weighing whether I mean it. Then she draws in a steady breath and squares her shoulders.

"Then I'll just have to show him," she says quietly. "I know it won't be overnight, but we'll get there."

And just like that, the vulnerability disappears.

She offers me a softer smile. "How are you feeling? You and the baby?"

"Well," I gesture vaguely at my body, "as you can see, I'm swelling in places I didn't even know could swell." I scrunch my nose. "Pretty sure even that's bigger."

The rest of the ride feels a little easier. Blaze even takes his headphones out to join after we were laughing at him doing a silent drum solo with his fingers.

She asks me about my life and tells me stories from a happier time.

It was actually... nice.

♡ ⚬⚬⚬⚬⚬ ♡

We finally make it to the game and we're sitting at a stadium that's way fancier than the high school games I'd been going to. It looks as nice as the field Lane plays on.

Kohen's team placed first in their district, so they were able to skip the first round of playoffs. So even though this is their first game, it's the second round. That's what they told me anyway.

The crowd is crazy and loud, with parents and classmates cheering on our team.

The other team scores right off the bat and we spend the rest of the night trying to catch up. We keep the score close but can't ever quite get ahead.

And just like that, after playing undefeated this whole time, Kohen's season is over.

Kohen comes off the field finding us in the crowd of people waiting on players.

"Hey honey. I'm sorry. You played so good though." Morgan gets to him first running a hand up and down his arm, soothing.

Kohen clears his throat, clearly still upset from the loss. "It's all right, Mom. We have next year." He shrugs like it doesn't matter, but he still hasn't looked at any of us directly.

"Of course. Next year y'all will get them." She squeezes him in a hug.

Kohen nods his head in my direction. "You talk to Lane?"

I quickly pull out my phone and see a text from him.

> Tell Kohen I watched the whole game. He played hard. Nothing else they could've done. I'll call when we get checked in.

I flip my phone around for him to see. He grips the collar of his jersey as he reads.

He gives a quick nod before stepping back.

I wink at him. "Probably would've won if they'd got the ball in your hands more."

He rolls his eyes but the corners of his mouth lift anyway.

"He probably would've just ran to the wrong end zone." Blaze teases, and Morgan presses her lips together to hold back a laugh.

Kohen glares at him. "You're so annoying. It was one time. And it was Pee Wee."

"He was so cute, though." Morgan chimes in. "Biggest smile I'd ever seen."

I crack up. "Oh no. How many yards?"

Blaze is laughing right along with me when Kohen's glare finds me.

"It was over half the field." Kohen admits. "It was my first year!"

Even Morgan lets a few laughs slip when Blaze and I start a whole new round.

"You done?" Kohen asks when we settle. He turns to his mom. "Coach wants us all to ride the bus back together. So I guess I'll see y'all when we get back."

"Okay, honey. We'll be there waiting on you." She smiles up at him like he's her whole world.

For just a split second, he just looks at her. Something unreadable flickers across his face, then it's gone, replaced by a rare, full smile.

"Sounds good." He pulls her into a hug. "Thanks for coming, Mom."

We all get back to my car and start the hour long trip back. It's another quiet ride but this time it's comfortable. The only sounds are the low music and a snoring Blaze.

I pull into the school parking lot, feeling the night closing in on me. I let out a big yawn.

"Why don't you just stay in Lane's room tonight? No need for you to drive all the way back to the campus tonight, and we can all watch Lane's game tomorrow."

I give her a sleepy smile. "Are you sure?"

"Of course. You look like you're about to pass out."

"Thank you. That sounds good to me."

"When I was pregnant, I was *always* tired. I don't know how you're doing it all."

"My allowance of one cup of coffee helps the most." I say seriously, making her chuckle softly.

The lights of the bus finally turn into the parking lot and the team files out one by one.

Kohen has a duffle bag thrown over his shoulder as he steps off the bus, searching for my car.

He shuffles over after he finds it, opens up the backdoor and swings his bag around and hits Blaze with it as he slides in.

"What the hell?" Blaze shoots awake, looking around in confusion.

"Blaze Michael! Language!" Morgan snaps. "Kohen Gray, tell your brother you're sorry."

I watch them in the rearview mirror when they both go still and stare at her, unsure how to respond.

Blaze's eyes are wide while Kohen has a brow arched before they both slowly turn to look at each other.

They bust out laughing.

Morgan rolls her eyes and faces the front again. "Get me home before I beat them." She mutters, teasing.

I meet their gaze in the mirror and share a conspiratorial grin with them before sliding the car into drive and pulling out.

♡ ⚬⚬⚬⚬⚬ ♡

"I really hope you all took a shower before you hopped in my bed." Lane says from the screen of my phone while Blaze and Kohen huddle on either side of me to be seen.

"Slumber party in here tonight," I cheer. "Popcorn, candy, and dirty feet all right here in your bed."

"If I find one single speck of anything in my sheets when I get back..." he warns.

"What are you going to do" I taunt. "Can't threaten me, I'm the holder of the baby. I'll just take blame for anything they do."

"Yeah," Kohen says with a wicked grin. "Wouldn't want to stress out your precious baby mama. Blaze... don't you have some Pixy Stix?"

Blaze perks up. "Oh yeah. A stack of them."

Lane's eyes narrow. "Out of my room now."

We snicker at his fear for his sheets.

"Yeah, I'm going to get to bed." Kohen announces, pushing

himself off the bed. "We'll be watching tomorrow, so don't fuck up."

Lane snorts. "Thanks for your support."

Kohen says nothing back, just walks to his room until we hear his door shut.

"I should probably get some sleep, too." Lane's big yawn only emphasizes his words.

"Good night." Blaze and I say together.

"Night. Love y'all."

"Love you too. Good luck tomorrow." Blaze says smiling easily.

I swallow through the panic trying to rise.

"Good luck. You're going to do great tomorrow. Go, fight, win, and all that." I say with a nervous laugh.

A small, knowing grin spreads on his face.

"Thanks," he says quietly, giving me a reassuring wink before he ends the call.

I'm still staring at the screen, wondering why I can't just say the words.

What difference does it even make? Things aren't going to change. It's not going to start a doom-clock for us or anything.

If anything I'm probably dooming us from holding back.

A throat being cleared reminds me that Blaze is still in the room and just witnessed that entire awkward exchange.

"You know, I remember the night he met you." Blaze says with more seriousness than he usually shows.

"You do?" I question, wondering where he's going with this.

"Yeah," He nods, lips turned up on one side. "He never stays out all night unless it's because of a game."

"Oh," I grimace feeling a little guilty. "I'm sorry. Were you two really worried about him?"

He runs his hand down the back of his neck in a familiar gesture. "Honestly, I kinda just wondered if he'd had enough and just left." Like his mom did.

He doesn't say it, but I feel it.

I grab one of his hands with both of mine. "Lane would never leave you two. If there's one thing I know is true about him, it's that he loves you very much."

Blaze chuckles at me. "I know. I don't know why I was freaking out like that. My point," He looks at me intently. "...is that he doesn't do that. He doesn't stay out all night with girls." He puts his other hand on top of mine. "And he definitely doesn't bring them around here."

My heart constricts at the sweetness of this precious boy. Either for me or his brother, he just let me see a fragile part of himself to reassure me.

The protectiveness these brothers have for each other is truly a beautiful thing to witness.

I smile brightly at him and pull him in for a slightly clumsy hug as he tries to avoid pressing too hard on my belly.

"You're the best. You know that?" I squeeze him a little tighter. "Thank you." I whisper.

He pulls back from our hug.

"Obviously," he says with a cocky grin.

"But so is Lane. So don't let all this..." He waves a hand in the air. "...scare you off."

My brows knit together.

He starts watching his hands, popping his knuckles. "He's done it all on his own for so long. Before you showed up, he was just... resigned to live his life. Not that I think he resented us or anything. He just woke up and did what he had to do." He meets my gaze. "He's different now... happier. More like our brother again."

My chest tightens.

"Blaze... I'm not going anywhere, unless your brother wants me to."

He gulps. "You mean that?"

"I swear it." I say seriously, holding his gaze so he can see how much I mean it. Then hold up my pinky.

He rolls his eyes but carries out the pinky promise.

When we're done, I add, "You're stuck with me no matter what, punk. Little One's going to need her younger, cool uncle to have her back."

He smiles. "Good. I kinda like having you around."

I scrunch my nose up at him. "I kinda like having you around, too. You're the only one who laughs at my jokes."

He makes a face, sucking in air through his teeth. "About that…"

My eyes widen. "What?"

"It's pity laughs."

I gasp and slap him playfully on the shoulder. "You don't mean it!"

"I'm sorry. Your jokes are just terrible." He dodges another slap, rolling backwards off the bed and landing on his feet, cracking himself up the whole time.

I pull a pillow out from behind me and toss it at him. "Take it back." I pick up another and rear back with it. "Say it."

He holds up the one I just threw as a shield. "Okay fine. *Sometimes* it's a real laugh."

I toss it at him anyway, sending us both into another round of laughter.

"Would you two shut up and go to sleep?" Kohen yells from his room down the hall.

I slap a hand over my mouth while Blaze freezes, a shit-eating grin spreading across his face.

We stare at each other for one beat…and then completely lose it again.

CHAPTER 38

Dylan

The game doesn't start until three so we have some time to kill after we all get up and moving. We spend most of the morning learning how to play Texas Hold'em from Morgan.

I really don't have the poker face skill. Kohen, on the other hand, can straight face with the best of them.

Then we decide to go all out on game day snacks, much to my delight.

By the time we're done, we have their kitchen table covered in finger foods. Wings, chips and dip, wraps, sandwiches, a cheese ball, jalapeño poppers... the works.

I'm already disgustingly full by the time it's kick off for Lane's game.

We receive the ball first, and special teams get us out to the forty-yard line. The offense stalls on the first couple of downs, but then the quarterback launches a deep pass downfield, and we end up in the end zone.

Our tiny little group freaks out, hoping it's a good sign for how the rest of the game's going to go.

We're able to hold them to a field goal—because my man is awesome at his job—but nobody scores again in the first half.

We're all getting up for another round of food during half-time when Morgan gets a call and walks out of the room.

I listen to Blaze and Kohen talk game as I steal the last two poppers and add them to my plate.

"As long as Lane and the rest of the defense can hold them and our offense could do anything, we should be able to win this," Kohen huffs out.

Blaze nods his head in agreement. "Yeah, our offense is really hurting without Nate, plus their defense is really good, too."

"I hate that Nate can't play. It hurts my heart for him. You can tell he's dying to be out there from the sidelines."

Morgan walks back into the room, smoothing her hands down the front of her shirt.

She clears her throat.

"Who's Nate?"

All of us pause.

"That's Lane's best friend," Blaze says carefully. "The one that got hurt."

Something flickers across her face, recognition trying to catch up.

"Oh," she lets out a soft laugh. "Right... right. I'm sorry."

She moves to sit, eyes locking on the television as if she's avoiding the rest of us.

She didn't even know her son's best friend? Lane's gone at least twice this week to see him.

I didn't realize how uninvolved she actually was in their lives. I wonder how much is actually going on inside her head. How often she's battling, even right here in front of us.

There's a stretch of silence where we look at each other with varying looks of concern.

"Mom, do you want anything while I'm still in the kitchen?" Kohen asks.

She jerks her head in his direction. "Oh, umm...sure. I'll take some wings and some ranch, please."

Kohen grabs a paper plate off the top of the stack in the middle of their table. "Anything to drink?"

She smiles warmly at him. "No thank you, honey. I still have some tea."

We settle back into our spots in the living room. Kohen surprisingly didn't take the recliner today, and is sitting next to me on the couch.

I try not to let my thoughts linger on Morgan, but she seems more tense since she had that phone call. Maybe it's just the fact that she didn't know who Nate was that has me in my head about it all.

I mean, she's currently laughing at something Blaze is telling her so I don't know why I fell so uncertain.

But Kohen's gaze is cut to the side, watching her subtly. So I know I'm not the only one that feels the change.

Half-time's finally over and the boys are running back on the field. It's our turn to kick the ball to them, but they only get to the twenty-five yard line.

We hold them to another field goal, but now they're only one point behind us. Our quarterback tries a couple more times to land another long pass like his first one, but can't ever get anyone open downfield to pull it off.

We manage to keep our one point lead the rest of the game and we have the ball. Just have to keep the ball and run down the clock.

Our offense needs to get one more first down and we can kneel it from there, but we still have seven yards to go.

We try to run it but lose a yard. The next snap the quarterback fakes a handoff then pulls back for a pass. Unfortunately he gets sacked mid throw. Hard.

The ball flies in the air and is caught by their defense.

Turnover.

Our guys try their best but they were already in field goal range when they got the ball back and my heart sinks when their kicker shoots it clean in the middle of the posts... ending Lane's game, season, and possibly his entire football career.

The boys are pissed off and yelling at the screen. I wish we would've gone to the game in person so I could see Lane right now. I just want to hold him and tell him how great he played.

Morgan just sits there shoulders sinking and head lowered. She *does* know how much this meant to him and is heartbroken for her son. "They were so close," she says so quietly I wouldn't have even heard it if I weren't already watching her.

♡ ⚛ ♡

After the loss, we hung out for a little while but I didn't want to overstay my welcome so that's how I find myself waking up alone the next morning.

I'm a little disappointed I'd expected him to call me when he got home or a text, but my phone has no notifications.

It's a little selfish of me to expect him to contact me when he's the one that had the long night so I send him a text asking if he made it home.

I watch it for a minute but it never shows it's read. He's probably still asleep.

I try to push it aside and do some studying since finals are this week.

Hours later, I'm surrounded by books and flashcards when I get a call. To my surprise, it's Kohen's name flashing across the screen.

"Hey what's up?"

"Hey Lane isn't answering my calls," he says without preamble. "Can I talk to him? It's important."

I instantly go on alert.

"I thought Lane was with you." I say slowly trying not to panic. "He didn't come home last night?"

"He came home, but he left early this morning. He didn't go to your place?" Kohen sounds just as confused as I feel.

Fear tingles up my spine.

"Maybe he went to Nate's. Call him and text me if he answers."

"Yeah. Okay. Give me a minute." The line cuts off.

My fingers are drumming on the notebook in front of me as I wait.

Instead of the text I was waiting for, Kohen's call lights up my phone again.

"He hasn't seen him either." Kohen rushes out as soon as I answer.

My fingers are trembling, but I don't want to scare Kohen, so I force my voice to stay steady. "Okay, I'll drive around to his usual spots. He may have gone to the gym or to talk to the coach or something."

"Let me know if you find him. I'll tell you if he comes back here."

"I will and okay I'll keep my phone close."

"Thanks, Dylan." For the first time, Kohen sounds like a scared kid.

"He's fine. I'm sure of it." I tell him, praying that I'm right.

"Yeah." He says with little confidence. His hard tone slips back in place. "Keep me updated."

Then the line goes dead.

I drive around the campus searching any place he might be. Nothing.

I've been driving around over an hour and I can't find him anywhere.

I'm completely at a loss.

What could he possibly have needed to do this morning?

I'd like to think if he needed comfort, he'd have come to me, but maybe there's someone else... wait.

Not some*one*, you idiot. Some*where*.

I turn my car around and head out of town.

I can hear the crunch of my tires on the rocks as I pull my car up beside his truck.

I'm relieved to find him but want to make sure he's okay before I text Kohen.

I walk out to our spot by the lake and he's sitting on the ground propped against the log. His sad green eyes find mine, and he forces a small smile.

"You scared the shit out of us." I say crouching down to sit beside him.

"I just figured y'all would call if anybody needed something." He replies looking back over the lake.

"We did. You didn't answer."

He looks back confused and pulls his phone out of his pocket. "Shit. It died. I'm sorry."

I give him a small smile. "It's okay. We just panicked a little." I look out over the lake pulling my jacket tighter around myself. "You okay?"

He sucks in a deep breath before releasing it. "Yeah. Just crazy thinking that was it. My last game." He wraps an arm around my shoulders and I lean into him.

"You don't know that. You had scouts asking about you before, I bet they're still interested. Don't give up hope yet."

"I'm not but..." he shrugs his shoulders. "Odds are it's over. And that's fine, it was always my plan to end it here. I just needed a bit to wrap my head around it."

I lace my fingers into his. "Well, I don't think it is," I say with all the confidence I feel. "But, if that was your last game, you still have us. All of us. And maybe one day we can give Little One a brother and you can be the sexiest damn Pee Wee coach I've ever seen."

His deep chuckle soothes something inside of me. "You wanting more kids from me already?"

I'm so glad he can't see my face right now. "No.. well.. I don't know. One day... maybe." I groan out loud when he's shaking uncontrollably from his laughter. "I need to call Kohen. I told him I'd let him know when I found you."

He's still laughing at my expense while I pull my phone out and search for Kohen's name. My phone rings before I can dial, and all I see is police department and answer it quickly.

"Hello?"

"Is this Dylan Whitlock?" A man's voice asks over the line.

"This is her. How can I help you?"

"This is Officer Chandler from County Sheriff's Department. We're looking for Lane Kemp. Is he with you by chance?"

My stomach drops.

"He is," I say carefully. "Can I ask what this is about?"

"It would be better if we could speak to him directly." His voice is professional, but stern.

I hand the phone to Lane and he takes it, head tilted in confusion.

"Yes sir. I'm Lane Kemp."

I watch the confusion leave his face and turn to one of panic. "You have the boys?"

He stands up as the voice I can't understand anymore continues.

He stands there quietly listening, but he's shaking with rage.

"Let me guess," he says voice sharp. "My mother."

Holy shit. What the fuck is happening? Are the boys okay?

"What does that mean?"

Another pause, and pure terror takes over his face. "I'll be right there."

He ends the phone call.

"Fuck!" He shouts before letting his head fall into his palms.

"What is it? Are the boys okay?" I ask, terrified.

"They took them." He runs a hand through his hair, shifting back and forth.

He finally meets my gaze and there are tears in his eyes. Fury and fear shine there, making him look as close to breaking as I've ever seen.

"They took the boys...because of *her*."

CHAPTER 39

Lane

"**A**m I speaking with a Lane Kemp?"

"Yes sir. I'm Lane Kemp," I say cautiously.

"We have Kohen and Blaze Kemp up here at the station…"

"You have the boys?"

What the fuck?

"We got a call today about a woman causing problems at a bar. When we showed up to take her in she was screaming about her kids."

"Let me guess. My mother." I feel a rage start to build inside of me.

"Yes sir. With her being the only living guardian on file we had to conduct a welfare check."

"What does that mean?"

"It means we showed up to the residence we have on file

and they were there alone. Social services had to be called. We need you to come in and speak with them."

"I'll be there soon." Is the only thing I can manage to get out.

I press end and let it out.

"Fuck!" I scream, feeling like I'm about to explode.

I let my head fall to my hands. Devastation is crashing through me right now, I can't lose them.

"What is it? Are the boys okay?" Dylan asks, voice shaky.

"They took them." I don't even know what to do with myself right now. I need to go but I can't make myself move either.

It wasn't enough for her to fail. She had to take the boys down with her. *My* boys.

"They took the boys," Anger replaces my fear. "...because of *her*."

I hate her.

"Let me take you up there. I don't think you should be driving." Dylan suggests hesitantly.

"Yeah, okay. Let's go." I'm nodding my head but I still haven't moved.

Her warm hand takes my cold one, and she starts leading me where I need to go.

I don't remember much of how we got here. My brain has been a mess of worry. Am I going to lose them? Are they going to be separated?

If I wouldn't have been whining about football, I would've fucking been there.

They're probably so scared.

I'm here now, though and bursting through the doors in a frantic search to find them.

An officer I recognize because he's covered for me in the past walks up to me. "Look at me, son. They're fine. Social Services has them in a room together back here, talking to them. I can bring you back right now."

I nod frantically, and I don't know if it's because I see him as an ally in this moment or because I just need someone to tell me it's going to be okay, I ask him. "Officer Hayes, they aren't going to take them from me, are they?"

"I've told you before just call me Mark. I'm not completely sure how it all works, but I'm sure it'll all be fine."

Dylan steps up beside me and in a voice that is steady she tells me, "You're the next of kin. You own the house and have been providing for them financially for years. It's most likely they'll want you to take over guardianship. They always look to family before anywhere else." She's speaking to me calmly and with an assurance that I desperately need. "Make sure you explain all of that to them. Have the boys back you up if they need it."

I nod my head taking in every bit of advice she can hand me.

She breaks her composure and leans in to wrap her arms around me and I use the moment to draw some strength. "We aren't going to lose them, okay?" She says where only I can hear.

"Come on follow me. I'll bring you to them." Officer Hayes glances at Dylan apologetically. "Only you, though."

Dylan releases me. "I'll wait out here. Go."

Everything in me wants to pull her back and take her with me. Have her by my side through all of this.

Mark starts walking past the front desk.

"It's not the first time we've been called about her. Mostly just disturbance calls, nothing really criminal. Usually we just let her sleep it off for the night and cut her loose the next morning. But when she started spouting off about how all she does is hurt her kids, it was out of my hands. We had to do a follow-up with that, and now they're talking about negligent charges."

I look at the middle-aged man who'd shown up at my house several times over the years. Knowing my father and the situation we were in, he protected us from being looked at too closely for years. Once we all got older, I guess the random calls of concern from teachers and town do-gooders stopped coming. It'd been a few years since he'd been around.

"I get it. Thanks for trying."

Mark leads me further down the hallway, but we're intercepted before we get to the room the boys are in. "Are you Gavin Kemp?"

"It's Lane," I tell him. "But yes."

"Lane, we need to ask you a few questions if you don't mind following me this way."

"I just want to make sure my brothers are okay." I insist.

"I'm sorry, sir. It's protocol to speak with you first."

I deflate. "Okay. Can we make it quick, please?"

I'm led to a room where I'm basically fucking interrogated, like it's my fault for having an alcoholic for a mother.

Am I aware of my mother's history with alcohol?

Do I leave them alone in her care often?

How often do I leave them alone?

Then the cop leaves and a social worker comes in and asks me all the same questions.

When I've had enough I finally ask, "Is there a reason why I'm being questioned when my mom is the fucking problem? Everything I do is for them, and I'm not going to sit here and listen to anymore insinuations that this is somehow my fault."

The case worker sits there unaffected by my outburst. "I'm sorry these are routine questions. We just need to determine that it's safe for them to return home with you."

"I've been taking care of them for years. I own the house they're living in. I keep them fed, clothed, and I pay all of their bills. They're perfectly safe with me."

All she does is write down notes and I'm sure after my meltdown I'm not looking good on paper.

I sag back into the office chair and wait for her gaze to lift to mine.

"All I want right now is to see them and make sure they're okay." I say more softly.

"We understand this is upsetting. I'm going to step out and confirm a few details. Once that's done, you'll be able to see your brothers." She gets up and holds the door open for me. "Please wait in the waiting room for me to return."

Mark's waiting for me when I step out the door.

"I was wondering if you wanted to see your mom."

I look at him a moment. "Not really."

"I can understand that," He slips his hands in his pockets. "She was asking for you earlier, is all."

"Well, I don't have much to say to her."

"Fair enough." He nods his head and starts to walk off.

I hesitate but decide, fuck it. "Where is she?"

"Follow me."

I get in the room and sit across from her. She won't even look at me. Just sits there glassy eyed and defeated. Her hands are cuffed sitting on the table.

I hope she feels just as bad as she looks.

"If I lose them because of you. I'll never forgive you for it."

She just sniffles and turns her head away from me.

"They're saying I either need to go to rehab or I'm getting charged with negligence."

"Yeah, just a few years too late on that." I scoff. "You were home this morning, what the hell happened?"

"I got a phone call yesterday from the job I was supposed to get. They said they didn't want a woman with my background. I knew I'd never be anything but a burden to you."

"It was one place. One job that turned you down. You barely even tried." I say with disgust.

I watch as tears start rolling down her face but all I can think about is that my brothers have been scared and interrogated all evening because... what? She couldn't handle rejection?

"And then you lost your game. And it just felt like everything was worse for y'all with me home. I watched you leave this morning, hurt and alone. I followed right behind you and went to the only bar I knew was open."

"My brothers are alone at a police station because you felt sorry for yourself. Jesus Christ."

"I'm sorry. I'm sorry if I ruined everything for good this time. I'm sorry if you can't get them back. I'm sorry..." She chokes up. "For being a sorry excuse of a mother." Her face crumples. "I just don't know how to stop."

"Then just stay away. Because they can't tell you no, and I won't make them choose." I lean forward, looking her directly in the eyes. "Go to rehab. Fix your shit. Until then... Stay. The fuck. Away."

She drops her head and makes herself small. "I will. I'll do the rehab and I'll be better. This was just a slip-up."

"A pretty catastrophic slip-up, Mom." I deadpan.

The chains of her cuffs rattle as she reaches for a Kleenex. "I know." She whispers.

"You're so selfish. I've begged you to go to rehab. For yourself. For us. I guess a potential felony is all it took to finally get your attention. Wouldn't be able to get your precious drink from behind bars, could you?"

She starts sobbing again. "I just didn't want to burden you anymore..."

"This is being a burden. Don't you dare sit there and act like you're concerned for anyone but yourself."

She's crying into her hands now, her small body shaking.

I let out a slow breath, the fight draining out of me.

"I hope it all works out for you. I really do." I say softer now. "You just have to do it by yourself. If they're coming home with me, I won't risk losing them again."

I don't wait for a reply. I get up and walk out of the room.

I can't sit there anymore and listen to her excuses.

I try to navigate my way through this maze to find Dylan. She's been waiting out there for what has to be hours.

I'm not even sure what time it is.

An exit sign with an arrow pointing to the right sits at the end of the hallway. Before I can figure out if it's the exit I'm looking for I'm stopped by the social worker.

"Mr. Kemp, I've been looking for you. Can you follow me, please?"

My shoulders sag. It's like no matter what I do I can't manage to get to any of my people.

We get back in the office and I take the same seat I had before.

She sits down in front of me and folds her hands together on the desk.

"Mr. Kemp, we've reviewed the situation."

I suck in a breath.

"Based on your age, your financial responsibility for the household, and statements from your brothers, we're placing them in your care effective immediately."

It takes a moment for her words to register.

"For now," she adds. "This is considered temporary guardianship pending further review. There will be follow-up visits. We'll also need documentation of income and proof of residency."

"That's fine," I say immediately. "I have it."

She nods. "Your mother will be required to enter a treatment program if she wishes to regain custodial consideration. If she refuses, charges may proceed."

"So she can still get them back?"

"Reunification is always the goal when it's safe and appropriate," she says evenly. "However, that would require documented completion of an inpatient treatment program, ongoing sobriety, compliance with court recommendations, and a formal custody review."

"But they're coming home with me? Tonight?"

"Yes."

My head falls back in the chair and my vision blurs, the tension that's been holding me upright finally cracking.

I drag a hand over my face and sit back up to face her. "When can I see them?"

"I just need you to sign some paperwork and I can bring you right to them."

She slides over a stack of paperwork and starts flipping through the pages. She tells me where to sign, where to initial, and brief summaries of what each signature is for.

She pulls the stack back to herself and slides it into her bag. "You can email me all the required forms we previously talked about. I'm giving you my card, and I've already written what I need on the back. If you could send that over as soon as possible, that would be great." She smiles warmly at me. "Let's get you and your brothers home."

My hand shakes as I reach for the handle. I've been trying to get to them since I got that phone call, and now I'm scared of what I'll find on the other side.

I push the door open.

They're sitting close together, talking quietly, until the sound of the door makes them look up.

Blaze slides off the table he's sitting on.

Kohen stands straight up out of the rolling chair he's in, shoulder squared like he's bracing for something.

Their eyes are red rimmed and tired but... they're okay. They're together. *We're* together.

I don't think, I just move. I pull them both to me bringing our heads together like we're in a huddle.

I can see Blaze's body start to shake and he makes a fist in my shirt like he'd been holding it together until this moment. "Is everything okay? Can we go home now?" He asks voice raw.

Kohen's worried gaze meets mine and waits for my response.

I swallow past the lump in my throat.

"We're okay." I say hoarsely. "Let's go home."

CHAPTER 40

Dylan

31 WEEKS

It's been a month since Lane walked out of that station with both boys tucked under his arms like someone might steal them if he even lessened his grip.

There have been court dates, CPS visits, evaluations...

It was chaos.

At first, I tried to hang back, just be there if they needed help with rides or watch them when Lane couldn't be there —he's terrified to leave them alone again. I didn't want to get in the way or make things harder for any of them with my presence.

There was one afternoon that I had surprised them with pizza for lunch and a social worker showed up for a surprise visit.

"If you don't mind, can I ask who you are to them?"

I started stammering, not sure how to explain.

"My name's Dylan Whitlock... I'm... He's.."

"She's with us," Lane says simply.

"Is she a permanent part of the household?" She asks writing notes on a clipboard.

"I have my own place." I rush to explain.

"She will eventually, so you might as well add her to whatever you're doing there. We're having a kid together, but that changes absolutely nothing with the boys," Lane tells her assuredly.

Lisa—the social worker—gives him an amused smile. "Okay. Well then, I'm going to have a few questions for you as well, Ms. Whitlock."

I laugh a little nervously. "Please, just call me Dylan."

I was scared the boys—Kohen especially—would push back.

But aside from the tension between him and Lane about how to handle their mom, he's been surprisingly steady through all of this, if not a little reserved.

We made it through finals; I tried to talk Lane into asking for extensions, but he said he didn't want it to seem like he couldn't handle the situation and passed them all with ease.

The only time I've ever seen him close to breaking through all of this was when he thought he lost them. I'll never forget the look of terror when the officer told him they had the boys.

It was nice that we all had a Christmas break together. I thought it was going to be hollow for them, but this is their normal. They're used to working around the absence.

We exchanged gifts with each other for Christmas, then I may have borrowed my dad's emergency credit card and went a little crazy with fireworks for New Year's, but we had a blast.

I even talked them all into wearing the party hats.

It was a night to forget about everything for a while and just have fun together.

Maybe a little hope for new beginnings for everyone.

Today is Morgan's first day in rehab.

After her court date, she got public intoxication charges, and the judge gave her thirty days inpatient if she wants a chance at custodial review.

There was a huge argument last night about whether they'd see her beforehand. Lane and Kohen were snapping at each other back and forth when Blaze stepped in and suggested they put it to a vote.

Two to Kohen's one, they agreed to let her go and do this on her own and be there when she gets out.

Kohen wasn't happy about it, but when the vote was over, he didn't fight it.

Lane and I are sitting on the couch watching—you guessed it—Sunday football.

"Well, tomorrow we go back to normal. School and work. You ready for it?" I ask him as he rubs my poor, swollen feet.

"Yeah. No more practice, so I have a little more free time."

"Oh, I like the sound of that." I say rubbing my free foot up his leg.

He laughs stopping my foot before it gets a little too high. "You won't, though. Swapping majors... You nervous about that?"

My head falls back with a groan when his thumb presses deeply in the arch of my foot. "Not at all. I'm actually really excited."

"How did your mom take it?" He asks, sliding his hand up my calf to massage there. "Or have you told her yet?"

I scoot down where he has easier access."She didn't sound thrilled about it but she never said anything. Just said 'If that's what you want you should do it.' I'll take it."

"I'm glad y'all worked everything out."

"Me too." He switches feet and I sneak a peek at him. "What about your mom?"

"What about her?" He says never pausing his movements.

"What are you going to do when she gets out?" I ask quietly.

"First she has to get through it," He glances over pressing his lips together. "Then stay sober."

"And if she does?"

"I asked about making the guardianship permanent." He keeps his eyes on my leg. "But if she checks all the boxes and her case worker clears her... I can't stop it."

He lets out a heavy breath and brings my feet together in his lap.

"I'll still be here," he adds. "No matter what."

I nod my head, wondering if he even believes she'll finish the program.

I sit up and lean into his side and he wraps an arm around my shoulders without a second thought.

"They won't let you get pushed out. Blaze and Kohen would fight for you same as you would for them."

"Yeah. I'm not going to worry about it until I have to."

I just nod my head and breathe in his comforting scent.

He's right. Though I'm surprised how well he's handling it.

"I guess I'm going to head home soon. I have work and school tomorrow and I need more clothes." I wrap him up tighter betraying my words of needing to leave.

"I'm about to just slowly bring your things over here so you don't have that excuse anymore." He jokes.

"Oh yeah? Just skip right over asking me and just move me in secret?" I look up at him expecting to see humor in his face but it's serious.

"Is that what you're waiting for? A formal question?" His brow is arched in question.

I shift to sit up. "Don't be ridiculous. I can't move in right *now*."

"Are you hesitant because of the situation? Because if you're not ready and just don't want to I'll drop it. But..." He trails off.

Is he actually serious right now?

I gulp before I answer. "I wouldn't mind living with you if that's what you're asking... but all of this is happening and I still have my lease... the boys. It just feels like bad timing."

"Take all of my mom's bullshit out of the equation. It's just me asking you if you want to live with me and my brothers. What's your answer?"

I press my lips together to fight a smile. "Of course I do."

A cocky grin spreads across his face that I haven't seen in a while, and my heart picks up speed.

"Blaze! Kohen!" He yells out suddenly, making me jump.

My eyes widen. "What are you doing?"

"You'll see." He says, standing up at the sound of heavy footsteps coming down the stairs.

They both look around trying to figure out what's going on, when they make it all the way down.

"What is it?" Kohen asks.

"I need to have another vote," Lane announces.

They both hesitate, but slowly shuffle into the room with us.

"Okay. I know this probably isn't the best timing, and if ya'll aren't ready for it, just say so. It won't be a big deal." Lane starts off by saying.

Oh my God. He's really doing this. Should I be here for this?

Do I want to be here for this?

"Oh-kay." Blaze says hesitantly.

"You both know I wanted Dylan living with us when the baby was born," He talked to them about this? "But what if she moved in before that?"

Blaze rolls his eyes but smiles. "I thought this was something serious. I don't care."

Kohen snorts. "Yeah she basically already lives here."

"You're not going to hurt my feelings if you don't want me to. Really!" I say to both of them, but my heart's already racing from their response.

Blaze laughs. "You're an idiot. I already think of you as a sister." He says it so easily it shocks me. "And you're here all the time, anyway. Might as well make it official."

My eyes start to tear up and I have a big goofy smile on my face. "Really?"

"Yes." He tells me with a duh look.

I slide my gaze to Kohen and my smile slips.

He's looking down like he can't meet my gaze. "Kohen, I really do understand if you want more time. I get it."

I glance at Lane and he has a concerned look for him.

Kohen finally lifts his head. "It's not that... I was just thinking." He pauses. Clears his throat. "I think you should take the big room."

I'm not sure what I thought he was thinking, but it wasn't that. His mom's room?

The whole room is quiet.

"Why do you say that?" Lane is the first to speak up.

"Little One will be here soon. You need the extra space." Kohen shrugs his shoulder and I smile at the use of our nickname. "Just makes sense."

He looks at Lane. "If Mom comes back, she can take your room."

And there it is. The reason all of this feels too fast. They have so much they still have to get through together.

"I don't know that feels like..." I begin but get interrupted.

"Trust me, I think we'll *all* want you to be downstairs when your kid's crying all night and stuff." He adds gruffly, like this isn't a big deal. "Plus, you moving in saves us all from Lane's moping around when you're gone."

I search his face to make sure he means it. He rolls his eyes, but gives me a small, encouraging nod.

I glance up at Lane, and his eyes are bright with emotion as he watches his brother.

Blaze raises a hand up beside him. "Alright. Well, you have my vote." He looks to Kohen.

He looks annoyed but raises a hand. "And mine."

Lane looks at them as if they just handed him the world, then raises his own hand.

"Mine was decided a long time ago." He looks at me expectantly. "Only one more to go."

I giggle at the absurdity of all this. But I stand up and raise my hand too. "Alright, I'm in. Looks like I'm stuck with you dorks."

Blaze immediately looks offended. "You think we're the dorks?"

I laugh, giddy from their not only their acceptance of me but how they made space for me.

"Come here. Bring it in, you guys."

They awkwardly accept my group hug, and when I sniffle, Kohen calls me out. "Are you crying right now?"

"I can't help it. It's the hormones." I choke out a laugh.

"Oh geez. It's going to be so weird having a girl around all the time," Blaze says, patting my back like he has absolutely no idea what to do with me.

They slowly pull away like I'm a ticking time bomb. "I'm just going to go back upstairs. This feels like a Lane thing to deal with." Kohen says, looking at me like I'm insane.

"Okay," I laugh again, wiping uselessly at the streams on my cheeks. "Thanks for your votes."

They scramble away quickly as soon as they get the all-clear and Lane watches them disappear up the stairs before stepping in front of me.

"I hope those are happy hormonal tears," he tells me, pressing a kiss into my hair and running his hands down my back.

A fresh wave of emotion hits me, so I just nod against his chest.

"I'm sorry." I mumble eventually. "I'm sure they'll go away in a minute. Just pretend like they aren't there. That's what I do."

He chuckles softly. "I knew they weren't going to care about you moving in. I think they claimed you that first day at your apartment."

"I don't know about me, but they certainly claimed all the snacks I had." I laugh thinking about how easily they made themselves at home in my apartment.

He laughs with me before letting his hand settle on the back of my neck. He gives a small squeeze—a silent request—and I lift my gaze to meet his.

"I'm not sure how you did it," he says quietly, "but you became family to all of us."

His thumb brushes against my skin.

"Like you were always meant to be here."

I wish I could explain to him how much they all mean to me. But I can't, so I lift myself up as high as a can on my toes. When his lips meet mine, I do my best to show him everything I can't say.

When I finally pull away, I whisper, "Hey Lane."

"Yeah?" He rests his head on mine.

"I'm really glad I picked that room to hide in."

CHAPTER 41

Dylan

35 WEEKS

I t took us over a month, but I'm finally looking at an empty apartment.

Bexley is helping me clean everything before I leave it behind for good.

It took us a while to get everything out with all of our busy schedules. Lane was picking up extra work on the weekends when he could, and I couldn't move anything big on my own.

Even when I tried picking up boxes, I had one of the boys on my case. So it's been a slow moving process.

I don't think I've ever been this happy in my life. Every day, I come home to a house that's full of life. The boys complain about their day at school. We eat together, hang out together, and laugh together.

And then I spend my nights in the arms of the best man in the world.

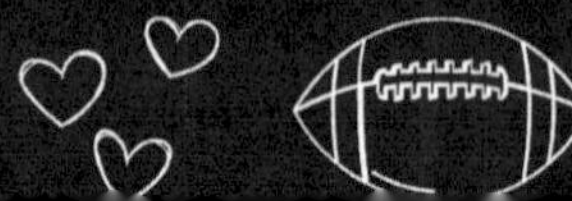

It's the home I didn't realize I spent my whole life searching for.

Not the house itself—but the people in it. They're my home.

I truly love all of them.

Kohen's quiet protectiveness, Blaze's contagious joy, and Lane at the center of it all is just... my everything.

Today's the day the boys pick up their mom. We haven't really heard anything from her since she left so I'm nervous how their reunion is going to go.

I figured this would keep me distracted for most of the day, but when I got here Bexley had most of it done. All I've managed to do is sweep, mop, and vacuum, but honestly, just that has my stomach cramping, so I'm a little glad she got the jump on me.

"Well, this went smoothly. What should we do for the rest of the day?" Bex asks leaning against the door, checking her phone.

"Well, I can't go anywhere looking like this." I wave a hand down myself, showcasing the pair of maternity leggings and one of Lane's old t-shirts I'm wearing.

"Yeah me either." She looks down at the clothes she's wearing. "Let's pop over to my place real quick... I bet I have a dress you can wear."

"For what? Whatcha got in mind?" I follow her out my door into the hallway.

She twists her doorknob, turning to me with a suspicious smile. "You'll see."

When the door swings open and I see what's waiting inside, I'm frozen in shock.

"Surprise."

Bexley grins. "Didn't think I'd let you get away with no baby shower, did you?"

"Sierra? Mom?"

Sierra runs up to me and we wrap each other up. "Holy crap. You're so pregnant!" She pulls away and rubs at my belly like it was her own. "Hello in there, no-named little girl. I'm Aunt Sierra."

I laugh at her familiar antics. "What are y'all doing here?"

I look over to my politely smiling mother before she finally caves and pulls me in for her own hug.

"Bexley and Sierra have been planning this for a little while now." Mom tells me.

"Oh my gosh. You guys! I can't believe you did this." I look at my best friend and mother in awe. "I'm just so happy to see both of you."

"I know. I've never gone this long without you." Sierra whines. "And hello Bexley, it's nice to officially meet you." She and Bexley start chatting like they've known each other forever.

"How are you feeling, honey?" My mom runs a hand down the side of my face. "Any pains?"

"I don't get much sleep. It's impossible to get comfortable. But other than that it's not so bad."

She nods her head. "That's good. I can't believe in a month my baby's going to have her own baby."

I smile at her blubbering. "I can't believe it either. I can't wait to meet her."

My mom gives me a once-over. "I bought you an outfit for the occasion. Please go put it on before anyone else shows up."

She points to the dress laid out on the back of the couch.

"Thank you." I groan. "There's no way anything Bex had was going to fit me right."

"I'm going to finish up decorating in here. You girls go get ready." Mom announces and Bexley leads us to her room.

I'd already put my hair into a bun, so my natural curls are a no-go at this point. I have to run Bex's straightener through it and leave it down.

"So...how's living together going?" Bex asks, looking at me in the mirror while she does her makeup.

"Yes spill." Sierra adds.

"I was scared it was going to be too much too soon but..." A big goofy grin spreads across my whole face. "It's so easy being with him. And I can't wait to see him at the end of the day."

Sierra squeals. "Oh my God. You love him so hard."

"She does." Bex deadpans. "Have you told him yet or still too chicken?"

I stick my tongue out at her. "I'm not a chicken."

"So no."

"What do you need? The ring?" Sierra bursts from Bex's bed.

"It wouldn't surprise me if he had one ready." Bex says to Sierra.

"No way," Sierra gasps.

I roll my eyes at the two of them. "He doesn't have a ring. We *just* moved in together. And we're both perfectly happy where we are."

"Yeah, I'm sure he's perfectly happy waiting months for you to say it back to him. Real confidence boost, Dyl-licious," Sierra says, lips pursed.

"I should've never even told you he said it you serial romantic." I turn to Bexley. "I want to tell him, but now it just feels like it's never the right time. Like it should be something special or it'll just feel like I'm saying it because he did."

"He's a dude. He doesn't need flowers and candles." Bexley finishes up wings on her eyes and hands me the eyeliner.

"I know I just feel like now I've let it turn into this whole thing in my head." I huff, adding wings of my own. "Probably just being dramatic."

"Definitely overthinking it," Sierra snarks. "It's like you two started out with this whole-ass family and kicked-ass at all the hard parts while you're over there fumbling the fun and easy ones."

Bexley snorts and busts out laughing.

I scoff fighting a smile. "You two are no help. I'll figure it out."

When I give in and join them laughing at my discomfort, a pain shoots through my belly and hangs around for a minute before easing up.

"Ow, ow, ow." I hold my tightened belly sucking air through my teeth.

They immediately go from humor to concern.

"Are you okay?" Bexley steps up beside me, rubbing circles on my back while Sierra jumps up off the bed.

"Yeah," I grunt. "As pathetic as it sounds, I think all the floor cleaning gave me some cramps or something." They're both watching me, with brows drawn. "Swear I'm fine. I think laughing too hard just set it off again."

"Are you sure?" Sierra watches me rub my abdomen and I let my hands drop to my sides.

"Yep. All better now." I take step away from them grabbing the dress my mom brought to put on and change the subject. "How did you even find enough people to invite to throw me one of these parties anyway?" I let out a self deprecating laugh. "Basically everyone I know is already here."

Bexley relaxes a little. "It wasn't easy. I invited some people from your work, some girls we met at all the football games. Remember Daphne? She's coming."

"Aww yeah I did like her. The quarterback's sister, right?"

"Yep. Mom's coming... Wes...." She pauses, thinking. "And yeah, that's about it." She raises her hands in a small shrug.

"I'd planned on Nate, Lane, Blaze and Kohen to come today but then they had the stuff with their mom, and Nate said he wasn't coming without Lane."

"Makes sense," I say, changing into the hunter-green long-sleeve dress. It clings to the top of me, floral lace making up the sleeves, but loosens into a soft, flowy skirt once it reaches the swell of my belly and falls all the way to the floor.

It's beautiful. I love it so much.

"Wow, that looks so good on you."

"Thank you." I turn to face her stand up mirror. It does look really good. Probably a touch too fancy for the occasion, but who cares.

When we finally leave Bex's bedroom, Mom has all of the decorations finished up and a small food table set up with baby themed snacks.

Susan's talking to Mom on the couch while they sip out of a plastic cup that says "It's a girl!" on the side.

Slowly but surely the room fills with so many people I hadn't realized I actually talk to on a regular basis.

We did the crazy games; Sniffing chocolate smeared diapers, stealing clothespins when someone said baby, and—much to my embarrassment— the toilet paper game where you guess how big I am.

I didn't want to freak anyone out but I couldn't get the cramps to go away. I snuck off at one point to scrounge through Bex's cabinets for some acetaminophen, but an hour later and I think they're getting worse not better.

Finally, we're opening presents, and I can sit while I open them. I'm gritting my teeth to hide the fact that pain is ripping through me while I'm the center of everyone's attention.

I'm truly so appreciative of all the gifts everyone has brought me but all I can think about is getting everyone out of here so I can go lie down somewhere.

Mom surprises me when she tells everyone that the party's over and starts shuffling people—almost rudely—out the door.

She politely excuses the last guest, her prim smile staying perfectly in place until the door finally clicks shut.

"What was all that about?" Bex asks, sounding a little put out.

Mom doesn't even answer. She walks straight over to me and presses a hand to my forehead.

"You're sweaty and hurting. What's going on?"

"How did you know I was hurting?" I ask, stunned. I thought I'd done an excellent job of faking enthusiasm the entire time.

"You've been rubbing your feet together the whole time you were sitting there," she says calmly. "You do that every time you get sick."Her eyes narrow slightly. "What's wrong?"

I glance around the room at the people still there—Susan, Sierra, and Bex. Every one of them is watching me now, concern written across their faces.

I look back at my mom's worried face and I finally crack.

"I think something's wrong." I whisper. "I've been having terrible cramps, and they won't go away. I even took some medicine. Do you think I did something wrong? Is she okay?"

Mom swipes her hand down my face again. "I'm sure everything's fine, probably just Braxton Hicks," she says calmly. "But let's bring you to the hospital. Just to make sure and give us some peace of mind."

I sniffle and nod. "Okay."

"I can drive." Bex says, already reaching for her keys.

We get to the hospital and they eventually take us back to a room that has several beds set up separated by curtains. They only let one person come with me so I take Mom while Sierra and Bexley sit in the waiting room.

I thought about calling Lane but unless this turns out to be serious I don't want to bother them.

Even though I really wish he was here.

They hook me up to a bunch of monitors. Small disks connected to bands that wrap around me to hold them in place. They also hook me up to an IV and start running liquids through it.

After a while a nurse finally walks in.

"Hi, my name is Tanya. I'll be your nurse today." She glances over at the monitor beside me. "It looks like you're having some pretty strong contractions about three to four minutes apart." She looks back at me with a small smile. "If you don't mind, I'd like to check your cervix."

Slowly, I nod my head. "Okay. Is it going to hurt?"

"Yes," my mom answers for her.

Tanya gives me a sympathetic smile. "It can be a little uncomfortable."

She moves to the foot of the bed and helps me scoot down. "Go ahead and spread your legs for me."

When she checks me, I seriously consider kicking her.

Uncomfortable my ass.

A moment later she stands and pulls off her gloves.

"Alright," she says calmly. "I'm going to go ahead and get you moved into a delivery room."

My stomach drops.

"You're about five centimeters dilated, and your contractions are coming strong every few minutes. It doesn't look like they're slowing down." She gives me a small, reassuring smile.

"It looks like we're having a baby today, Ms. Whitlock."

I shake my head in horror. "But it's too early."

"From what I've seen, you're 36 weeks tomorrow." She gives me a reassuring smile. "That's considered late preterm. Babies born around this time usually do really well."

"But she's supposed to be in there another month."

"Ideally, yes," she says gently. "But sometimes babies have their own schedule. Right now, your contractions are strong and consistent, and you're already five centimeters. Our job is to make sure both of you stay safe and healthy."

She walks out of the small space and I look at my mom in a panic.

"Call Lane." I point to my phone in my pile of clothes sitting beside her. "NOW!"

CHAPTER 42

Lane

"I'm not going to lie. I'm not mad about missing the baby shower," Blaze says from the passenger seat.

I find Kohen in the rearview mirror, and he's not even listening as he watches cars pass out the window.

He's been quiet ever since we started this forty-five minute drive to Clearview Recovery Center.

"I feel bad we weren't there to help her finish clean the apartment this morning." I reply to Blaze.

"I don't, considering I've been a victim to the musical beds y'all have been playing lately. First you want your bed down there, then she wants her bed in there. Don't forget about Little One's bed. I'm not helping with anymore." He tells me defiantly.

I chuckle. "I think we have everything settled now. Shouldn't be a problem."

"Thank God." He goes back to drumming his fingers on

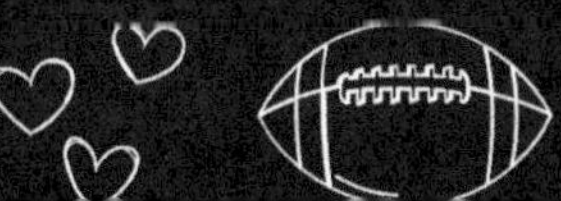

the dash then checking his phone, then fiddling with the radio.

"Are y'all nervous?" I ask quietly, and I see Kohen's gaze jerk to meet mine in the mirror before he looks back out the window again.

"A little." Blaze admits. "I feel like a lot has happened, and I don't know what she's going to be like... or what she's going to want."

I run a hand through my hair before letting it fall back to the wheel.

"I don't know either, honestly. But lucky for her, the court said she can come back and live in the house with us so she at least has her normal home to go back to, even if things are going to be a little different."

"Are you nervous about telling her about Dylan moving in?" He looks up at me curiously. "Because I don't think she'll mind. She liked Dylan."

I don't want to sound cruel so I don't tell him that I couldn't give two shits what she thinks about Dylan moving in. As far as I'm concerned it's more her place now than Mom's.

"I think she liked her too." I check Kohen again. "What about you?"

He doesn't even look at me, just shrugs his shoulders.

"I'm sure there's a reason she never wrote back. Maybe it's part of her process." I try to reassure him.

"She's supposed to be allowed letters after two weeks." His jaw clenches. "I called and checked."

"Maybe she just wanted to wait until she was ready. When we see her today, she can clear it all up." Blaze tells him, turned around in his seat.

Kohen just nods his head.

The rest of the drive is quiet, other than Blaze's fidgeting and my music.

I pull up in the parking lot and put the truck in park, but none of us make a move. We sit there, car idling, waiting for one of us to make the first move.

Now that we're here, the pit in my stomach has grown into a full-on wave of dread. I'm not sure what to expect or how I'm going to hold back the gnawing anger I feel for her.

But for them, I'll figure it out.

Both of them just keep staring at the brick building sitting in front of us and I realize I'm going to have to be the one to get this ball rolling.

I turn off the ignition and open my door and not too long after that, I have a brother standing on either side of me.

I walk through the white doors with fancy glass that distorts the view of what's going on inside and find the front desk.

I clear my throat, and the lady behind the desk looks up.

"Hi, how can I help you?"

"We're here to pick up Morgan Kemp." I tell her, voice way steadier than I feel.

Something flickers across her face before she stands. "Give me one moment, please."

I nod my head, and she disappears into another room.

I lean an elbow on the desk, crossing my arms so the boys can't see my trembling hands.

I take in all the pictures on the walls trying to busy myself while we wait.

Eventually the lady comes back, being led by another guy who must work here.

"Sir, I'm sorry for any confusion. Morgan Kemp checked out early this morning."

My stomach dips. What does he mean? Is she already at the house? We called yesterday to set this up.

The man pulls a manila envelope out and holds it toward me.

"But she left this behind if you don't mind taking it for her."

I take it from him. "Thank you."

"Again. Sorry for any confusion."

I turn to head outside, never taking my eyes off the envelope that has only one word written on it.

Lane

I look up at the sound of the door and it's Kohen slamming the door on his way out. Blaze flinches beside me at the sound.

I open it and find a small stack of Kohen's unopened letters and one written note left out.

I pull it out to read it.

Lane,

I'm sure this isn't the best way to handle this, but I guess that's the one thing you can always count on from me.

I wish you could count on me to be the mom you all deserve. I just don't think I'm capable of it anymore.

One thing I learned through this process is that I'll never be good for any of you until I face everything in the past and fix myself. And the truth is, I don't know if I'll ever be able to do that.

The day we lost your dad and your sister, something inside of me died, too. I've spent years trying to pretend it didn't, but I think we all know that isn't true.

I spoke with the case worker yesterday and filled out all the paperwork. The boys are yours now. They've been yours for a long time, but now it's official.

You don't have to worry about me showing up and screwing things up again. I won't put that on you anymore.

This is the only way I know how to make sure I don't fail any of you again.

Tell Blaze and Kohen that I love them. I

always have, even when I wasn't strong enough to be the mother they needed. Maybe someday they'll understand why I had to do this.

Take care of them the way you always have. I know they'll be safe with you.

I'm sorry for everything.

—Mom

My hands shake as I lower the note, and Blaze is staring at it like it's a bomb about to detonate.

"What does it say?" he asks, his voice breaking.

"She's gone." I croak.

His eyes go wide. "What do you mean?"

I let my head fall back and blow out a breath. "I don't think she's coming back this time."

Blaze stands there in shock.

"Let's go find Kohen." I say, grabbing him by the shoulders and leading him away from this place.

I walk outside, finding Kohen sitting on the tailgate of the truck, staring off in the distance.

I walk around to the back and see a steady stream of tears going down his face, and my heart breaks.

"She left, didn't she?" He asks angrily.

There's nothing to say but the truth. "Yeah, Kohen. She's gone."

He huffs out a bitter laugh. "I guess you got what you wanted, didn't you?"

"You think I wanted any of this?"

He drops his gaze to mine, every ounce of pain he feels shining there. "You wanted her gone."

"I wanted you safe. There's a difference." I try to keep my cool.

"I just wanted her back. I wanted my mom." His voice cracks as he shouts the words. "I thought this was her chance. To get better. To just—" His shoulders sag. "Want us back."

"Kohen, she always *wanted* you." I say softly. "Why do you think she came back so many times to try?" I look at Blaze, who's standing beside the truck, tears tracking down his face too. "She tried for y'all so many times. She hated that house. Hated walking into all of those memories she could never get back."

I put a hand on both of their shoulders. "Both of you were worth walking back into her personal hell for, over and over again."

Kohen sniffles and wipes his face. "Just not enough."

I grit my teeth and my fingers clench a little.

"That's not because of you." I say firmly. "It's because of her. Please tell me you know that."

Kohen looks away. "Yeah. I guess."

Blaze looks down at his shoes, kicking at the gravel.

I let my head fall.

Fuck. I don't know what to say to make this better for them. The only thing I can do is tell them how I see it. Tell them my truth.

"I know it hurts. Trust me, I get it. A small piece of me wondered if this was going to magically fix everything. She'd get the help she needed and come back to us. But it didn't... or maybe it did, and we just weren't the answer. I don't know. We may never know." I lift my head to find them watching me. "But I do know I have y'all. And that's all I need. As long as I have the two of you, I know it's going to be okay."

Blaze gives me a small smile and nods his head in agreement.

Kohen shoves my hand off of him before hopping off the tailgate.

"Yeah, I guess we never needed her." Something hardens in his face, and I'm not sure if it's for worse or better.

He looks me straight in the face. "We did just fine, didn't we?"

I swallow back my concern and slowly nod my head.

"Thanks to you, I guess."

Blaze's eyes widen slightly and they bounce between the two of us.

My breath stutters at his confession.

"It wasn't just me." I admit quietly. "I couldn't have done it without either of you."

Blaze's smile takes over his face, a dimple flashing, reminding me of the woman we're leaving behind.

Kohen clears his throat. "Let's get back to it then." He starts walking to the back seat of the truck. "You know how Dylan gets when you're gone too long."

A chuckle escapes Blaze as he walks around to the passenger seat. "Yeah, she can get pretty whiny when you're not there to pamper her."

I smile at the turn our conversation has taken.

"She gets whiny?" I ask sliding into the driver's seat.

"Whiny might not be the best word, but she's definitely in a better mood when you come home." Blaze teases.

"I like the sound of that." I admit.

"Yeah, Yeah. You two are annoyingly in love and shit. Can we just go?" Kohen says, but I catch a small grin on his face in the mirror.

I start the ignition and reach to put it in gear.

My phone starts ringing in my pocket, and I see that it's Dylan.

Blaze peeks over and says with a smirk. "See?"

I chuckle and answer the phone. "Missing me already?"

"Hardly," Dylan's mother tells me over the phone. "You need to get to the hospital as fast as you can."

No. Not her.

"What is it? What's wrong?" My heart starts to beat out of my chest.

"It's the baby. She's in labor. And I'm not sure how much time you'll have to get here."

I throw the truck in gear and hurriedly pull out of the parking lot, tires screeching.

"Well, please don't kill yourself getting here. She's fine. The baby's fine."

My grip tightens on the steering wheel. "But it's too soon."

I hear her sigh over the line. "I know, honey. But the doctors are saying that everyone should be fine." She's keeping her tone steady, but I can hear the tremble of fear for her daughter underneath it. "She's asking for you so get here soon, but with all of you in one piece, okay?"

I can't say anything past the lump in my throat. All I can do is nod.

"Everything's going to be fine."

But I know from experience that nothing is ever guaranteed.

CHAPTER 43

Dylan

35 WEEKS

I let my feet slide together under the scratchy hospital blanket as another wave of intense tightening pulls at my insides.

When the contraction passes, Tanya continues, "We can artificially break your water and it should progress the labor much faster."

I shake my head frantically. "No, I want to wait for Lane. Is the baby in trouble or something?"

"Right now, everything looks good. But if we see signs that you or the baby are in distress, we may need to move things along," Tanya warns gently. "How's your pain? Would you like me to call for an epidural?"

I look at Bex and Sierra, who are watching me from their chairs, and then my mom, who's waiting for my answer. She must see the question on my face.

"Honey, babies are born every day from moms who take the epidural. I certainly did. And they turn out just fine. Not

taking the epidural isn't going to get you any points in an imaginary competition to be the best mom." She reaches over and squeezes my hand. "If you're hurting, get the epidural."

Another contraction starts rolling through me taking my breath so I just nod my head.

Tanya must have left the room while I was mid-contraction because when I finally relax back into the bed, she's gone.

"Mom, how long has it been? Why isn't he here yet?" I moan trying not to cry.

"He's coming, honey. He said they were less than an hour away."

"Kohen and Blaze are texting me. They said they're about twenty minutes away. I've been keeping them updated. I hope that's okay." Bexley tells me.

"Of course. Thank you." I lay my head back, preparing myself for the next attack from my body. "And thank you both for the baby shower today, if I haven't said it. It was perfect!"

"And apparently, just in the nick of time," Sierra jokes, chewing on her thumbnail.

I can only laugh halfheartedly because I'm honestly terrified.

Dr. Mendez came in earlier to let me know she was here and not to worry because babies being born this early is normal, especially for first-time moms.

It didn't help.

I'm definitely worried. Worried for my baby. Worried for myself. Worried Lane won't make it in time.

I know this is everyday for the people that work here but my entire world's changing today.

There's a knock at the door. "Hello, Ms. Whitlock. I'm Dr. Patel, the anesthesiologist. I'm here to place your epidural for you." He glances at my mom and friends. "I apologize, but I'm going to have to ask you to leave the room."

I squeeze my mom's hand with mine, and she swipes a hand down my face. "It's okay. We'll be right outside."

A tear slips free and I nod my head at her before she gets up and follows Bexley and Sierra out the door.

Getting an epidural is *not* a pleasant experience, but when it's all done and I'm laid back in the bed I have to admit I feel much less tense.

My fear is still there, but my body isn't as coiled tight.

Tanya walks in with everyone else in tow. "How are you feeling?"

"A little more relaxed, but still scared to death." I admit.

She chuckles. "That's to be expected. It's a big day for you, Momma." She takes a step forward to the end of the bed. "If you don't mind, I'd like to check you again and see how you're progressing."

"Okay," I tell her reluctantly.

I scoot down the bed and spread my legs, because apparently the day you give birth there's no such thing as modesty.

She pops on her latex gloves and takes her place at the end of the bed. I feel the pressure for just a second when all of a sudden a gush of warmth rushes out of me.

"Oh dear. Well that answers that question, and you're eight centimeters dilated."

"Did you just pee all over her?" Sierra shrieks from beside me.

Bex slaps her. "Her water broke."

"Right, sorry. I'm just shocked by the amount of my best friend I'm seeing today. I think we're closer now than we've ever been."

"Just wait until it's your turn!" I shoot her a vicious look.

"Sorry." She holds her hands up, then mimes locking up her lips. "I'll be quiet again."

"I don't think it's going to be long now." Tanya announces. "I'm going to go find Dr. Mendez."

"Oh God." I groan. "Where's Lane?"

"He should be here any minute." Bex tells me typing away on her phone.

I need him beside me, telling me everything's going to be okay. He needs to be here to see our baby take her first breath.

"I can't do this without him." I plead with my mom like she can fix this.

She sucks in a deep breath. "He hasn't let you down yet. He won't start now." She reassures, surprising me.

"You think so?" I whisper.

She smiles warmly at me and nods.

I don't feel the pain of the contractions anymore, but I can feel from the tightening of my stomach when I'm having one, and there's an intense pressure like she's already trying to break free.

"Mom, I think it's happening." I cry.

"I'll go get the nurse." Sierra says as she rushes out the door.

"Mom, if he doesn't make it I want you in here."

"Of course—"

"But," I cut her off. "If he gets here in time. I want it to be just the two of us." I tell her softly.

Her brows draw together and her eyes squeeze shut a moment. "Alright." She croaks.

"Thank you."

The door swings open so hard it hits the wall.

"Dylan?!"

He runs in the room with Blaze and Kohen flanking him. His hair is disheveled and he looks how I feel.

But the second our eyes meet it's like I'm safe again and every emotion I feel comes pouring out of me.

My mom squeezes my hand one last time before leaving her spot at my side and shuffling everyone else out of the room.

Lane rushes to my side. "Are you okay? How are you feeling?"

I just nod my head and grab his shirt, pulling him down to me.

"I love you." The words rush out before I can stop them. "I don't know why it took me this long to say it, but I do."

He pulls back just enough to look at me, his expression somewhere between shock and disbelief.

"I've had the craziest day," I continue, my voice shaking. "And every step of the way I wanted you there beside me. I needed you here telling me everything was going to be okay. Because even if it isn't... I know that as long as you're with me, we'll figure it out."

I swallow hard.

"I know we weren't in my plan, but you're the best thing that's ever happened to me."

He crushes his mouth into mine and even in the middle of this chaos everything feels right.

"I love you too, baby." He cradle my face with one hand and places the other one over mine sitting on my tight stomach. "More than anything in this world." His mouth lifts on one side. "Until Little One gets here...safe and sound."

We hear a throat clearing.

"I hear it's time to have a baby." Dr. Mendez says shuffling around the room.

Lane takes my hand in his but moves to stand beside me.

Tanya walks into the room, followed by several other nurses and doctors that I don't recognize.

"You must be Lane. You made it." Tanya smiles politely at him.

"Barely." He chuckles nervously

Dr. Mendez lifts up the blanket to see how everything's going I guess and suddenly I'm a little nervous.

"Under no circumstances are you allowed to look down there at any point in this process. Got it?" I tell Lane, fixing him with a serious look.

He just nods his head, paler than I've ever seen him. "Yes, Ma'am."

I shift uncomfortably as my doctor pulls out stirrups for me to put my feet in. "Oh yeah. You're fully dilated."

"Holy shit," I breathe. "This is really happening."

Lane is shaking like a leaf while everyone around us scurries around to the doctor's instructions.

Tanya leans closer to us.

"After she's born the neonatal team will check her over. Since she's a little early, we just want to make sure her breathing and temperature look good."

I hold on to Lane for dear life and pray that our little girl will be okay.

"Dylan, when I tell you, I'm going to need you to push. Okay?" She tells me, and I nod my head vigorously.

"Okay, Dylan, here it comes. Deep breath and... push."

And I do.

Over and over again until it feels like I have nothing left to give.

I'm sweaty, out of breath, and every limb on my body is shaking.

"One more push, Dylan. She's right there."

I fall back into Lane's hold from behind me.

"I can't. I'm so tired."

"Come on, baby. One more, you can do it." He tells me, and I feel his hands tense on my neck and around my hand.

I twist my head to meet his gaze and the encouragement shining there. Drawing strength from him, I suck in a shaky breath, grit my teeth, and push with everything I have left.

"Keep going." My doctor urges. "We're almost there."

My body trembles and I'm half screaming as I buckle down to finish bringing my little girl into this world.

"You have a baby girl!" My doctor finally announces, and I collapse.

I can barely keep my eyes open, but I still can't hear her cry, and I know that's not a good sign.

"Where is she? Why isn't she crying?" I croak out as loud as I can.

They cut the cord, and I see glimpses of my baby as they hustle her over to a bed across the room with the neonatal team.

They use a small suction to clear her mouth and then I finally hear it. Her pitiful little cry fills the room.

Lane pulls me into his arms.

"You did it. She's here. She's okay." He tells me dropping kisses all over my damp face.

"Five pounds and twelve ounces, eighteen inches long. She's tiny, but everything looks great on her. Lungs definitely sound great. I think she was just ready to meet you Momma and Daddy." Tanya tells me with a big smile.

I'm crying for the hundredth time today. "Can I hold her now?"

"They're just doing a few more things, and she'll be all yours."

Her cries are still going strong, and while I'm glad to know she's good, it's still building anxiety inside of me to help her.

I see them wrap her in a blanket and finally carry her toward me. I hold my breath the whole time until they lay her on my chest.

"Hi, Little One," I cry cradling her tiny, screaming body to me.

"Everything looks good so far, but since she's a little early, we'll come back several times to check on her temperature and blood sugar." One of the neonatal doctors tells me. "Congratulations, Momma."

"She's so tiny." Lane whispers staring down at her.

I watch her while her screams slowly subside as she nestles into my skin. She's so beautiful.

A little messy. And puffy.

But she's absolutely…

"Perfect." Lane says in awe as he reaches down and rests his hand on her back covering up the entire thing.

His thumb hides her entire ear when he uses it to lift up her tiny hat to reveal shining red hair.

"Just like her momma," he murmurs to me with a smile, never taking his eyes off her.

A happy sob escapes me as I take in the tiny baby resting comfortably on my chest, Lane's hand still sitting beside mine because he's just as taken by her as I am.

We did it.

Our baby girl is here.

CHAPTER 44

Dylan

SHE'S HERE

"I can't believe you're a dad," I hear Nate tell Lane, who's proudly pacing the room with our baby tucked in his arms.

"Come on. It's my turn." My mom insists, reaching for her.

"You just had a turn." Sierra complains. "I still haven't gotten to hold her."

Bexley smirks. "That's what happens when you sneak off to Starbucks instead of just taking the hospital coffee."

"Who knew a baby could make people turn on each other like this," Blaze whispers, leaning an elbow on the back of my raised hospital bed.

"I know," I agree. "We could just put her in the middle of them and watch them all fight to the death."

Blaze snickers at my terrible joke before dropping his voice into a dramatic rumble.

"Are you not entertained?"

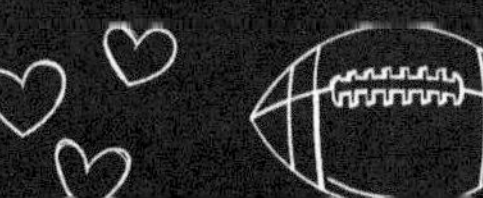

I gasp. "I'm so proud of you for making a *Gladiator* reference." Then I hold my hand up for a high five, which he accepts enthusiastically.

"Pretty sure your mom would win," Kohen says dryly from beside him.

Lane told me about their mom. I hate that they had so much happen today. The boys haven't even really had time to process their loss.

Blaze seems fine, but Kohen has kept himself on the outskirts all evening. I want to ask him how he's doing, but I know he won't want to talk about it. Especially in front of everybody.

"Have you gotten to hold her yet?" I ask instead.

"Nah. That's okay though. I don't want to drop her or something."

"Kohen's turn." I announce loudly.

"But I just got her." Sierra whines.

"That's what happens when you sneak away and don't get *me* Starbucks." I scrunch my nose at her playfully.

Lane carefully steals our baby back and starts walking to Kohen.

"You can't even have coffee." Sierra reminds me.

I whip my gaze toward her sharply. "I can have one cup a day."

She starts giggling. "Don't look at me like that. I did bring you food, Miss Hangry."

I smile gratefully at her. "You did, and it was amazing."

Kohen acts like Lane's handing him a porcupine. His eyes are wide, and he can't figure out what to do with his arms.

"Nate, I see you lost the brace." I say, hoping everyone will stop watching Kohen so he can get comfortable.

"Yeah," Nate says, stretching out his leg in front of him. "Now we just need it to be summer again so I can show these pretty legs off."

"You'd look great in a bikini." Sierra winks at him.

Nate immediately turns his charms to my oldest friend. "I look great in anything, sweetheart."

"Nope." Bex steps in between them. "Absolutely not."

I chuckle at their nonsense and turn my attention back to my guys talking amongst themselves as they huddle around Little One.

Kohen lets her wrap her tiny fingers around his and I'm melting at the scene.

"So?" My mom hedges.

"What?" I ask hesitantly.

"Have you two finally picked out a name, or is *Little One* going on the birth certificate?"

I glance at Lane, and he must feel it because he looks up to see what I need.

"She asked about her name." I look at him knowingly. "I think you should take this one."

He looks back at his brother with a sad smile.

"We want to use Claire as her middle name," he says quietly. "But wanted to see what y'all thought about it first."

The room goes still as we wait for their answers.

They both look down at her sleeping peacefully in Kohen's arms.

Blaze nods his head smiling down at her. "Yeah... I think that'll be a good name for her."

Kohen pulls her a little closer, never looking up. "Yeah... I think she'd like that."

Lane clears his throat.

"Okay. Everyone," He turns dramatically to include the whole room. "Meet Mila Claire Kemp."

Cheers and soft awws ripple around the room.

Mila stirs in Kohen's arms, letting out tiny grunts and squeaks.

"Oh shit. Take her back. Hurry." Kohen panics, handing her back to Lane, and we all laugh.

Sierra runs to finish up her turn, and Bex and Mom surround her.

They all take turns holding her while we laugh and chat well into the evening. Even Nate takes a turn holding her, telling her in a goofy baby voice that he's going to be the favorite uncle.

I'm not sure how I imagined having my first child...

but I know it couldn't have been better than this.

♡ ⚬⚬⚬⚬ ♡

Eventually, a nurse comes to let us know that visiting hours are over and everyone has to head out.

Mom and Sierra have to catch their flight back home in the morning, so they spent a little extra time with their goodbyes.

Bexley and Nate take Blaze and Kohen back home and promise they'll stay with them until we're discharged from the hospital.

Lane kept getting in trouble for squeezing into the hospital bed with me, so he finally gave up and turned the couch into a bed. Now we're sitting together, his arm laid draped over my shoulders while I nurse Mila.

"Geez. I didn't realize this was going to hurt so bad," I complain, watching my tiny baby attack my boob like a feral animal. I didn't expect to feel like I was going through labor all over again every time she sucks me dry.

Lane twists around so he can see her better. "She does look a little aggressive when she's trying to latch."

"Right?!" I laugh softly. "Like calm down, kid. I swear I'm not going to let you go hungry."

His shoulders shake. "She makes the exact face you do before you bite into a burger."

"Hey." I elbow him as carefully as I can without disturbing Mila, but she still lets out a tiny grunt of protest.

Lane chuckles, then his expression softens as he looks down at her.

"It's still amazing to me that she's here and everything's okay," he says quietly. "I was terrified when I got that phone call."

"I was terrified you weren't going to make it in time. Everything happened so fast."

He watches her for a moment, awe written all over his face.

"I guess the hard part's over now. We all survived... and now we have this perfect, beautiful little girl."

"Lane," I say, giving him a look. "I don't think that was the hard part."

He raises an eyebrow.

"Now we have to raise her," I continue, glancing down at the tiny human attached to me. "And make sure we don't mess her up."

"I'm sure we won't be perfect, but we'll do alright." He leans down and kisses me on the cheek. "She'll be spoiled rotten, but she won't have any doubts about how much she's loved. She's going to be independent but caring, like her mom."

I smile up at him. "And protective and tough like her daddy."

"She will, but she won't need to be."

"What do you mean?"

He shrugs to the quiet hallway outside our room. "Look at the family she's got. We've got backup all over the place."

"That's true. She has way more people to look to than I ever did."

"Me too." Lane agrees.

We sit in comfortable silence as Mila slowly drifts off to sleep again. I fix my clothes and lay her over my shoulder to pat on her back.

Lane leans over and presses a kiss to her tiny head, making my heart squeeze in my chest.

"I know another thing she'll always know." He says when he looks back at me.

I smile at the crooked grin he's giving me. "What's that?"

"How in love I am with her mom."

My chest warms as I take in the man who gave me everything.

This wasn't the life I planned, but it turned out to be exactly the one I needed.

I lean up and kiss him softly, careful not to squish Little One between us.

"I love you too, Lane." I whisper. "And everything that came with you."

Epilogue

DYLAN- 3 MONTHS LATER

I've got Mila decked out in the cutest little onesie for the occasion. It says "The Cutest Catch" and I got her the cutest little sun hat to put on.

I'm dancing around with her while I wait for the boys to unload everything from the truck.

Lane just got back from a team minicamp he had to fly out to.

I'll never forget his face when his name was called on draft day as a fourth-round pick for the Denver Broncos.

Everyone showed up that day to celebrate with him.

Nate and Bex, the boys, all of us crammed into the living room, staring at the TV like we might miss it if we look away.

All of us lost it when he got that call.

We decided when practice starts he'd get an apartment out there, and we'd all fly back and forth to see each other while

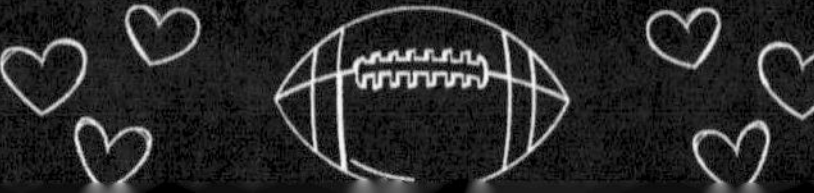

Kohen and I finish out our senior years, and we'll move there with him after that.

"Make sure you set up her playpen in the shade." I tell Kohen.

"I don't know why you even brought this thing. It's not like she ever gets put down." He shouts, fighting the clasps to get them to spread out right.

Mila wraps her chubby little fist around my finger and starts chewing on it. "Is Uncle Kohen right? Do you get held too much?" I ask her in a silly voice.

She gives me a gummy smile, her bright green eyes squinting in the light.

"Just wait, it won't be long, and I'll get you your own tiny fishing pole, and Daddy will teach you so you won't feel left out," Lane tells her, walking up beside me and dropping a kiss on her tiny head, his arms full of fishing gear.

"Are Nate and Bex coming?" Blaze asks, dragging an ice chest behind him.

"Yeah, Nate just texted and said they're pulling up right now."

"Does he have the bait?" Kohen asks with a little more concern than I felt was necessary.

"Yep," Lane tells him never even looking up from setting up the poles.

"There she is! The prettiest little girl in the whole wide world!" Bex chirps as she walks up from out of the trees holding an armful of lawn chairs.

"I love the way you greet me. Really keeps our friendship strong." I snicker at my joke.

She tosses the chairs down in a heap and stalks toward me with her hands held up expectantly.

"Your momma's crazy. Isn't she?" Bex continues with her baby talk, while Mila's arms are flailing in her direction. "Come see Auntie Bex."

Bexley scoops her up out of my arms and wraps her up, nuzzling in her neck to make her laugh. It's one of my most favorite sounds in the world.

I walk up behind Lane, who's tying hooks in our poles and sigh dramatically. "It's like we don't even exist anymore. Everyone just visits us for the kid."

He smiles up at me. "It's one of the few cons of having the prettiest little girl in the world."

I chuckle, wrapping my arms around him from behind. "What other cons are there?"

He twists to look at me with a serious expression on his face. "Boys."

I bust out laughing and smack a kiss on his mouth. "We have some time before we have to worry about that."

"Don't worry, Laney. I'll have your back when those little bastards start showing up." Nate tells him as he walks up holding the rest of the lawn chairs and a little foam box that I know is holding slimy worms.

Gross.

"You going to help at all today or just keep walking around avoiding labor?" Blaze asks, elbowing me as he walks by.

I giggle. "Caught that, did ya? Alright, I'm coming. What do you need?"

We finally get everything set up, lawn chairs lined up for all of us while Bexley sits back in the shade with Mila.

Lane baits my hook—as promised—and I cast my line and wait.

Blaze catches on almost immediately and then Kohen follows right behind him.

"Looks like we're in the lead." Kohen taunts, and I'm ashamed to admit that it works on me because I reel my line in and recast it, hoping for better results.

Finally I see my bobber dip under the water with a bite and I squeal in excitement as I set the hook.

"I got one!" I yell as I reel it in.

I finally get it to the bank and hold it up by the string so it doesn't touch me.

"Hang on, I'll get my phone out and take a picture." Bex shouts excitedly.

"I'm pretty sure mine's bigger than y'alls." I look at Blaze and Kohen, sticking my tongue out.

Blaze raises an amused eyebrow. "Did she just say y'all?"

"Looks like we're rubbing off on her. Pretty soon she'll have an accent too." Kohen says with a grin.

Bexley takes my picture but never puts her phone down the whole time Lane's helping me take off the fish.

And by helping, I mean doing it for me.

"Well, I think that's everything," Lane announces.

"What do you mean?"

He releases my catch back into the water. "I baited your hook, dealt with your fish... You in love with me yet?"

I laugh at the joke he told that very first night we met, almost a year ago to date. So much has happened since that night, it feels like a lifetime ago. I reach up on my toes and smack a kiss on his cheek.

"You know, it's weird, but it wasn't until the exact moment I saw you handling that slimy fish that I knew for sure. But you have to keep the bait coming, or it'll never last."

"Well, let me get on it then." He leans over and picks up the foam box full of worms to pull one out for me. "That's weird." He tilts the box back and forth as if he's looking at something.

"What is it?" I ask him curiously.

He closes the lid and tosses me the box. I start opening it slowly.

"Lane, if this is some kind of weird prank..." I gasp when I see what's inside.

My head snaps up...

and find Lane on one knee in front of me.

Holy shit! Is he doing what I think he's doing?

"Dylan Sterling Whitlock, a year ago I thought I let an almost perfect girl get away from me." My heart's racing in my chest and my vision's getting a little blurry. "And I don't ever want to let that happen again. Could you do me a favor and marry me?"

I pull the ring out and slip it on my finger, watching it sparkle in the sun.

"Gavin Lane Kemp, there's nothing else I want more than to be your wife." I hurl myself at him, wrapping my arms and legs around him.

Everyone around us cheers as he stands, still holding me and never breaking our kiss.

Behind us, Mila lets out a happy little squeal like she's cheering with us too.

I pull back, laying my forehead on his.

"I love you so much." I say only for him to hear.

"I love you too. And now I get to keep you... forever."

Epilogue

LANE- 5 YEARS LATER

"**B**laze Kemp." The principal goes on but we can't hear it over the sounds of our group screaming and yelling as he walks across the stage.

Mila claps from my lap as she yells, "Go Blazey!"

Her little wild curls catch on my face when she whips them around to look at me. "Look, Daddy. There's Uncle Blazey."

A proud smile shoots across my face as I glance from her to the boy who's fist-pumping his diploma in the air, looking right at us in the stands.

"I see him." I tell her with more meaning than she understands.

"He's so silly." She squeals with laughter, and I wrangle her in before she squirms right off my lap.

Dylan squeezes my hands with hers, and I look up to find her wiping tears off her cheeks.

"I can't believe he's graduating from high school." She chokes out.

I watch him smiling with the same boyish grin he's had since he was little, and I swear it's like taking a hit out on the field.

My vision blurs just a little before I can shut it down. "It's pretty crazy."

♡ ⊰⊱ ♡

Later on, after we all celebrate with a giant barbecue together, Blaze took off to a party with his friends.

I'm getting Little One out of the bath while her momma takes a shower downstairs.

"Alright squirt. What PJs are we wearing?" I ask her, searching through her drawers in a room that used to be mine.

"Cowboys," she yells at me from on top of her bed that she's jumping on.

Kohen got to her while she was little and got her to be a Cowboys super fan.

It was a little awkward for about a year there when she kept getting mad that I wasn't on her favorite team.

Luckily, at the end of my rookie contract, they picked me up. Now my baby girl gets to watch her favorite team—me just being a perk—live and in person.

She's our biggest fan in the stadium, every time she comes to one of our games.

I grab her favorite pajamas and start wrestling her into them.

"Come on, crazy pants. It's time to settle down and go night, night." I tell her, picking her up high in the air and pretending to slam her down on the bed.

She giggles uncontrollably and shuffles under her unicorn blanket.

"I like when Uncle Nate and Aunt Bex get to come over. I missed Uncle Kohen too."

"Me too. Did you like seeing everyone today?" I ask, tucking her in.

She lets out a big yawn. "Yeah, it makes me happy when everyone's here."

"Me too," I tell her, leaning over to give her a kiss. "Good night, Little One."

"Good night, Daddy." She says already rolling over. I watch her for a second before switching off the light and closing the door.

I go back downstairs to find Dylan already dressed for bed.

"You already got her down?" Dylan asks me, surprised.

I watch her as she rubs lotion up and down her arms as she lies down in our bed. "Yeah, didn't take much after all the excitement from today. Once I got her to be still for longer than two seconds, she was done for."

She chuckles and I fall down on top of her, laying my head in her lap. She immediately starts running her fingers through my scalp exactly how I wanted her to.

"It's kinda sad. First Kohen, now Blaze. The house just feels so... empty."

"Mmmhmmm." I hum.

"So... I was thinking..."

Oh shit.

"That's never good." I say, never even opening my eyes, and she smacks me on the head.

I sit up, narrowing my eyes at her. "What are you thinking, dear wife?"

"That's much better." She smiles, satisfied. "I was think-ing... Things have been going pretty smoothly at work... and you seem pretty settled with the team... and when Blaze leaves for college, it'll just be us."

"And... are you ever gonna get to your point, woman?"

Her eyes light up, "Let's have another baby."

"Really?" I perk up, eyes wide.

She nods her head. "Yeah, I don't want Mila to grow up without siblings like I did. And she's already five-"

"Let's do it."

"Yeah?" She asks excitedly.

"Hell yeah," I grin. "Let's do it right now," I tell her, lifting up and yanking her underneath me.

Dylan squeals. "I'm still on birth control. It's not going to work right now."

I lean down and start kissing up her neck. "We can practice."

She wraps her arms and legs around me, tiny moans already escaping her. "It's been a while since our last baby. I guess it couldn't hurt to do some practicing."

"See," I say, nibbling into her skin. "We both have good ideas tonight."

Dylan laughs softly, dragging my face to hers and pulling me in for a heated kiss.

I can't believe there was a time when this place was so broken. A house I came home to every day and fought like hell to keep in one piece.

Now it holds all of my favorite memories—and all of my favorite people.

Everything I thought I'd never get back, we built it together inside these walls.

And we aren't even finished yet.

Hell... we're just getting started.

Afterword

When I started writing this story, it began as an idea—just a few scenes, a couple of characters that wouldn't leave me alone. Somewhere along the way, these characters stopped being just words on a page and started feeling like people I knew... people I cared about.

This book was written in the middle of real life—busy days, long nights, and a house that's never quiet. I'm a mom to five incredible kids (and two very opinionated weenie dogs), so writing didn't always look pretty.

Luckily, I have a pretty amazing husband at my side to help me pick up the slack.

Thank you to my family that listened to me drone on about my book all the time and took the time to read it along the way.

If you made it all the way to the end, thank you. Truly. There are a million books you could've picked up, and the fact that you chose to spend your time with my first one means more than I can really put into words.

I hope this story made you feel something—whether it was comfort, excitement, frustration, or even just a moment of escape.

And most of all, I hope it reminded you that sometimes the life you didn't plan... ends up being exactly the one you needed.

About the Author

G. Kespa is an indie author who writes in the middle of a busy life with five kids and two weenie dogs. Her stories are shaped by the small moments, the messy ones, and everything in between.

Join her on Facebook or TikTok to stay up to date on any books she's releasing.

www.ingramcontent.com/pod-product-compliance
Lightning Source LLC
Chambersburg PA
CBHW071443140726
47997CB00005B/1579